GIGOLO

EDNA FERBER

*erenity
Publishers, LLC

ROCKVILLE, MARYLAND
2009

ISBN: 978-1-60450-673-0

Published by Serenity Publishers
An Arc Manor Company
P. O. Box 10339
Rockville, MD 20849-0339
www.SerenityPublishers.com

Printed in the United States of America/United Kingdom

GIGOLO

CONTENTS

THE AFTERNOON OF A FAUN

Though he rarely heeded its summons—cagy boy that he was—the telephone rang oftenest for Nick. Because of the many native noises of the place, the telephone had a special bell that was a combination buzz and ring. It sounded above the roar of outgoing cars, the splash of the hose, the sputter and hum of the electric battery in the rear. Nick heard it, unheeding. A voice—Smitty's or Mike's or Elmer's—answering its call. Then, echoing through the grey, vaulted spaces of the big garage: "Nick! Oh, Ni-ick!"

From the other side of the great cement-floored enclosure, or in muffled tones from beneath a car: "Whatcha want?"

"Dame on the wire."

"I ain't in."

The obliging voice again, dutifully repeating the message: "He ain't in.... Well, it's hard to say. He might be in in a couple hours and then again he might not be back till late. I guess he's went to Hammond on a job—" (Warming to his task now.) "Say, won't I do?... Who's fresh! Aw, say, *lady!*"

You'd think, after repeated rebuffs of this sort, she could not possibly be so lacking in decent pride as to leave her name for Smitty or Mike or Elmer to bandy about. But she invariably did, baffled by Nick's elusiveness. She was likely to be any one of a number. Miss Bauers phoned: Will you tell him, please? (A nasal voice, and haughty, with the hauteur that seeks to conceal secret fright.) Tell him it's important. Miss Ahearn phoned: Will you tell him, please? Just say Miss Ahearn. A-h-e-a-r-n. Miss Olson: Just Gertie. But oftenest Miss Bauers.

Cupid's messenger, wearing grease-grimed overalls and the fatuous grin of the dalliant male, would transmit his communication to the uneager Nick.

"'S wonder you wouldn't answer the phone once yourself. Says you was to call Miss Bauers any time you come in between one and six at Hyde Park—wait a min't'—yeh—Hyde Park 6079, and any time after six at—"

"Wha'd she want?"

"Well, how the hell should I know! Says call Miss Bauers any time between one and six at Hyde Park 6—"

"Swell chanst. *Swell* chanst!"

Which explains why the calls came oftenest for Nick. He was so indifferent to them. You pictured the patient and persistent Miss Bauers, or the oxlike Miss Olson, or Miss Ahearn, or just Gertie hovering within hearing distance of the telephone listening, listening—while one o'clock deepened to six—for the call that never came; plucking up fresh courage at six until six o'clock dragged on to bedtime. When next they met: "I bet you was there all the time. Pity you wouldn't answer a call when a person leaves their name. You could of give me a ring. I bet you was there all the time."

"Well, maybe I was."

Bewildered, she tried to retaliate with the boomerang of vituperation.

How could she know? How could she know that this slim, slick young garage mechanic was a woodland creature in disguise—a satyr in store clothes—a wild thing who perversely preferred to do his own pursuing? How could Miss Bauers know—she who cashiered in the Green Front Grocery and Market on Fifty-third Street? Or Miss Olson, at the Rialto ticket window? Or the Celtic, emotional Miss Ahearn, the manicure? Or Gertie the goof? They knew nothing of mythology; of pointed ears and pug noses and goat's feet. Nick's ears, to their fond gaze, presented an honest red surface protruding from either side of his head. His feet, in tan laced shoes, were ordinary feet, a little more than ordinarily expert, perhaps, in the convolutions of the dance at Englewood Masonic Hall, which is part of Chicago's vast South Side. No; a faun, to Miss Bauers, Miss Olson, Miss Ahearn, and just Gertie, was one of those things in the Lincoln Park Zoo.

Perhaps, sometimes, they realized, vaguely, that Nick was different. When, for example, they tried—and failed—to picture him looking interestedly at one of those three-piece bedroom sets glistening like pulled taffy in the window of the installment furniture store, while they, shy yet proprietary, clung to his arm and eyed the price ticket. Now $98.50. You couldn't see Nick interested in bedroom sets, in price tickets, in any of those settled, fixed, everyday things. He was fluid, evasive, like quicksilver, though they did not put it thus.

Miss Bauers, goaded to revolt, would say pettishly: "You're like a mosquito, that's what. Person never knows from one minute to the other where you're at."

"Yeh," Nick would retort. "When you know where a mosquito's at, what do you do to him? Plenty. I ain't looking to be squashed."

Miss Ahearn, whose public position (the Hygienic Barber Shop. Gent's manicure, 50c.) offered unlimited social opportunities, would assume a gay indifference. "They's plenty boys begging to take me out every hour in the day. Swell lads, too. I ain't waiting round for any greasy mechanic like you. Don't think it. Say, lookit your nails! They'd queer you with me, let alone what else all is wrong with you."

In answer Nick would put one hand—one broad, brown, steel-strong hand with its broken discoloured nails—on Miss Ahearn's arm, in its flimsy georgette sleeve. Miss Ahearn's eyelids would flutter and close, and a little shiver would run with icy-hot feet all over Miss Ahearn.

Nick was like that.

Nick's real name wasn't Nick at all—or scarcely at all. His last name was Nicholas, and his parents, long before they became his parents, traced their origin to some obscure Czechoslovakian province—long before we became so glib with our Czechoslovakia. His first name was Dewey, knowing which you automatically know the date of his birth. It was a patriotic but unfortunate choice on the part of his parents. The name did not fit him; was too mealy; not debonair enough. Nick. Nicky in tenderer moments (Miss Bauers, Miss Olson, Miss Ahearn, just Gertie, et al.).

His method with women was firm and somewhat stern, but never brutal. He never waited for them if they were late. Any girl who assumed that her value was enhanced in direct proportion to her tardiness in keeping an engagement with Nick found herself standing disconsolate on the corner of Fifty-third and Lake trying to look as if she were merely waiting for the Lake Park car and not peering wistfully up and down the street in search of a slim, graceful, hurrying figure that never came.

It is difficult to convey in words the charm that Nick possessed. Seeing him, you beheld merely a medium-sized young mechanic in reasonably grimed garage clothes when working; and in tight pants, tight coat, silk shirt, long-visored green cap when at leisure. A rather pallid skin due to the nature of his work. Large deft hands, a good deal like the hands of a surgeon, square, blunt-fingered, spatulate. Indeed, as you saw him at work, a wire-netted electric bulb held in one hand, the other plunged deep into the vitals of the car on which he was engaged, you thought of a surgeon performing a major operation. He wore one of those round skullcaps characteristic of his craft (the brimless crown of an old felt hat). He would deftly remove the transmission case and plunge his hand deep into the car's guts, feeling expertly about with his engine-wise fingers as a surgeon feels for liver, stomach, gall bladder, intestines, appendix. When he brought up his hand, all dripping with grease (which is the warm blood of the car), he invariably had put his finger on the sore spot.

All this, of course, could not serve to endear him to the girls. On the contrary, you would have thought that his hands alone, from which he could never quite free the grease and grit, would have caused some feeling of repugnance among the lily-fingered. But they, somehow, seemed always to be finding an excuse to touch him: his tie, his hair, his coat sleeve. They seemed even to derive a vicarious thrill from holding his hat or cap when on an outing. They brushed imaginary bits of lint from his coat lapel. They tried on his seal ring, crying: "Oo, lookit, how big it is for me, even my thumb!" He called this "pawing a guy over"; and the lint ladies he designated as "thread pickers."

No; it can't be classified, this powerful draw he had for them. His conversation furnished no clue. It was commonplace conversation, limited, even dull. When astonished, or impressed, or horrified, or amused, he said: "Ken yuh feature that!" When emphatic or confirmatory, he said: "You *tell*'em!"

It wasn't his car and the opportunities it furnished for drives, both country and city. That motley piece of mechanism represented such an assemblage of unrelated parts as could only have been made to cooerdinate under Nick's expert guidance. It was out of commission more than half the time, and could never be relied upon to furnish a holiday. Both Miss Bauers and Miss Ahearn had twelve-cylinder opportunities that should have rendered them forever unfit for travel in Nick's one-lung vehicle of locomotion.

It wasn't money. Though he was generous enough with what he had, Nick couldn't be generous with what he hadn't. And his wage at the garage was $40 a week. Miss Ahearn's silk stockings cost $4.50.

His unconcern should have infuriated them, but it served to pique. He wasn't actually as unconcerned as he appeared, but he had early learned that effort in their direction was unnecessary. Nick had little imagination; a gorgeous selfishness; a tolerantly contemptuous liking for the sex. Naturally, however, his attitude toward them had been somewhat embittered by being obliged to watch their method of driving a car in and out of the Ideal Garage doorway. His own manipulation of the wheel was nothing short of wizardry.

He played the harmonica.

Each Thursday afternoon was Nick's half day off. From twelve until seven-thirty he was free to range the bosky highways of Chicago. When his car—he called it "the bus"—was agreeable, he went awheel in search of amusement. The bus being indisposed, he went afoot. He rarely made plans in advance; usually was accompanied by some successful telephonee. He rather liked to have a silken skirt beside him fluttering and flirting in the breeze as he broke the speed regulations.

On this Thursday afternoon in July he had timed his morning job to a miraculous nicety so that at the stroke of twelve his workaday garments dropped from him magically, as though he were a male (and reversed) Cinderella. There was a wash room and a rough sort of sleeping room containing two cots situated in the second story of the Ideal Garage. Here Nick shed the loose garments of labour for the fashionably tight habiliments of leisure. Private chauffeurs whose employers housed their cars in the Ideal Garage used this nook for a lounge and smoker. Smitty, Mike, Elmer, and Nick snatched stolen siestas there in the rare absences of the manager. Sometimes Nick spent the night there when forced to work overtime. His home life, at best, was a sketchy affair. Here chauffeurs, mechanics, washers lolled at ease exchanging soft-spoken gossip, motor chat, speculation, comment, and occasional verbal obscenity. Each possessed a formidable knowledge of that neighbourhood section of Chicago known as Hyde Park. This knowledge was not confined to car costs and such impersonal items, but included meals, scandals, relationships, finances, love affairs, quarrels, peccadillos. Here Nick often played his harmonica, his lips sweeping the metal length of it in throbbing rendition of such sure-fire sentimentality as The Long, Long Trail, or Mammy, while the others talked, joked, kept time with tapping feet or wagging heads.

To-day the hot little room was empty except for Nick, shaving before the cracked mirror on the wall, and old Elmer, reading a scrap of yesterday's newspaper as he lounged his noon hour away. Old Elmer was thirty-seven, and Nicky regarded him as an octogenarian. Also, old Elmer's conversation bored Nick to the point of almost sullen resentment. Old Elmer was a family man. His talk was all of his family—the wife, the kids, the flat. A garrulous person, lank, pasty, dish-faced, and amiable. His half day off was invariably spent tinkering about the stuffy little flat—painting, nailing up shelves, mending a broken window shade, puttying a window, playing with his pasty little boy, aged sixteen months, and his pasty little girl, aged three years. Next day he regaled his fellow workers with elaborate recitals of his holiday hours.

"Believe me, that kid's a caution. Sixteen months old, and what does he do yesterday? He unfastens the ketch on the back-porch gate. We got a gate on the back porch, see." (This frequent "see" which interlarded Elmer's verbiage was not used in an interrogatory way, but as a period, and by way of emphasis. His voice did not take the rising inflection as he uttered it.) "What does he do, he opens it. I come home, and the wife says to me: 'Say, you better get busy and fix a new ketch on that gate to the back porch. Little Elmer, first thing I know, he'd got it open to-day and was crawling out almost.' Say, can you beat that for a kid sixteen months—"

Nick had finished shaving, had donned his clean white soft shirt. His soft collar fitted to a miracle about his strong throat. Nick's sartorial effects were a triumph—on forty a week. "Say, can't you talk about nothing but that kid of yours? I bet he's a bum specimen at that. Runt, like his pa."

Elmer flung down his newspaper in honest indignation as Nick had wickedly meant he should. "Is that so! Why, we was wrastling round— me and him, see—last night on the floor, and what does he do, he raises his mitt and hands me a wallop in the stomick it like to knock the wind out of me. That's all. Sixteen months—"

"Yeh. I suppose this time next year he'll be boxing for money."

Elmer resumed his paper. "What do *you* know." His tone mingled pity with contempt.

Nick took a last critical survey of the cracked mirror's reflection and found it good. "Nothing, only this: you make me sick with your kids and your missus and your place. Say, don't you never have no fun?"

"Fun! Why, say, last Sunday we was out to the beach, and the kid swum out first thing you know—"

"Oh, shut up!" He was dressed now. He slapped his pockets. Harmonica. Cigarettes. Matches. Money. He was off, his long-visored cloth cap pulled jauntily over his eyes.

Elmer, bearing no rancour, flung a last idle query: "Where you going?"

"How should I know? Just bumming around. Bus is outa commission, and I'm outa luck."

He clattered down the stairs, whistling.

Next door for a shine at the Greek bootblack's. Enthroned on the dais, a minion at his feet, he was momentarily monarchial. How's the boy? Good? Same here. Down, his brief reign ended. Out into the bright noon-day glare of Fifty-third Street.

A fried-egg sandwich. Two blocks down and into the white-tiled lunchroom. He took his place in the row perched on stools in front of the white slab, his feet on the railing, his elbows on the counter. Four white-aproned vestals with blotchy skins performed rites over the steaming nickel urns, slid dishes deftly along the slick surface of the white slab, mopped up moisture with a sly grey rag. No nonsense about them. This was the rush hour. Hungry men from the shops and offices and garages of the district were bent on food (not badinage). They ate silently, making a dull business of it. Coffee? What kinda pie do you want? No fooling here. "Hello, Jessie."

As she mopped the slab in front of him you noticed a slight softening of her features, intent so grimly on her task. "What's yours?"

"Bacon-and-egg sandwich. Glass of milk. Piece of pie. Blueberry."

Ordinarily she would not have bothered. But with him: "The blueberry ain't so good to-day, I noticed. Try the peach?"

"All right." He looked at her. She smiled. Incredibly, the dishes ordered seemed to leap out at her from nowhere. She crashed them down on the glazed white surface in front of him. The bacon-and-egg sandwich was served open-faced, an elaborate confection. Two slices of white bread, side by side. On one reposed a fried egg, hard, golden, delectable, indigestible. On the other three crisp curls of bacon. The ordinary order held two curls only. A dish so rich in calories as to make it food sufficient for a day. Jessie knew nothing of calories, nor did Nick. She placed a double order of butter before him—two yellow pats, moisture-beaded. As she scooped up his milk from the can you saw that the glass was but three quarters filled. From a deep crock she ladled a smaller scoop and filled the glass to the top. The deep crock held cream. Nick glanced up at her again. Again Jessie smiled. A plain damsel, Jessie, and capable. She went on about her business. What's yours? Coffee with? White or rye? No nonsense about her. And yet: "Pie all right?"

"Yeh. It's good."

She actually blushed.

13

He finished, swung himself off the stool, nodded to Jessie. She stacked his dishes with one lean, capable hand, mopped the slab with the other, but as she made for the kitchen she flung a glance at him over her shoulder.

"Day off?"

"Yeh."

"Some folks has all the luck."

He grinned. His teeth were strong and white and even. He walked toward the door with his light quick step, paused for a toothpick as he paid his check, was out again into the July sunlight. Her face became dull again.

Well, not one o'clock. Guessed he'd shoot a little pool. He dropped into Moriarty's cigar store. It was called a cigar store because it dealt in magazines, newspapers, soft drinks, golf balls, cigarettes, pool, billiards, chocolates, chewing gum, and cigars. In the rear of the store were four green-topped tables, three for pool and one for billiards. He hung about aimlessly, watching the game at the one occupied table. The players were slim young men like himself, their clothes replicas of his own, their faces lean and somewhat hard. Two of them dropped out. Nick took a cue from the rack, shed his tight coat. They played under a glaring electric light in the heat of the day, yet they seemed cool, aloof, immune from bodily discomfort. It was a strangely silent game and as mirthless as that of the elfin bowlers in Rip Van Winkle. The slim-waisted shirted figures bent plastically over the table in the graceful postures of the game. You heard only the click of the balls, an occasional low-voiced exclamation. A solemn crew, and unemotional.

Now and then: "What's all the shootin' fur?"

"In she goes."

Nick, winner, tired of it in less than an hour. He bought a bottle of some acidulous drink just off the ice and refreshed himself with it, drinking from the bottle's mouth. He was vaguely restless, dissatisfied. Out again into the glare of two o'clock Fifty-third Street. He strolled up a block toward Lake Park Avenue. It was hot. He wished the bus wasn't sick. Might go in swimming, though. He considered this idly. Hurried steps behind him. A familiar perfume wafted to his senses. A voice nasal yet cooing. Miss Bauers. Miss Bauers on pleasure bent, palpably, being attired in the briefest of silks, white-strapped slippers, white silk stockings, scarlet hat. The Green Front Grocery and Market closed for a half day each Thursday afternoon during July and August. Nicky had not availed himself of the knowledge.

"Well, if it ain't Nicky! I just seen you come out of Moriarty's as I was passing." (She had seen him go in an hour before and had waited a patient hour in the drug store across the street.) "What you doing around loose this hour the day, anyway?"

"I'm off 'safternoon."

"Are yuh? So'm I." Nicky said nothing. Miss Bauers shifted from one plump silken leg to the other. "What you doing?"

"Oh, nothing much."

"So'm I. Let's do it together." Miss Bauers employed the direct method.

"Well," said Nick, vaguely. He didn't object particularly. And yet he was conscious of some formless programme forming mistily in his mind—a programme that did not include the berouged, be-powdered, plump, and silken Miss Bauers.

"I phoned you this morning, Nicky. Twice."

"Yeh?"

"They said you wasn't in."

"Yeh?"

A hard young woman, Miss Bauers, yet simple: powerfully drawn toward this magnetic and careless boy; powerless to forge chains strong enough to hold him. "Well, how about Riverview? I ain't been this summer."

"Oh, that's so darn far. Take all day getting there, pretty near."

"Not driving, it wouldn't."

"I ain't got the bus. Busted."

His apathy was getting on her nerves. "How about a movie, then?" Her feet hurt. It was hot.

His glance went up the street toward the Harper, down the street toward the Hyde Park. The sign above the Harper offered Mother o' Mine. The lettering above the Hyde Park announced Love's Sacrifice.

"Gawd, no," he made decisive answer.

Miss Bauers's frazzled nerves snapped. "You make me sick! Standing there. Nothing don't suit you. Say, I ain't so crazy to go round with you. Cheap guy! Prob'ly you'd like to go over to Wooded Island or something, in Jackson Park, and set on the grass and feed the squirrels. That'd be a treat for me, that would." She laughed a high, scornful tear-near laugh.

"Why—say—" Nick stared at her, and yet she felt he did not see her. A sudden peace came into his face—the peace of a longing fulfilled. He turned his head. A Lake Park Avenue street car was roaring its way toward them. He took a step toward the roadway. "I got to be going."

Fear flashed its flame into Miss Bauers's pale blue eyes. "Going! How do you mean, going? Going where?"

"I got to be going." The car had stopped opposite them. His young face was stern, implacable. Miss Bauers knew she was beaten, but she clung to hope tenaciously, piteously. "I got to see a party, see?"

"You never said anything about it in the first place. Pity you wouldn't say so in the first place. Who you got to see, anyway?" She knew it was useless to ask. She knew she was beating her fists against a stone wall, but she must needs ask notwithstanding: "Who you got to see?"

"I got to see a party. I forgot." He made the car step in two long strides; had swung himself up. "So long!" The car door slammed after him. Miss Bauers, in her unavailing silks, stood disconsolate on the hot street corner.

He swayed on the car platform until Sixty-third Street was reached. There he alighted and stood a moment at the curb surveying idly the populous corner. He purchased a paper bag of hot peanuts from a vender's glittering scarlet and nickel stand, and crossed the street into the pathway that led to Jackson Park, munching as he went. In an open space reserved for games some boys were playing baseball with much hoarse hooting and frenzied action. He drew near to watch. The ball, misdirected, sailed suddenly toward him. He ran backward at its swift approach, leaped high, caught it, and with a long curving swing, so easy as to appear almost effortless, sent it hurtling back. The lad on the pitcher's mound made as if to catch it, changed his mind, dodged, started after it.

The boy at bat called to Nick: "Heh, you! Wanna come on and pitch?"

Nick shook his head and went on.

He wandered leisurely along the gravel path that led to the park golf shelter. The wide porch was crowded with golfers and idlers. A foursome was teed up at the first tee. Nick leaned against a porch pillar waiting for them to drive. That old boy had pretty good practise swing ... Stiff, though ... Lookit that dame. Je's! I bet she takes fifteen shots before she ever gets on to the green ... There, that kid had pretty good drive. Must of been hundred and fifty, anyway. Pretty good for a kid.

Nick, in the course of his kaleidoscopic career, had been a caddie at thirteen in torn shirt and flapping knickers. He had played the smooth, expert, scornful game of the caddie with a natural swing from the lithe waist and a follow-through that was the envy of the muscle-bound men who watched him. He hadn't played in years. The game no longer interested him. He entered the shelter lunchroom. The counters were lined with lean, brown, hungry men and lean, brown, hungry women. They were eating incredible dishes considering that the hour was 3 P. M. and the day a hot one. Corned-beef hash with a poached egg on top; wieners and potato salad; meat pies; hot roast beef sandwiches; steaming cups of coffee in thick white ware; watermelon. Nick slid a leg over a stool as he had done earlier in the afternoon. Here, too, the Hebes were of stern stuff, as they needs must be to serve these ravenous hordes of club swingers who swarmed upon them from dawn to dusk. Their task it was to wait upon the golfing male, which is man at his simplest—reduced to the least common denominator and shorn of all attraction for the female eye and heart. They represented merely hungry mouths, weary muscles, reaching fists. The waitresses served them as a capable attendant serves another woman's child—efficiently and without emotion.

"Blueberry pie à la mode," said Nick—"with strawberry ice cream."

Inured as she was to the horrors of gastronomic miscegenation, the waitress—an old girl—recoiled at this.

"Say, I don't think you'd like that. They don't mix so very good. Why don't you try the peach pie instead with the strawberry ice cream—if you want strawberry?" He looked so young and cool and fresh.

"Blueberry," repeated Nick sternly, and looked her in the eye. The old waitress laughed a little and was surprised to find herself laughing. "'S for you to say." She brought him the monstrous mixture, and he devoured it to the last chromatic crumb.

"Nothing the matter with that," he remarked as she passed, dish-laden.

She laughed again tolerantly, almost tenderly. "Good thing you're young." Her busy glance lingered a brief moment on his face. He sauntered out.

Now he took the path to the right of the shelter, crossed the road, struck the path again, came to a rustic bridge that humped high in the middle, spanning a cool green stream, willow-bordered. The cool green stream was an emerald chain that threaded its way in a complete circlet about the sylvan spot known as Wooded Island, relic of World's Fair days.

The little island lay, like a thing under enchantment, silent, fragrant, golden, green, exquisite. Squirrels and blackbirds, rabbits and pigeons mingled in AEsopian accord. The air was warm and still, held by the encircling trees and shrubbery. There was not a soul to be seen. At the far north end the two Japanese model houses, survivors of the exposition, gleamed white among the trees.

Nick stood a moment. His eyelids closed, languorously. He stretched his arms out and up deliciously, bringing his stomach in and his chest out. He took off his cap and stuffed it into his pocket. He strolled across the thick cool nap of the grass, deserting the pebble path. At the west edge of the island a sign said: "No One Allowed in the Shrubbery." Ignoring it, Nick parted the branches, stopped and crept, reached the bank that sloped down to the cool green stream, took off his coat, and lay relaxed upon the ground. Above him the tree branches made a pattern against the sky. Little ripples lipped the shore. Scampering velvet-footed things, feathered things, winged things made pleasant stir among the leaves. Nick slept.

He awoke in half an hour refreshed. He lay there, thinking of nothing—a charming gift. He found a stray peanut in his pocket and fed it to a friendly squirrel. His hand encountered the cool metal of his harmonica. He drew out the instrument, placed his coat, folded, under his head, crossed his knees, one leg swinging idly, and began to play rapturously. He was perfectly happy. He played Gimme Love, whose jazz measures are stolen from Mendelssohn's Spring Song. He did not know this. The leaves rustled. He did not turn his head.

"Hello, Pan!" said a voice. A girl came down the slope and seated herself beside him. She was not smiling.

Nick removed the harmonica from his lips and wiped his mouth with the back of his hand. "Hello who?"

"Hello, Pan."

"Wrong number, lady," Nick said, and again applied his lips to the mouth organ. The girl laughed then, throwing back her head. Her throat was long and slim and brown. She clasped her knees with her arms and looked at Nick amusedly. Nick thought she was a kind of homely little thing.

"Pan," she explained, "was a pagan deity. He played pipes in the woods."

"'S all right with me," Nick ventured, bewildered but amiable. He wished she'd go away. But she didn't. She began to take off her shoes and stockings. She went down to the water's edge, then, and paddled her feet. Nick sat up, outraged. "Say, you can't do that."

She glanced back at him over her shoulder. "Oh, yes, I can. It's so hot." She wriggled her toes ecstatically.

The leaves rustled again, briskly, unmistakably this time. A heavy tread. A rough voice. "Say, looka here! Get out of there, you! What the—" A policeman, red-faced, wroth. "You can't do that! Get outa here!"

It was like a movie, Nick thought.

The girl turned her head. "Oh, now, Mr. Elwood," she said.

"Oh, it's you, miss," said the policeman. You would not have believed it could be the same policeman. He even giggled. "Thought you was away."

"I was. In fact, I am, really. I just got sick of it and ran away for a day. Drove. Alone. The family'll be wild."

"All the way?" said the policeman, incredulously. "Say, I thought that looked like your car standing out there by the road; but I says no, she ain't in town." He looked sharply at Nick, whose face had an Indian composure, though his feelings were mixed. "Who's this?"

"He's a friend of mine. His name's Pan." She was drying her feet with an inadequate rose-coloured handkerchief. She crept crabwise up the bank, and put on her stockings and slippers.

"Why'n't you come out and set on a bench?" suggested the police-man, worriedly.

The girl shook her head. "In Arcadia we don't sit on benches. I should think you'd know that. Go on away, there's a dear. I want to talk to this—to Pan."

He persisted. "What'd your pa say, I'd like to know!" The girl shrugged her shoulders. Nick made as though to rise. He was worried. A nut, that's what. She pressed him down again with a hard brown hand.

"Now it's all right. He's going. Old Fuss!" The policeman stood a brief moment longer. Then the foliage rustled again. He was gone. The girl sighed, happily. "Play that thing some more, will you? You're a wiz at it, aren't you?"

"I'm pretty good," said Nick, modestly. Then the outrageousness of her conduct struck him afresh. "Say, who're you, anyway?"

"My name's Berry—short for Bernice.... What's yours, Pan?"

"Nick—that is—Nick."

"Ugh, terrible! I'll stick to Pan. What d'you do when you're not Pan-ning?" Then, at the bewilderment in his face: "What's your job?"

"I work in the Ideal Garage. Say, you're pretty nosey, ain't you?"

"Yes, pretty.... That accounts for your nails, h'm?" She looked at her own brown paws. "'Bout as bad as mine. I drove one hundred and fifty miles to-day."

"Ya-as, you did!"

"I did! Started at six. And I'll probably drive back to-night."

"You're crazy!"

"I know it," she agreed, "and it's wonderful.... Can you play the Tommy Toddle?"

"Yeh. It's kind of hard, though, where the runs are. I don't get the runs so very good." He played it. She kept time with head and feet. When he had finished and wiped his lips:

"Elegant!" She took the harmonica from him, wiped it brazenly on the much-abused, rose-coloured handkerchief and began to play, her cheeks puffed out, her eyes round with effort. She played the Tommy Toddle, and her runs were perfect. Nick's chagrin was swallowed by his admiration and envy.

"Say, kid, you got more wind than a factory whistle. Who learned you to play?"

She struck her chest with a hard brown fist. "Tennis ... Tim taught me."

"Who's Tim?"

"The—a chauffeur."

Nick leaned closer. "Say, do you ever go to the dances at Englewood Masonic Hall?"

"I never have."

"'Jah like to go some time?"

"I'd love it." She grinned up at him, her teeth flashing white in her brown face.

"It's swell here," he said, dreamily. "Like the woods?"

"Yes."

"Winter, when it's cold and dirty, I think about how it's here summers. It's like you could take it out of your head and look at it whenever you wanted to."

"Endymion."

"Huh?"

"A man said practically the same thing the other day. Name of Keats."

"Yeh?"

"He said: 'A thing of beauty is a joy forever.'"

"That's one way putting it," he agreed, graciously.

Unsmilingly she reached over with one slim forefinger, as if compelled, and touched the blond hairs on Nick's wrist. Just touched them. Nick remained motionless. The girl shivered a little, deliciously. She glanced at him shyly. Her lips were provocative. Thoughtlessly, blindly, Nick suddenly flung an arm about her, kissed her. He kissed her as he had never kissed Miss Bauers—as he had never kissed Miss Ahearn, Miss Olson, or just Gertie. The girl did not scream, or push him away, or slap him, or protest, or giggle as would have the above-mentioned young ladies. She sat breathing rather fast, a tinge of scarlet showing beneath the tan.

"Well, Pan," she said, low-voiced, "you're running true to form, any-way." She eyed him appraisingly. "Your appeal is in your virility, I sup-pose. Yes."

"My what?"

She rose. "I've got to go."

Panic seized him. "Say, don't drive back to-night, huh? Wherever it is you've got to go. You ain't driving back to-night?"

She made no answer; parted the bushes, was out on the gravel path in the sunlight, a slim, short-skirted, almost childish figure. He fol-lowed. They crossed the bridge, left the island, reached the roadway almost in silence. At the side of the road was a roadster. Its hood was the kind that conceals power. Its lamps were two giant eyes rimmed in precious metal. Its line spelled strength. Its body was foreign. Nick's engine-wise eyes saw these things at a glance.

"That your car?"

"Yes."

"Gosh!"

She unlocked it, threw in the clutch, shifted, moved. "Say!" was wrung from Nick helplessly. She waved at him. "Good-bye, Pan." He stared, stricken. She was off swiftly, silently; flashed around a corner; was hidden by the trees and shrubs.

He stood a moment. He felt bereaved, cheated. Then a little wave of exaltation shook him. He wanted to talk to someone. "Gosh!" he said again. He glanced at his wrist. Five-thirty. He guessed he'd go home. He guessed he'd go home and get one of Ma's dinners. One of Ma's din-ners and talk to Ma. The Sixty-third Street car. He could make it and back in plenty time.

Nick lived in that section of Chicago known as Englewood, which is not so sylvan as it sounds, but appropriate enough for a faun. Not only that; he lived in S. Green Street, Englewood. S. Green Street, near Seventieth, is almost rural with its great elms and poplars, its frame cottages, its back gardens. A neighbourhood of thrifty, foreign-born fa-thers and mothers, many children, tree-lined streets badly paved. Nick turned in at a two-story brown frame cottage. He went around to the back. Ma was in the kitchen.

Nick's presence at the evening meal was an uncertain thing. Sometimes he did not eat at home for a week, excepting only his hurried early breakfast. He rarely spent an evening at home, and when he did used the opportunity for making up lost sleep. Pa never got home from work until after six. Nick liked his dinner early and hot. On his rare visits his mother welcomed him like one of the Gracchi. Mother and son understood each other wordlessly, having much in common. You would not have thought it of her (forty-six bust, forty waist, measureless hips), but Ma was a nymph at heart. Hence Nick.

"Hello, Ma!" She was slamming expertly about the kitchen.

"Hello, yourself," said Ma. Ma had a line of slang gleaned from her numerous brood. It fell strangely from her lips. Ma had never quite lost a tinge of foreign accent, though she had come to America when a girl. A hearty, zestful woman, savouring life with gusto, undiminished by child-bearing and hard work. "Eating home, Dewey?" She alone used his given name.

"Yeh, but I gotta be back by seven-thirty. Got anything ready?"

"Dinner ain't, but I'll get you something. Plenty. Platter ham and eggs and a quick fry. Cherry cobbler's done. I'll fix you some." (Cherry cobbler is shortcake with a soul.)

He ate enormously at the kitchen table, she hovering over him.

"What's the news, Dewey?"

"Ain't none." He ate in silence. Then: "How old was you when you married Pa?"

"Me? Say, I wasn't no more'n a kid. I gotta laugh when I think of it."

"What was Pa earning?"

She laughed a great hearty laugh, dipping a piece of bread sociably in the ham fat on the platter as she stood by the table, just to bear him company.

"Say, earn! If he'd of earned what you was earning now, we'd of thought we was millionaires. Time Etty was born he was pulling down thirteen a week, and we saved on it." She looked at him suddenly, sharply. "Why?"

"Oh, I was just wondering."

"Look what good money he's getting now! If I was you, I wouldn't stick around no old garage for what they give you. You could get a good job in the works with Pa; first thing you know you'd be pulling down big money. You're smart like that with engines.... Takes a lot of money nowadays for feller to get married."

"You *tell* 'em," agreed Nick. He looked up at her, having finished eating. His glance was almost tender. "How'd you come to marry Pa, anyway? You and him's so different."

The nymph in Ma leaped to the surface and stayed there a moment, sparkling, laughing, dimpling. "Oh, I dunno. I kept running away and he kept running after. Like that."

He looked up again quickly at that. "Yeh. That's it. Fella don't like to have no girl chasing him all the time. Say, he likes to do the chasing himself. Ain't that the truth?"

"You *tell* 'em!" agreed Ma. A great jovial laugh shook her. Heavy-footed now, but light of heart.

Suddenly: "I'm thinking of going to night school. Learn something. I don't know nothing."

"You do, too, Dewey!"

"Aw, wha'd I know? I never had enough schooling. Wished I had."

"Who's doings was it? You wouldn't stay. Wouldn't go no more than sixth reader and quit. Nothing wouldn't get you to go."

He agreed gloomily. "I know it. I don't know what nothing is. Uh—Arcadia—or—now—vitality or nothing."

"Oh, that comes easy," she encouraged him, "when you begin once."

He reached for her hand gratefully. "You're a swell cook, Ma." He had a sudden burst of generosity, of tenderness. "Soon's the bus is fixed I'll take you joy-riding over to the lake."

Ma always wore a boudoir cap of draggled lace and ribbon for motoring. Nick almost never offered her a ride. She did not expect him to.

She pushed him playfully. "Go on! You got plenty young girls to take riding, not your ma."

"Oh, girls!" he said, scornfully. Then in another tone: "Girls."

He was off. It was almost seven. Pa was late. He caught a car back to Fifty-third Street. Elmer was lounging in the cool doorway of the garage. Nick, in sheer exuberance of spirits, squared off, doubled his fists, and danced about Elmer in a semicircle, working his arms as a prizefighter does, warily. He jabbed at Elmer's jaw playfully.

"What you been doing," inquired that long-suffering gentleman, "makes you feel so good? Where you been?"

"Oh, nowheres. Bumming round. Park."

He turned in the direction of the stairway. Elmer lounged after him. "Oh, say, dame's been calling you for the last hour and a half. Like to busted the phone. Makes me sick."

"Aw, Bauers."

"No, that wasn't the name. Name's Mary or Berry, or something like that. A dozen times, I betcha. Says you was to call her as soon as you come in. Drexel 47—wait a min't'—yeh—that's right—Drexel 473—"

"Swell chanst," said Nick. Suddenly his buoyancy was gone. His shoulders drooped. His cigarette dangled limp. Disappointment curved his lips, burdened his eyes. "*Swell* chanst!"

OLD MAN MINICK

His wife had always spoiled him outrageously. No doubt of that. Take, for example, the matter of the pillows merely. Old man Minick slept high. That is, he thought he slept high. He liked two plump pillows on his side of the great, wide, old-fashioned cherry bed. He would sink into them with a vast grunting and sighing and puffing expressive of nerves and muscles relaxed and gratified. But in the morning there was always one pillow on the floor. He had thrown it there. Always, in the morning, there it lay, its plump white cheek turned reproachfully up at him from the side of the bed. Ma Minick knew this, naturally, after forty years of the cherry bed. But she never begrudged him that extra pillow. Each morning, when she arose, she picked it up on her way to shut the window. Each morning the bed was made up with two pillows on his side of it, as usual.

Then there was the window. Ma Minick liked it open wide. Old man Minick, who rather prided himself on his modernism (he called it being up to date) was distrustful of the night air. In the folds of its sable mantle lurked a swarm of dread things—colds, clammy miasmas, fevers.

"Night air's just like any other air," Ma Minick would say, with some asperity. Ma Minick was no worm; and as modern as he. So when they went to bed the window would be open wide. They would lie there, the two old ones, talking comfortably about commonplace things. The kind of talk that goes on between a man and a woman who have lived together in wholesome peace (spiced with occasional wholesome bickerings) for more than forty years.

"Remind me to see Gerson to-morrow about that lock on the basement door. The paper's full of burglars."

"If I think of it." She never failed to.

"George and Nettie haven't been over in a week now."

"Oh, well, young folks.... Did you stop in and pay that Koritz the fifty cents for pressing your suit?"

"By golly, I forgot again! First thing in the morning."

A sniff. "Just smell the Yards." It was Chicago.

"Wind must be from the west."

Sleep came with reluctant feet, but they wooed her patiently. And presently she settled down between them and they slept lightly. Usually, some time during the night, he awoke, slid cautiously and with infinite stealth from beneath the covers and closed the wide-flung window to within a bare two inches of the sill. Almost invariably she heard him; but she was a wise old woman; a philosopher of parts. She knew better than to allow a window to shatter the peace of their marital felicity. As she lay there, smiling a little grimly in the dark and giving no sign of being awake, she thought, "Oh, well, I guess a closed window won't kill me either."

Still, sometimes, just to punish him a little, and to prove that she was nobody's fool, she would wait until he had dropped off to sleep again and then she, too, would achieve a stealthy trip to the window and would raise it slowly, carefully, inch by inch.

"How did that window come to be open?" he would say in the morning, being a poor dissembler.

"Window? Why, it's just the way it was when we went to bed." And she would stoop to pick up the pillow that lay on the floor.

There was little or no talk of death between this comfortable, active, sound-appearing man of almost seventy and this plump capable woman of sixty-six. But as always, between husband and wife, it was understood wordlessly (and without reason) that old man Minick would go first. Not that either of them had the slightest intention of going. In fact, when it happened they were planning to spend the winter in California and perhaps live there indefinitely if they liked it and didn't get too lonesome for George and Nettie, and the Chicago smoke, and Chicago noise, and Chicago smells and rush and dirt. Still, the solid sum paid yearly in insurance premiums showed clearly that he meant to leave her in comfort and security. Besides, the world is full of widows. Everyone sees that. But how many widowers? Few. Widows there are by the thousands; living alone; living in hotels; living with married daughters and sons-in-law or married sons and daughters-in-law. But of widowers in a like situation there are bewilderingly few. And why this should be no one knows.

So, then. The California trip never materialized. And the year that followed never was quite clear in old man Minick's dazed mind. In the first place, it was the year in which stocks tumbled and broke their backs. Gilt-edged securities showed themselves to be tinsel. Old man Minick had retired from active business just one year before, meaning to live comfortably on the fruit of a half-century's toil. He now saw that fruit rotting all about him. There was in it hardly enough nourishment to sustain them. Then came the day when Ma Minick went downtown to see Matthews about that pain right here and came home looking shrivelled, talking shrilly about nothing, and evading Pa's eyes. Followed months that were just a jumble of agony, X-rays, hope, despair, morphia, nothingness.

After it was all over: "But I was going first," old man Minick said, dazedly.

The old house on Ellis near Thirty-ninth was sold for what it would bring. George, who knew Chicago real-estate if any one did, said they might as well get what they could. Things would only go lower. You'll see. And nobody's going to have any money for years. Besides, look at the neighbourhood!

Old man Minick said George was right. He said everybody was right. You would hardly have recognized in this shrunken figure and wattled face the spruce and dressy old man whom Ma Minick used to spoil so delightfully. "You know best, George. You know best." He who used to stand up to George until Ma Minick was moved to say, "Now, Pa, you don't know everything."

After Matthews' bills, and the hospital, and the nurses and the medicines and the thousand and one things were paid there was left exactly five hundred dollars a year.

"You're going to make your home with us, Father," George and Nettie said. Alma, too, said this would be the best. Alma, the married daughter, lived in Seattle. "Though you know Ferd and I would be only too glad to have you."

Seattle! The ends of the earth. Oh, no. No! he protested, every fibre of his old frame clinging to the accustomed. Seattle, at seventy! He turned piteous eyes on his son George and his daughter-in-law Nettie. "You're going to make your home with us, Father," they reassured him. He clung to them gratefully. After it was over Alma went home to her husband and their children.

So now he lived with George and Nettie in the five-room flat on South Park Avenue, just across from Washington Park. And there was no extra pillow on the floor.

Nettie hadn't said he couldn't have the extra pillow. He had told her he used two and she had given him two the first week. But every morning she had found a pillow cast on the floor.

"I thought you used two pillows, Father."

"I do."

"But there's always one on the floor when I make the bed in the morning. You always throw one on the floor. You only sleep on one pillow, really."

"I use two pillows."

But the second week there was one pillow. He tossed and turned a good deal there in his bedroom off the kitchen. But he got used to it in time. Not used to it, exactly, but—well—

The bedroom off the kitchen wasn't as menial as it sounds. It was really rather cosy. The five-room flat held living room, front bedroom, dining room, kitchen, and maid's room. The room off the kitchen was intended as a maid's room but Nettie had no maid. George's business had suffered with the rest. George and Nettie had said, "I wish there was a front room for you, Father. You could have ours and we'd move back here, only this room's too small for twin beds and the dressing table and the chiffonier." They had meant it—or meant to mean it.

"This is fine," old man Minick had said. "This is good enough for anybody." There was a narrow white enamel bed and a tiny dresser and a table. Nettie had made gay cretonne covers and spreads and put a little reading lamp on the table and arranged his things. Ma Minick's picture on the dresser with her mouth sort of pursed to make it look small. It wasn't a recent picture. Nettie and George had had it framed for him as a surprise. They had often urged her to have a picture taken, but she had dreaded it. Old man Minick didn't think much of that photograph, though he never said so. He needed no photograph of Ma Minick. He had a dozen of them; a gallery of them; thousands of them. Lying on his one pillow he could take them out and look at them one by one as they passed in review, smiling, serious, chiding, praising, there in the dark. He needed no picture on his dresser.

A handsome girl, Nettie, and a good girl. He thought of her as a girl, though she was well past thirty. George and Nettie had married late. This was only the third year of their marriage. Alma, the daughter, had married young, but George had stayed on, unwed, in the old house on Ellis until he was thirty-six and all Ma Minick's friends' daughters had had a try at him in vain. The old people had urged him to marry, but it had been wonderful to have him around the house, just the same.

Somebody young around the house. Not that George had stayed around very much. But when he was there you knew he was there. He whistled while dressing. He sang in the bath. He roared down the stairway, "Ma, where's my clean shirts?" The telephone rang for him. Ma Minick prepared special dishes for him. The servant girl said, "Oh, now, Mr. George, look what you've done! Gone and spilled the grease all over my clean kitchen floor!" and wiped it up adoringly while George laughed and gobbled his bit of food filched from pot or frying pan.

They had been a little surprised about Nettie. George was in the bond business and she worked for the same firm. A plump, handsome, eye-glassed woman with fine fresh colouring, a clear skin that old man Minick called appetizing, and a great coil of smooth dark hair. She wore plain tailored things and understood the bond business in a way that might have led you to think hers a masculine mind if she hadn't been so feminine, too, in her manner. Old man Minick had liked her better than Ma Minick had.

Nettie had called him Pop and joked with him and almost flirted with him in a daughterly sort of way. He liked to squeeze her plump arm and pinch her soft cheek between thumb and forefinger. She would laugh up at him and pat his shoulder and that shoulder would straighten spryly and he would waggle his head doggishly.

"Look out there, George!" the others in the room would say. "Your dad'll cut you out. First thing you know you'll lose your girl, that's all."

Nettie would smile. Her teeth were white and strong and even. Old man Minick would laugh and wink, immensely pleased and flattered. "We understand each other, don't we, Pop?" Nettie would say.

During the first years of their married life Nettie stayed home. She fussed happily about her little flat, gave parties, went to parties, played bridge. She seemed to love the ease, the relaxation, the small luxuries. She and George were very much in love. Before her marriage she had lived in a boarding house on Michigan Avenue. At mention of it now she puckered up her face. She did not attempt to conceal her fondness for these five rooms of hers, so neat, so quiet, so bright, so cosy. Overstuffed velvet in the living room, with silk lampshades, and small tables holding books and magazines and little boxes containing cigarettes or hard candies. Very modern. A gate-legged table in the dining room. Caramel-coloured walnut in the bedroom, rich and dark and smooth. She loved it. An orderly woman. Everything in its place. Before eleven o'clock the little apartment was shining, spotless; cushions plumped, crumbs brushed, vegetables in cold water. The telephone. "Hello!... Oh, hello, Bess! Oh, hours ago ... Not a thing ... Well, if George is willing ... I'll call him up and ask him. We haven't seen a show in two weeks. I'll call you back within the next half hour ... No, I haven't done my marketing yet.... Yes, and have dinner downtown. Meet at seven."

Into this orderly smooth-running mechanism was catapulted a bewildered old man. She no longer called him Pop. He never dreamed of squeezing the plump arm or pinching the smooth cheek. She called him Father. Sometimes George's Father. Sometimes, when she was telephoning, there came to him—"George's father's living with us now, you know. I can't."

They were very kind to him, Nettie and George. "Now just you sit right down here, Father. What do you want to go poking off into your own room for?"

He remembered that in the last year Nettie had said something about going back to work. There wasn't enough to do around the house to keep her busy. She was sick of afternoon parties. Sew and eat, that's all, and gossip, or play bridge. Besides, look at the money. Business was awful. The two old people had resented this idea as much as George had—more, in fact. They were scandalized.

"Young folks nowdays!" shaking their heads. "Young folks nowdays. What are they thinking of! In my day when you got married you had babies."

George and Nettie had had no babies. At first Nettie had said, "I'm so happy. I just want a chance to rest. I've been working since I was seventeen. I just want to rest, first." One year. Two years. Three. And now Pa Minick.

Ma Minick, in the old house on Ellis Avenue, had kept a loose sort of larder; not lavish, but plentiful. They both ate a great deal, as old people are likely to do. Old man Minick, especially, had liked to nibble. A handful of raisins from the box on the shelf. A couple of nuts from the dish on the sideboard. A bit of candy rolled beneath the tongue. At dinner (sometimes, toward the last, even at noon-time) a plate of steaming soup, hot, revivifying, stimulating. Plenty of this and plenty of that. "What's the matter, Jo? You're not eating." But he was, amply. Ma Minick had liked to see him eat too much. She was wrong, of course.

But at Nettie's things were different. Hers was a sufficient but stern ménage. So many mouths to feed; just so many lamb chops. Nettie knew about calories and vitamines and mysterious things like that, and talked about them. So many calories in this. So many calories in that. He never was quite clear in his mind about these things said to be lurking in his food. He had always thought of spinach as spinach, chops as chops. But to Nettie they were calories. They lunched together, these two. George was, of course, downtown. For herself Nettie would have one of those feminine pick-up lunches; a dab of apple sauce, a cup of tea, and a slice of cold toast left from breakfast. This she would eat while old man Minick guiltily supped up his cup of warmed-over broth, or his coddled egg. She always pressed upon him any bit of cold meat that was left from the night before, or any remnants of vegetable or spaghetti. Often there was quite a little fleet of saucers and sauce plates grouped about his main plate. Into these he dipped and swooped uncomfortably, and yet with a relish. Sometimes, when he had finished, he would look about, furtively.

"What'll you have, Father? Can I get you something?"

"Nothing, Nettie, nothing. I'm doing fine." She had finished the last of her wooden toast and was waiting for him, kindly.

Still, this balanced and scientific fare seemed to agree with him. As the winter went on he seemed actually to have regained most of his former hardiness and vigour. A handsome old boy he was, ruddy, hale, with the zest of a juicy old apple, slightly withered but still sappy. It should be mentioned that he had a dimple in his cheek which flashed unexpectedly when he smiled. It gave him a roguish—almost boyish— effect most appealing to the beholder. Especially the feminine beholder. Much of his spoiling at the hands of Ma Minick had doubtless been due to this mere depression of the skin.

Spring was to bring a new and welcome source of enrichment into his life. But these first six months of his residence with George and Nettie were hard. No spoiling there. He missed being made much of. He got kindness, but he needed love. Then, too, he was rather a gabby old man. He liked to hold forth. In the old house on Ellis there had been visiting back and forth between men and women of his own age, and Ma's. At these gatherings he had waxed oratorical or argumentative, and they had heard him, some in agreement, some in disagreement, but always respectfully, whether he prated of real estate or social depravity; prohibition or European exchange.

"Let me tell you, here and now, something's got to be done before you can get a country back on a sound financial basis. Why, take Russia alone, why ..." Or: "Young people nowdays! They don't know what respect means. I tell you there's got to be a change and there will be, and it's the older generation that's got to bring it about. What do they know of hardship! What do they know about work—real work. Most of 'em's never done a real day's work in their life. All they think of is dancing and gambling and drinking. Look at the way they dress! Look at ..."

Ad lib.

"That's so," the others would agree. "I was saying only yesterday ..."

Then, too, until a year or two before, he had taken active part in business. He had retired only at the urging of Ma and the children. They said he ought to rest and play and enjoy himself.

Now, as his strength and good spirits gradually returned he began to go downtown, mornings. He would dress, carefully, though a little shakily. He had always shaved himself and he kept this up. All in all, during the day, he occupied the bathroom literally for hours, and this annoyed Nettie to the point of frenzy, though she said nothing. He liked the white cheerfulness of the little tiled room. He puddled about in the water endlessly. Snorted and splashed and puffed and snuffled and blew. He was one of those audible washers who emerge dripping and whose ablutions are distributed impartially over ceiling, walls, and floor.

Nettie, at the closed door: "Father, are you all right?"

Splash! Prrrf! "Yes. Sure. I'm all right."

"Well, I didn't know. You've been in there so long."

He was a neat old man, but there was likely to be a spot or so on his vest or his coat lapel, or his tie. Ma used to remove these, on or off him, as the occasion demanded, rubbing carefully and scolding a little, making a chiding sound between tongue and teeth indicative of great impatience of his carelessness. He had rather enjoyed these sounds, and this rubbing and scratching on the cloth with the fingernail and a moistened rag. They indicated that someone cared. Cared about the way he looked. Had pride in him. Loved him. Nettie never removed spots. Though infrequently she said, "Father, just leave that suit out, will you? I'll send it to the cleaner's with George's. The man's coming to-morrow morning." He would look down at himself, hastily, and attack a spot here and there with a futile fingernail.

His morning toilette completed, he would make for the Fifty-first Street L. Seated in the train he would assume an air of importance and testy haste; glance out of the window; look at his watch. You got the impression of a handsome and well-preserved old gentleman on his way downtown to consummate a shrewd business deal. He had been familiar with Chicago's downtown for fifty years and he could remember when State Street was a tree-shaded cottage district. The noise and rush and clangour of the Loop had long been familiar to him. But now he seemed to find the downtown trip arduous, even hazardous. The roar of the elevated trains, the hoarse hoots of the motor horns, the clang of the street cars, the bedlam that is Chicago's downtown district bewildered him, frightened him almost. He would skip across the street like a harried hare, just missing a motor truck's nose and all unconscious of the stream of invective directed at him by its charioteer. "Heh! Whatcha!... Look!"—Sometimes a policeman came to his aid, or attempted to, but he resented this proffered help.

"Say, look here, my lad," he would say to the tall, tired, and not at all burly (standing on one's feet directing traffic at Wabash and Madison for eight hours a day does not make for burliness) policeman, "I've been coming downtown since long before you were born. You don't need to help me. I'm no jay from the country."

He visited the Stock Exchange. This depressed him. Stocks were lower than ever and still going down. His five hundred a year was safe, but the rest seemed doomed for his lifetime, at least. He would drop in at George's office. George's office was pleasantly filled with dapper, neat young men and (surprisingly enough) dapper, slim young women, seated at desks in the big light-flooded room. At one corner of each desk stood a polished metal placard on a little standard, and bearing the name of the desk's occupant. Mr. Owens. Mr. Satterlee. Mr. James. Miss Rauch. Mr. Minick.

"Hello, Father," Mr. Minick would say, looking annoyed. "What's bringing you down?"

"Oh, nothing. Nothing. Just had a little business to tend to over at the Exchange. Thought I'd drop in. How's business?"

"Rotten."

"I should think it was!" Old man Minick would agree. "I—should—think—it—was! Hm."

George wished he wouldn't. He couldn't have it, that's all. Old man Minick would stroll over to the desk marked Satterlee, or Owens, or James. These brisk young men would toss an upward glance at him and concentrate again on the sheets and files before them. Old man Minick would stand, balancing from heel to toe and blowing out his breath a little. He looked a bit yellow and granulated and wavering, there in the cruel morning light of the big plate glass windows. Or perhaps it was the contrast he presented with these slim, slick young salesmen.

"Well, h'are you to-day, Mr.—uh—Satterlee? What's the good word?"

Mr. Satterlee would not glance up this time. "I'm pretty well. Can't complain."

"Good. Good."

"Anything I can do for you?"

"No-o-o. No. Not a thing. Just dropped in to see my son a minute."

"I see." Not unkindly. Then, as old man Minick still stood there, balancing, Mr. Satterlee would glance up again, frowning a little. "Your son's desk is over there, I believe. Yes."

George and Nettie had a bedtime conference about these visits and Nettie told him, gently, that the bond house head objected to friends and relatives dropping in. It was against office rules. It had been so when she was employed there. Strictly business. She herself had gone there only once since her marriage.

Well, that was all right. Business was like that nowdays. Rush and grab and no time for anything.

The winter was a hard one, with a record snowfall and intense cold. He stayed indoors for days together. A woman of his own age in like position could have occupied herself usefully and happily. She could have hemmed a sash-curtain; knitted or crocheted; tidied a room; taken a hand in the cooking or preparing of food; ripped an old gown; made over a new one; indulged in an occasional afternoon festivity with women of her own years. But for old man Minick there were no small tasks. There was nothing he could do to make his place in the household justifiable. He wasn't even particularly good at those small jobs of hammering, or painting, or general "fixing." Nettie could drive a nail more swiftly, more surely than he. "Now, Father, don't you bother. I'll do it. Just you go and sit down. Isn't it time for your afternoon nap?"

He waxed a little surly. "Nap! I just got up. I don't want to sleep my life away."

George and Nettie frequently had guests in the evening. They played bridge, or poker, or talked.

"Come in, Father," George would say. "Come in. You all know Dad, don't you, folks?" He would sit down, uncertainly. At first he had attempted to expound, as had been his wont in the old house on Ellis. "I want to say, here and now, that this country's got to ..." But they went on, heedless of him. They interrupted or refused, politely, to listen. So he sat in the room, yet no part of it. The young people's talk swirled and eddied all about him. He was utterly lost in it. Now and then Nettie or George would turn to him and with raised voice (he was not at all deaf and prided himself on it) would shout, "It's about this or that, Father. He was saying ..."

When the group roared with laughter at a sally from one of them he would smile uncertainly but amiably, glancing from one to the other in complete ignorance of what had passed, but not resenting it. He took to sitting more and more in his kitchen bedroom, smoking a comforting pipe and reading and re-reading the evening paper. During that winter he and Canary, the negro washwoman, became quite good friends. She washed down in the basement once a week but came up to the kitchen for her massive lunch. A walrus-waisted black woman, with a rich throaty voice, a rolling eye, and a kindly heart. He actually waited for her appearance above the laundry stairs.

"Weh, how's Mist' Minick to-day! Ah nev' did see a gemun spry's you ah fo' yo' age. No, suh! nev' did."

At this rare praise he would straighten his shoulders and waggle his head. "I'm worth any ten of these young sprats to-day." Canary would throw back her head in a loud and companionable guffaw.

Nettie would appear at the kitchen swinging door. "Canary's having her lunch, Father. Don't you want to come into the front room with me? We'll have our lunch in another half-hour." He followed her obediently enough. Nettie thought of him as a troublesome and rather pathetic child—a child who would never grow up. If she attributed any thoughts to that fine old head they were ambling thoughts, bordering, perhaps, on senility. Little did she know how expertly this old one surveyed her and how ruthlessly he passed judgment. She never suspected the thoughts that formed in the active brain.

He knew about women. He had married a woman. He had had children by her. He looked at this woman—his son's wife—moving about her little five-room flat. She had theories about children. He had heard her expound them. You didn't have them except under such and such circumstances. It wasn't fair otherwise. Plenty of money for their education. Well. He and his wife had had three children. Paul, the second, had died at thirteen. A blow, that had been. They had not always planned for the coming of the three but they always had found a way, afterward. You managed, somehow, once the little wrinkled red ball had fought its way into the world. You managed. You managed. Look at George! Yet when he was born, thirty-nine years ago, Pa and Ma Minick had been hard put to it.

Sitting there, while Nettie dismissed him as negligible, he saw her clearly, grimly. He looked at her. She was plump, but not too short, with a generous width between the hips; a broad full bosom, but firm; round arms and quick slim legs; a fine sturdy throat. The curve between arm and breast made a graceful gracious line ... Working in a bond office ...

35

Working in a bond office ... There was nothing in the Bible about working in a bond office. Here was a woman built for child-bearing.

She thought him senile, negligible.

In March Nettie had in a sewing woman for a week. She had her two or three times a year. A hawk-faced woman of about forty-nine, with a blue-bottle figure and a rapacious eye. She sewed in the dining room and there was a pleasant hum of machine and snip of scissors and murmur of conversation and rustle of silky stuff; and hot savoury dishes for lunch. She and old man Minick became great friends. She even let him take out bastings. This when Nettie had gone out from two to four, between fittings.

He chuckled and waggled his head. "I expect to be paid regular assistant's wages for this," he said.

"I guess you don't need any wages, Mr. Minick," the woman said. "I guess you're pretty well fixed."

"Oh, well, I can't complain." (Five hundred a year.)

"Complain! I should say not! If I was to complain it'd be different. Work all day to keep myself; and nobody to come home to at night."

"Widow, ma'am?"

"Since I was twenty. Work, work, that's all I've had. And lonesome! I suppose you don't know what lonesome is."

"Oh, don't I!" slipped from him. He had dropped the bastings.

The sewing woman flashed a look at him from the cold hard eye. "Well, maybe you do. I suppose living here like this, with sons and daughters, ain't so grand, for all your money. Now me, I've always managed to keep my own little place that I could call home, to come back to. It's only two rooms, and nothing to rave about, but it's home. Evenings I just cook and fuss around. Nobody to fuss for, but I fuss, anyway. Cooking, that's what I love to do. Plenty of good food, that's what folks need to keep their strength up." Nettie's lunch that day had been rather scant.

She was there a week. In Nettie's absence she talked against her. He protested, but weakly. Did she give him egg-nogs? Milk? Hot toddy? Soup? Plenty of good rich gravy and meat and puddings? Well! That's what folks needed when they weren't so young any more. Not that he looked old. My, no. Sprier than many young boys, and handsomer than his own son if she did say so.

He fed on it, hungrily. The third day she was flashing meaning glances at him across the luncheon table. The fourth she pressed his foot beneath the table. The fifth, during Nettie's afternoon absence, she got up, ostensibly to look for a bit of cloth which she needed for sewing, and, passing him, laid a caressing hand on his shoulder. Laid it there and pressed his shoulder ever so little. He looked up, startled. The glances across the luncheon had largely passed over his head; the foot beneath the table might have been an accident. But this—this was unmistakable. He stood up, a little shakily. She caught his hand. The hawk-like face was close to his.

"You need somebody to love you," she said. "Somebody to do for you, and love you." The hawk face came nearer. He leaned a little toward it. But between it and his face was Ma Minick's face, plump, patient, quizzical, kindly. His head came back sharply. He threw the woman's hot hand from him.

"Woman!" he cried. "Jezebel!"

The front door slammed. Nettie. The woman flew to her sewing. Old man Minick, shaking, went into his kitchen bedroom.

"Well," said Nettie, depositing her bundles on the dining room table, "did you finish that faggoting? Why, you haven't done so very much, have you!"

"I ain't feeling so good," said the woman. "That lunch didn't agree with me."

"Why, it was a good plain lunch. I don't see—"

"Oh, it was plain enough, all right."

Next day she did not come to finish her work. Sick, she telephoned. Nettie called it an outrage. She finished the sewing herself, though she hated sewing. Pa Minick said nothing, but there was a light in his eye. Now and then he chuckled, to Nettie's infinite annoyance, though she said nothing.

"Wanted to marry me!" he said to himself, chuckling. "Wanted to marry me! The old rip!"

At the end of April, Pa Minick discovered Washington Park, and the Club, and his whole life was from that day transformed.

He had taken advantage of the early spring sunshine to take a walk, at Nettie's suggestion.

"Why don't you go into the Park, Father? It's really warm out. And the sun's lovely. Do you good."

He had put on his heaviest shirt, and a muffler, and George's old red sweater with the great white "C" on its front, emblem of George's athletic prowess at the University of Chicago; and over all, his greatcoat. He had taken warm mittens and his cane with the greyhound's head handle, carved. So equipped he had ambled uninterestedly over to the Park across the way. And there he had found new life.

New life in old life. For the park was full of old men. Old men like himself, with greyhound's-head canes, and mufflers and somebody's sweater worn beneath their greatcoats. They wore arctics, though the weather was fine. The skin of their hands and cheek-bones was glazed and had a tight look though it lay in fine little folds. There were splotches of brown on the backs of their hands, and on the temples and forehead. Their heavy grey or brown socks made comfortable folds above their ankles. From that April morning until winter drew on the Park saw old man Minick daily. Not only daily but by the day. Except for his meals, and a brief hour for his after-luncheon nap, he spent all his time there.

For in the park old man Minick and all the old men gathered there found a Forum—a safety valve—a means of expression. It did not take him long to discover that the Park was divided into two distinct sets of old men. There were the old men who lived with their married sons and daughters-in-law or married daughters and sons-in-law. Then there were the old men who lived in the Grant Home for Aged Gentlemen. You saw its fine red-brick facade through the trees at the edge of the Park.

And the slogan of these first was:

"My son and my da'ter they wouldn't want me to live in any public Home. No, sirree! They want me right there with them. In their own home. That's the kind of son and daughter I've got!"

The slogan of the second was:

"I wouldn't live with any son or daughter. Independent. That's me. My own boss. Nobody to tell me what I can do and what I can't. Treat you like a child. I'm my own boss! Pay my own good money and get my keep for it."

The first group, strangely enough, was likely to be spotted of vest and a little frayed as to collar. You saw them going on errands for their daughters-in-law. A loaf of bread. Spool of white No. 100. They took their small grandchildren to the duck pond and between the two toddlers hand in hand—the old and infirm and the infantile and infirm—it was hard to tell which led which.

The second group was shiny as to shoes, spotless as to linen, dapper as to clothes. They had no small errands. Theirs was a magnificent leisure. And theirs was magnificent conversation. The questions they discussed and settled there in the Park—these old men—were not international merely. They were cosmic in scope.

The War? Peace? Disarmament? China? Free love? Mere conversational bubbles to be tossed in the air and disposed of in a burst of foam.

Strong meat for old man Minick who had so long been fed on pap. But he soon got used to it. Between four and five in the afternoon, in a spot known as Under The Willows, the meeting took the form of a club—an open forum. A certain group made up of Socialists, Free Thinkers, parlour anarchists, bolshevists, had for years drifted there for talk. Old man Minick learned high-sounding phrases. "The Masters ... democracy ... toil of the many for the good of the few ... the ruling class ... free speech ... the People...."

The strong-minded ones held forth. The weaker ones drifted about on the outskirts, sometimes clinging to the moist and sticky paw of a round-eyed grandchild. Earlier in the day—at eleven o'clock, say—the talk was not so general nor so inclusive. The old men were likely to drift into groups of two or three or four. They sat on sun-bathed benches and their conversation was likely to be rather smutty at times, for all they looked so mild and patriarchal and desiccated. They paid scant heed to the white-haired old women who, like themselves, were sunning in the park. They watched the young women switch by, with appreciative glances at their trim figures and slim ankles. The day of the short skirt was a grand time for them. They chuckled among themselves and made wicked comment. One saw only white-haired, placid, tremulous old men, but their minds still worked with belated masculinity like naughty small boys talking behind the barn.

Old man Minick early achieved a certain leadership in the common talk. He had always liked to hold forth. This last year had been one of almost unendurable bottling up. At first he had timidly sought the less assertive ones of his kind. Mild old men who sat in rockers in the pavilion waiting for lunch time. Their conversation irritated him. They remarked everything that passed before their eyes.

"There's a boat. Fella with a boat."

A silence. Then, heavily: "Yeh."

Five minutes.

"Look at those people laying on the grass. Shouldn't think it was warm enough for that.... Now they're getting up."

A group of equestrians passed along the bridle path on the opposite side of the lagoon. They made a frieze against the delicate spring greenery. The coats of the women were scarlet, vivid green, arresting, stimulating.

"Riders."

"Yes."

"Good weather for riding."

A man was fishing near by. "Good weather for fishing."

"Yes."

"Wonder what time it is, anyway." From a pocket, deep-buried, came forth a great gold blob of a watch. "I've got one minute to eleven."

Old man Minick dragged forth a heavy globe. "Mm. I've got eleven."

"Little fast, I guess."

Old man Minick shook off this conversation impatiently. This wasn't conversation. This was oral death, though he did not put it thus. He joined the other men. They were discussing Spiritualism. He listened, ventured an opinion, was heard respectfully and then combated mercilessly. He rose to the verbal fight, and won it.

"Let's see," said one of the old men. "You're not living at the Grant Home, are you?"

"No," old man Minick made reply, proudly. "I live with my son and his wife. They wouldn't have it any other way."

"Hm. Like to be independent myself."

"Lonesome, ain't it? Over there?"

"Lonesome! Say, Mr.—what'd you say your name was? Minick? Mine's Hughes—I never was lonesome in my life 'cept for six months when I lived with my daughter and her husband and their five children. Yes, sir. That's what I call lonesome, in an eight-room flat."

George and Nettie said, "It's doing you good, Father, being out in the air so much." His eyes were brighter, his figure straighter, his colour better. It was that day he had held forth so eloquently on the emigration question. He had to read a lot—papers and magazines and one thing and another—to keep up. He devoured all the books and pamphlets about bond issues and national finances brought home by George. In the Park he was considered an authority on bonds and banking. He and a retired real-estate man named Mowry sometimes debated a single question for weeks. George and Nettie, relieved, thought he ambled to the Park and spent senile hours with his drooling old friends discussing nothing amiably and witlessly. This while he was eating strong meat, drinking strong drink.

Summer sped. Was past. Autumn held a new dread for old man Minick. When winter came where should he go? Where should he go? Not back to the five-room flat all day, and the little back bedroom, and nothingness. In his mind there rang a childish old song they used to sing at school. A silly song:

Where do all the birdies go?
I know. I know.

40

But he didn't know. He was terror-stricken. October came and went. With the first of November the Park became impossible, even at noon, and with two overcoats and the sweater. The first frost was a black frost for him. He scanned the heavens daily for rain or snow. There was a cigar store and billiard room on the corner across the boulevard and there he sometimes went, with a few of his Park cronies, to stand behind the players' chairs and watch them at pinochle or rum. But this was a dull business. Besides, the Grant men never came there. They had card rooms of their own.

He turned away from this smoky little den on a drab November day, sick at heart. The winter. He tried to face it, and at what he saw he shrank and was afraid.

He reached the apartment and went around to the rear, dutifully. His rubbers were wet and muddy and Nettie's living-room carpet was a fashionable grey. The back door was unlocked. It was Canary's day downstairs, he remembered. He took off his rubbers in the kitchen and passed into the dining room. Voices. Nettie had company. Some friends, probably, for tea. He turned to go to his room, but stopped at hearing his own name. Father Minick. Father Minick. Nettie's voice.

"Of course, if it weren't for Father Minick I would have. But how can we as long as he lives with us? There isn't room. And we can't afford a bigger place now, with rents what they are. This way it wouldn't be fair to the child. We've talked it over, George and I. Don't you suppose? But not as long as Father Minick is with us. I don't mean we'd use the maid's room for a—for the—if we had a baby. But I'd have to have someone in to help, then, and we'd have to have that extra room."

He stood there in the dining room, quiet. Quiet. His body felt queerly remote and numb, but his mind was working frenziedly. Clearly, too, in spite of the frenzy. Death. That was the first thought. Death. It would be easy. But he didn't want to die. Strange, but he didn't want to die. He liked Life. The Park, the trees, the Club, the talk, the whole show.... Nettie was a good girl.... The old must make way for the young. They had the right to be born.... Maybe it was just another excuse. Almost four years married. Why not three years ago?... The right to live. The right to live....

He turned, stealthily, stealthily, and went back into the kitchen, put on his rubbers, stole out into the darkening November afternoon.

In an hour he was back. He entered at the front door this time, ringing the bell. He had never had a key. As if he were a child they would not trust him with one. Nettie's women friends were just leaving. In the air you smelled a mingling of perfume, and tea, and cakes, and powder. He sniffed it, sensitively.

"How do you do, Mr. Minick!" they said. "How are you! Well, you certainly look it. And how do you manage these gloomy days?"

He smiled genially, taking off his greatcoat and revealing the red sweater with the big white "C" on it. "I manage. I manage." He puffed out his cheeks. "I'm busy moving."

"Moving!" Nettie's startled eyes flew to his, held them. "Moving, Father?"

"Old folks must make way for the young," he said, gaily. "That's the law of life. Yes, sir! New ones. New ones."

Nettie's face was scarlet. "Father, what in the world—"

"I signed over at the Grant Home to-day. Move in next week." The women looked at her, smiling. Old man Minick came over to her and patted her plump arm. Then he pinched her smooth cheek with a quizzical thumb and forefinger. Pinched it and shook it ever so little.

"I don't know what you mean," said Nettie, out of breath.

"Yes, you do," said old man Minick, and while his tone was light and jesting there was in his old face something stern, something menacing. "Yes, you do."

❧

When he entered the Grant Home a group of them was seated about the fireplace in the main hall. A neat, ruddy, septuagenarian circle. They greeted him casually, with delicacy of feeling, as if he were merely approaching them at their bench in the Park.

"Say, Minick, look here. Mowry here says China ought to have been included in the four-power treaty. He says—"

Old man Minick cleared his throat. "You take China, now," he said, "with her vast and practically, you might say, virgin country, why—"

An apple-cheeked maid in a black dress and a white apron stopped before him. He paused.

"Housekeeper says for me to tell you your room's all ready, if you'd like to look at it now."

"Minute. Minute, my child." He waved her aside with the air of one who pays five hundred a year for independence and freedom. The girl turned to go. "Uh—young lady! Young lady!" She looked at him. "Tell the housekeeper two pillows, please. Two pillows on my bed. Be sure."

"Yes, sir. Two pillows. Yes, sir. I'll be sure."

GIGOLO

In the first place, *gigolo* is slang. In the second place (with no desire to appear patronizing, but one's French conversation class does not include the *argot*), it is French slang. In the third place, the gig is pronounced zhig, and the whole is not a respectable word. Finally, it is a term of utter contempt.

A gigolo, generally speaking, is a man who lives off women's money. In the mad year 1922 A. W., a gigolo, definitely speaking, designated one of those incredible and pathetic male creatures, born of the war, who, for ten francs or more or even less, would dance with any woman wishing to dance on the crowded floors of public tea rooms, dinner or supper rooms in the cafés, hotels, and restaurants of France. Lean, sallow, handsome, expert, and unwholesome, one saw them everywhere, their slim waists and sleek heads in juxtaposition to plump, respectable American matrons and slender, respectable American flappers. For that matter, feminine respectability of almost every nationality (except the French) yielded itself to the skilful guidance of the genus gigolo in the tango or fox-trot. Naturally, no decent French girl would have been allowed for a single moment to dance with a gigolo. But America, touring Europe like mad after years of enforced absence, outnumbered all other nations atravel ten to one.

By no feat of fancy could one imagine Gideon Gory, of the Winnebago, Wisconsin, Gorys, employed daily and nightly as a gigolo in the gilt and marble restaurants that try to outsparkle the Mediterranean along the Promenade des Anglais in Nice. Gideon Gory, of Winnebago, Wisconsin! Why any one knows that the Gorys were to Winnebago what the Romanoffs were to Russia—royal, remote, omnipotent. Yet the Romanoffs went in the cataclysm, and so, too, did the Gorys. To

43

appreciate the depths to which the boy Gideon had fallen one must have known the Gorys in their glory. It happened something like this:

The Gorys lived for years in the great, ugly, sprawling, luxurious old frame house on Cass Street. It was high up on the bluff overlooking the Fox River and, incidentally, the huge pulp and paper mills across the river in which the Gory money had been made. The Gorys were so rich and influential (for Winnebago, Wisconsin) that they didn't bother to tear down the old frame house and build a stone one, or to cover its faded front with cosmetics of stucco. In most things the Gorys led where Winnebago could not follow. They disdained to follow where Winnebago led. The Gorys had an automobile when those vehicles were entered from the rear and when Winnebago roads were a wallow of mud in the spring and fall and a snow-lined trench in the winter. The family was of the town, and yet apart from it. The Gorys knew about golf, and played it in far foreign playgrounds when the rest of us thought of it, if we thought of it at all, as something vaguely Scotch, like haggis. They had oriental rugs and hardwood floors when the town still stepped on carpets; and by the time the rest of the town had caught up on rugs the Gorys had gone back to carpets, neutral tinted. They had fireplaces in bedrooms, and used them, like characters in an English novel. Old Madame Gory had a slim patent leather foot, with a buckle, and carried a sunshade when she visited the flowers in the garden. Old Gideon was rumoured to have wine with his dinner. Gideon Junior (father of Giddy) smoked cigarettes with his monogram on them. Shroeder's grocery ordered endive for them, all blanched and delicate in a wicker basket from France or Belgium, when we had just become accustomed to head-lettuce.

Every prosperous small American town has its Gory family. Every small town newspaper relishes the savoury tid-bits that fall from the rich table of the family life. Thus you saw that Mr. and Mrs. Gideon Gory, Jr., have returned from California where Mr. Gory had gone for the polo. Mr. and Mrs. Gideon Gory, Jr., announce the birth, in New York, of a son, Gideon III (our, in a manner of speaking, hero). Mr. and Mrs. Gideon Gory, Jr., and son Gideon III, left to-day for England and the continent. It is understood that Gideon III will be placed at school in England. Mr. and Mrs. Gideon Gory, accompanied by Madame Gory, have gone to Chicago for a week of the grand opera.

Born of all this, you would have thought that young Giddy would grow up a somewhat objectionable young man; and so, in fact, he did, though not nearly so objectionable as he might well have been, considering things in general and his mother in particular. At sixteen, for example, Giddy was driving his own car—a car so exaggerated and low-slung and with such a long predatory and glittering nose that one marvelled at the expertness with which he swung its slim length around the corners of our narrow tree-shaded streets. He was a real Gory, was Giddy, with his thick waving black hair (which he tried for vain years to train into docility), his lean swart face, and his slightly hooked Gory nose. In appearance Winnebago pronounced him foreign looking—an attribute which he later turned into a doubtful asset in Nice. On the rare occasions when Giddy graced Winnebago with his presence you were likely to find him pursuing the pleasures that occupied other Winnebago boys of his age, if not station. In some miraculous way he had escaped being a snob. Still, training and travel combined to lead him into many innocent errors. When he dropped into Fetzer's pool shack carrying a malacca cane, for example. He had carried a cane every day for six months in Paris, whence he had just returned. Now it was as much a part of his street attire as his hat—more, to be exact, for the hatless head had just then become the street mode. There was a good game of Kelly in progress. Giddy, leaning slightly on his stick, stood watching it. Suddenly he was aware that all about the dim smoky little room players and loungers were standing in attitudes of exaggerated elegance. Each was leaning on a cue, his elbow crooked in as near an imitation of Giddy's position as the stick's length would permit. The figure was curved so that it stuck out behind and before; the expression on each face was as asinine as its owner's knowledge of the comic-weekly swell could make it; the little finger of the free hand was extravagantly bent. The players themselves walked with a mincing step about the table. And: "My deah fellah, what a pretty play. Mean to say, neat, don't you know," came incongruously from the lips of Reddy Lennigan, whose father ran the Lennigan House on Outagamie Street. He spatted his large hands delicately together in further expression of approval.

"Think so?" giggled his opponent, Mr. Dutchy Meisenberg. "Aw—fly sweet of you to say so, old thing." He tucked his unspeakable handkerchief up his cuff and coughed behind his palm. He turned to Giddy. "Excuse my not having my coat on, deah boy."

Just here Giddy might have done a number of things, all wrong. The game was ended. He walked to the table, and, using the offending stick as a cue, made a rather pretty shot that he had learned from Benoit in London. Then he ranged the cane neatly on the rack with the cues. He even grinned a little boyishly. "You win," he said. "My treat. What'll you have?"

Which was pretty sporting for a boy whose American training had been what Giddy's had been.

Giddy's father, on the death of old Gideon, proved himself much more expert at dispensing the paper mill money than at accumulating it. After old Madame Gory's death just one year following that of her husband, Winnebago saw less and less of the three remaining members of the royal family. The frame house on the river bluff would be closed for a year or more at a time. Giddy's father rather liked Winnebago and would have been content to spend six months of the year in the old Gory house, but Giddy's mother, who had been a Leyden, of New York, put that idea out of his head pretty effectively.

"Don't talk to me," she said, "about your duty toward the town that gave you your money and all that kind of feudal rot because you know you don't mean it. It bores you worse than it does me, really, but you like to think that the villagers are pulling a forelock when you walk down Normal Avenue. As a matter of fact they're not doing anything of the kind. They've got their thumbs to their noses, more likely."

Her husband protested rather weakly. "I don't care. I like the old shack. I know the heating apparatus is bum and that we get the smoke from the paper mills, but—I don't know—last year, when we had that punk pink palace at Cannes I kept thinking—"

Mrs. Gideon Gory raised the Leyden eyebrow. "Don't get sentimental, Gid, for God's sake! It's a shanty, and you know it. And you know that it needs everything from plumbing to linen. I don't see any sense in sinking thousands in making it livable when we don't want to live in it."

"But I do want to live in it—once in a while. I'm used to it. I was brought up in it. So was the kid. He likes it, too. Don't you, Giddy?" The boy was present, as usual, at this particular scene.

The boy worshipped his mother. But, also, he was honest. So, "Yeh, I like the ol' barn all right," he confessed.

Encouraged, his father went on: "Yesterday the kid was standing out there on the bluff-edge breathing like a whale, weren't you, Giddy? And when I asked him what he was puffing about he said he liked the smell of the sulphur and chemicals and stuff from the paper mills, didn't you, kid?"

Shame-facedly, "Yeh," said Giddy.

Betrayed thus by husband and adored son, the Leyden did battle. "You can both stay here, then," she retorted with more spleen than elegance, "and sniff sulphur until you're black in the face. I'm going to London in May."

46

They, too, went to London in May, of course, as she had known they would. She had not known, though, that in leading her husband to England in May she was leading him to his death as well.

"All Winnebago will be shocked and grieved to learn," said the Winnebago *Courier* to the extent of two columns and a cut, "of the sudden and violent death in England of her foremost citizen, Gideon Gory. Death was due to his being thrown from his horse while hunting."

... To being thrown from his horse while hunting. Shocked and grieved though it might or might not be, Winnebago still had the fortitude to savour this with relish. Winnebago had died deaths natural and unnatural. It had been run over by automobiles, and had its skull fractured at football, and been drowned in Lake Winnebago, and struck by lightning, and poisoned by mushrooms, and shot by burglars. But never had Winnebago citizen had the distinction of meeting death by being thrown from his horse while hunting. While hunting. Scarlet coats. Hounds in full cry. Baronial halls. Hunt breakfasts. *Vogue. Vanity Fair.*

Well! Winnebago was almost grateful for this final and most picturesque gesture of Gideon Gory the second.

The widowed Leyden did not even take the trouble personally to superintend the selling of the Gory place on the river bluff. It was sold by an agent while she and Giddy were in Italy, and if she was ever aware that the papers in the transaction stated that the house had been bought by Orson J. Hubbell she soon forgot the fact and the name. Giddy, leaning over her shoulder while she handled the papers, and signing on the line indicated by a legal forefinger, may have remarked:

"Hubbell. That's old Hubbell, the dray man. Must be money in the draying line."

Which was pretty stupid of him, because he should have known that the draying business was now developed into the motor truck business with great vans roaring their way between Winnebago and Kaukauna, Winnebago and Neenah, and even Winnebago and Oshkosh. He learned that later.

Just now Giddy wasn't learning much of anything, and, to do him credit, the fact distressed him not a little. His mother insisted that she needed him, and developed a bad heart whenever he rebelled and threatened to sever the apron-strings. They lived abroad entirely now. Mrs. Gory showed a talent for spending the Gory gold that must have set old Gideon to whirling in his Winnebago grave. Her spending of it was foolish enough, but her handling of it was criminal. She loved Europe. America bored her. She wanted to identify herself with foreigners,

47

with foreign life. Against advice she sold her large and lucrative interest in the Winnebago paper mills and invested great sums in French stocks, in Russian enterprises, in German shares.

She liked to be mistaken for a French woman.

She and Gideon spoke the language like natives—or nearly.

She was vain of Gideon's un-American looks, and cross with him when, on their rare and brief visits to New York, he insisted that he liked American tailoring and American-made shoes. Once or twice, soon after his father's death, he had said, casually, "You didn't like Winnebago, did you? Living in it, I mean."

"*Like* it!"

"Well, these English, I mean, and French—they sort of grow up in a place, and stay with it and belong to it, see what I mean? and it gives you a kind of permanent feeling. Not patriotic, exactly, but solid and native heathy and Scots-wha-hae-wi'-Wallace and all that kind of slop."

"Giddy darling, don't be silly."

Occasionally, too, he said, "Look here, Julia"—she liked this modern method of address—"look here, Julia, I ought to be getting busy. Doing something. Here I am, nineteen, and I can't do a thing except dance pretty well, but not as well as that South American eel we met last week; mix a cocktail pretty well, but not as good a one as Benny the bartender turns out at Voyot's; ride pretty well, but not as well as the English chaps; drive a car—"

She interrupted him there. "Drive a car better than even an Italian chauffeur. Had you there, Giddy darling."

She undoubtedly had Giddy darling there. His driving was little short of miraculous, and his feeling for the intricate inside of a motor engine was as delicate and unerring as that of a professional pianist for his pet pianoforte. They motored a good deal, with France as a permanent background and all Europe as a playground. They flitted about the continent, a whirl of glittering blue-and-cream enamel, tan leather coating, fur robes, air cushions, gold-topped flasks, and petrol. Giddy knew Como and Villa D'Este as the place where that pretty Hungarian widow had borrowed a thousand lires from him at the Casino roulette table and never paid him back; London as a pleasing potpourri of briar pipes, smart leather gloves, music-hall revues, and night clubs; Berlin as a rather stuffy hole where they tried to ape Paris and failed, but you had to hand it to Charlotte when it came to the skating at the Eis Palast. A pleasing existence, but unprofitable. No one saw the cloud gathering because of cloud there was none, even of the man's-hand size so often discerned as a portent.

When the storm broke (this must be hurriedly passed over because of the let's-not-talk-about-the-war-I'm-so-sick-of-it-aren't-you feeling) Giddy promptly went into the Lafayette Escadrille. Later he learned never to mention this to an American because the American was so likely to say, "There must have been about eleven million scrappers in that outfit. Every fella you meet's been in the Lafayette Escadrille. If all the guys were in it that say they were they could have licked the Germans the first day out. That outfit's worse than the old Floradora Sextette."

Mrs. Gory was tremendously proud of him, and not as worried as she should have been. She thought it all a rather smart game, and not at all serious. She wasn't even properly alarmed about her European money, at first. Giddy looked thrillingly distinguished and handsome in his aviation uniform. When she walked in the Paris streets with him she glowed like a girl with her lover. But after the first six months of it Mrs. Gory, grown rather drawn and haggard, didn't think the whole affair quite so delightful. She scarcely ever saw Giddy. She never heard the drum of an airplane without getting a sick, gone feeling at the pit of her stomach. She knew, now, that there was more to the air service than a becoming uniform. She was doing some war work herself in an incompetent, frenzied sort of way. With Giddy soaring high and her foreign stocks and bonds falling low she might well be excused for the panic that shook her from the time she opened her eyes in the morning until she tardily closed them at night.

"Let's go home, Giddy darling," like a scared child.

"Where's that?"

"Don't be cruel. America's the only safe place now."

"Too darned safe!" This was 1915.

By 1917 she was actually in need of money. But Giddy did not know much about this because Giddy had, roughly speaking, got his. He had the habit of soaring up into the sunset and sitting around in a large pink cloud like a kid bouncing on a feather bed. Then, one day, he soared higher and farther than he knew, having, perhaps, grown careless through over-confidence. He heard nothing above the roar of his own engine, and the two planes were upon him almost before he knew it. They were not French, or English, or American planes. He got one of them and would have got clean away if the other had not caught him in the arm. The right arm. His mechanician lay limp. Even then he might have managed a landing but the pursuing plane got in a final shot. There followed a period of time that seemed to cover, say, six years but that was actually only a matter of seconds. At the end of that period

Giddy, together with a tangle of wire, silk, wood, and something that had been the mechanician, lay inside the German lines, and you would hardly have thought him worth the disentangling.

They did disentangle him, though, and even patched him up pretty expertly, but not so expertly, perhaps, as they might have, being enemy surgeons and rather busy with the patching of their own injured. The bone, for example, in the lower right arm, knitted promptly and properly, being a young and healthy bone, but they rather over-looked the matter of arm nerves and muscles, so that later, though it looked a perfectly proper arm, it couldn't lift four pounds. His head had emerged slowly, month by month, from swathings of gauze. What had been quite a crevasse in his skull became only a scarlet scar that his hair pretty well hid when he brushed it over the bad place. But the surgeon, perhaps being overly busy, or having no real way of knowing that Giddy's nose had been a distinguished and aristocratically hooked Gory nose, had remoulded that wrecked feature into a pure Greek line at first sight of which Giddy stood staring weakly into the mirror; reeling a little with surprise and horror and unbelief and general misery. "Can this be I?" he thought, feeling like the old man of the bramble bush in the Mother Goose rhyme. A well-made and becoming nose, but not so fine looking as the original feature had been, as worn by Giddy.

"Look here!" he protested to the surgeon, months too late. "Look here, this isn't my nose."

"Be glad," replied that practical Prussian person, "that you have any."

With his knowledge of French and English and German Giddy acted as interpreter during the months of his invalidism and later internment, and things were not so bad with him. He had no news of his mother, though, and no way of knowing whether she had news of him. With 1918, and the Armistice and his release, he hurried to Paris and there got the full impact of the past year's events.

Julia Gory was dead and the Gory money nonexistent.

Out of the ruins—a jewel or two and some paper not quite worthless—he managed a few thousand francs and went to Nice. There he walked in the sunshine, and sat in the sunshine, and even danced in the sunshine, a dazed young thing together with hundreds of other dazed young things, not thinking, not planning, not hoping. Existing only in a state of semi-consciousness like one recovering from a blinding blow. The francs dribbled away. Sometimes he played baccarat and won; oftener he played baccarat and lost. He moved in a sort of trance, feeling nothing. Vaguely he knew that there was a sort of Conference going on in Paris. Sometimes he thought of Winnebago, recalling it remotely, dimly, as one is occasionally conscious of a former unknown existence. Twice he went to Paris for periods of some months, but he was unhappy there and even strangely bewildered, like a child. He was still sick in mind and body, though he did not know it. Driftwood, like thousands of others, tossed up on the shore after the storm; lying there bleached and useless and battered.

Then, one day in Nice, there was no money. Not a franc. Not a centime. He knew hunger. He knew terror. He knew desperation. It was out of this period that there emerged Giddy, the gigolo. Now, though, the name bristled with accent marks, thus: Gédéon Goré.

This Gédéon Goré, of the Nice dansants, did not even remotely resemble Gideon Gory of Winnebago, Wisconsin. This Gédéon Goré wore French clothes of the kind that Giddy Gory had always despised. A slim, sallow, sleek, sad-eyed gigolo in tight French garments, the pants rather flappy at the ankle; effeminate French shoes with fawn-coloured uppers and patent-leather eyelets and vamps, most despicable; a slim cane; hair with a magnificent natural wave that looked artificially marcelled and that was worn with a strip growing down from the temples on either side in the sort of cut used only by French dandies and English stage butlers. No, this was not Giddy Gory. The real Giddy Gory lay in a smart but battered suitcase under the narrow bed in his lodgings. The suitcase contained:

Item; one grey tweed suit with name of a London tailor inside.

Item; one pair Russia calf oxfords of American make.

Item; one French aviation uniform with leather coat, helmet, and gloves all bearing stiff and curious splotches of brown or rust-colour which you might not recognize as dried blood stains.

Item; one handful assorted medals, ribbons, orders, etc.

All Europe was dancing. It seemed a death dance, grotesque, convulsive, hideous. Paris, Nice, Berlin, Budapest, Rome, Vienna, London writhed and twisted and turned and jiggled. St. Vitus himself never imagined contortions such as these. In the narrow side-street dance rooms of Florence, and in the great avenue restaurants of Paris they were performing exactly the same gyrations—wiggle, squirm, shake. And over all the American jazz music boomed and whanged its syncopation. On the music racks of violinists who had meant to be Elmans or Kreislers were sheets entitled Jazz Baby Fox Trot. Drums, horns, cymbals, castanets, sandpaper. So the mannequins and marionettes of Europe tried to whirl themselves into forgetfulness.

The Americans thought Giddy was a Frenchman. The French knew him for an American, dress as he would. Dancing became with him a profession—no, a trade. He danced flawlessly, holding and guiding his partner impersonally, firmly, expertly in spite of the weak right arm—it served well enough. Gideon Gory had always been a naturally rhythmic dancer. Then, too, he had been fond of dancing. Years of practise had perfected him. He adopted now the manner and position of the professional. As he danced he held his head rather stiffly to one side, and a little down, the chin jutting out just a trifle. The effect was at the same time stiff and chic. His footwork was infallible. The intricate and imbecilic steps of the day he performed in flawless sequence. Under his masterly guidance the feet of the least rhythmic were suddenly endowed with deftness and grace. One swayed with him as naturally as with an elemental force. He danced politely and almost wordlessly unless first addressed, according to the code of his kind. His touch was firm, yet remote. The dance concluded, he conducted his partner to her seat, bowed stiffly from the waist, heels together, and departed. For these services he was handed ten francs, twenty francs, thirty francs, or more, if lucky, depending on the number of times he was called upon to dance with a partner during the evening. Thus was dancing, the most spontaneous and unartificial of the Muses, vulgarized, commercialized, prostituted. Lower than Gideon Gory, of Winnebago, Wisconsin, had fallen, could no man fall.

Sometimes he danced in Paris. During the high season he danced in Nice. Afternoon and evening found him busy in the hot, perfumed, overcrowded dance salons. The Negresco, the Ruhl, Maxim's, Belle Meunière, the Casina Municipale. He learned to make his face go a perfect blank—pale, cryptic, expressionless. Between himself and the other boys of his ilk there was little or no professional comradeship. A weird lot they were, young, though their faces were strangely lacking in the look of youth. All of them had been in the war. Most of them had been injured. There was Aubin, the Frenchman. The right side of Aubin's face was rather startlingly handsome in its Greek perfection. It was like a profile chiselled. The left side was another face—the same, and yet not the same. It was as though you saw the left side out of drawing, or blurred, or out of focus. It puzzled you—shocked you. The left side of Aubin's face had been done over by an army surgeon who, though deft and scientific, had not had a hand expert as that of the Original Sculptor. Then there was Mazzetti, the Roman. He parted his hair on the wrong side, and under the black wing of it was a deep groove into which you could lay a forefinger. A piece of shell had plowed it neatly. The Russian boy who called himself Orloff had the look in his eyes of one who has seen things upon which eyes never should have looked. He smoked constantly and ate, apparently, not at all. Among these there existed a certain unwritten code and certain unwritten signals.

You did not take away the paying partner of a fellow gigolo. If in too great demand you turned your surplus partners over to gigolos unemployed. You did not accept less than ten francs (they all broke this rule). Sometimes Gédéon Goré made ten francs a day, sometimes twenty, sometimes fifty, infrequently a hundred. Sometimes not enough to pay for his one decent meal a day. At first he tried to keep fit by walking a certain number of miles daily along the ocean front. But usually he was too weary to persist in this. He did not think at all. He felt nothing. Sometimes, down deep, deep in a long-forgotten part of his being a voice called feebly, plaintively to the man who had been Giddy Gory. But he shut his ears and mind and consciousness and would not listen.

The American girls were best, the gigolos all agreed, and they paid well, though they talked too much. Gédéon Goré was a favourite among them. They thought he was so foreign looking, and kind of sad and stern and everything. His French, fluent, colloquial, and bewildering, awed them. They would attempt to speak to him in halting and hackneyed phrases acquired during three years at Miss Pence's Select School at Hastings-on-the-Hudson. At the cost of about a thousand dollars a word they would enunciate, painfully:

"*Je pense que*—um—*que Nice est le plus belle*—uh—ville de France."

Giddy, listening courteously, his head inclined as though unwilling to miss one conversational pearl falling from the pretty American's lips, would appear to consider this gravely. Then, sometimes in an unexpected burst of pure mischief, he would answer:

"You said something! *Some* burg, I'm telling the world."

The girl, startled, would almost leap back from the confines of his arms only to find his face stern, immobile, his eyes sombre and reflective.

"Why! Where did you pick that up?"

His eyebrows would go up. His face would express complete lack of comprehension. "*Pardon?*"

Afterward, at home, in Toledo or Kansas City or Los Angeles, the girl would tell about it. "I suppose some American girl taught it to him, just for fun. It sounded too queer—because his French was so wonderful. He danced divinely. A Frenchman, and so aristocratic! Think of his being a professional partner. They have them over there, you know. Everybody's dancing in Europe. And gay! Why, you'd never know there'd been a war."

Mary Hubbell, of the Winnebago Hubbells, did not find it so altogether gay. Mary Hubbell, with her father, Orson J. Hubbell, and her mother, Bee Hubbell, together with what appeared to be practically the entire white population of the United States, came to Europe early in 1922, there to travel, to play, to rest, to behold, and to turn their good hard American dollars into cordwood-size bundles of German marks, Austrian kronen, Italian lires, and French francs. Most of the men regarded Europe as a wine list. In their mental geography Rheims, Rhine, Moselle, Bordeaux, Champagne, or Wuerzburg were not localities but libations. The women, for the most part, went in for tortoise-shell combs, fringed silk shawls, jade earrings, beaded bags, and coral neck chains. Up and down the famous thoroughfare of Europe went the absurd pale blue tweed tailleurs and the lavender tweed cape suits of America's wives and daughters. Usually, after the first month or two, they shed these respectable, middle-class habiliments for what they fondly believed to be smart Paris costumes; and you could almost invariably tell a good, moral, church-going matron of the Middle West by the fact that she was got up like a demimondaine of the second class, in the naive belief that she looked French and chic.

The three Hubbells were thoroughly nice people. Mary Hubbell was more than thoroughly nice. She was a darb. She had done a completely good job during the 1918-1918 period, including the expert driving of a wild and unbroken Ford up and down the shell-torn roads of France. One of those small-town girls with a big-town outlook, a well-trained mind, a slim boyish body, a good clear skin, and a steady eye that saw. Mary Hubbell wasn't a beauty by a good many measurements, but she had her points, as witness the number of bouquets, bundles, books, and bon-bons piled in her cabin when she sailed.

The well-trained mind and the steady seeing eye enabled Mary Hubbell to discover that Europe wasn't so gay as it seemed to the blind; and she didn't write home to the effect that you'd never know there'd been war.

The Hubbells had the best that Europe could afford. Orson J. Hubbell, a mild-mannered, grey-haired man with a nice flat waistline and a good keen eye (hence Mary's) adored his women-folk and spoiled them. During the first years of his married life he had been

Hubbell, the drayman, as Giddy Gory had said. He had driven one of his three drays himself, standing sturdily in the front of the red-painted wooden two-horse wagon as it rattled up and down the main business thoroughfare of Winnebago. But the war and the soaring freight-rates had dealt generously with Orson Hubbell. As railroad and shipping difficulties increased the Hubbell draying business waxed prosperous. Factories, warehouses, and wholesale business firms could be assured that their goods would arrive promptly, safely, and cheaply when conveyed by a Hubbell van. So now the three red-painted wooden horse-driven drays were magically transformed into a great fleet of monster motor vans that plied up and down the state of Wisconsin and even into Michigan and Illinois and Indiana. The Orson J. Hubbell Transportation Company, you read. And below, in yellow lettering on the red background:

Have HUBBELL *Do Your* HAULING.

There was actually a million in it, and more to come. The buying of the old Gory house on the river bluff had been one of the least of Orson's feats. And now that house was honeycombed with sleeping porches and linen closets and enamel fittings and bathrooms white and glittering as an operating auditorium. And there were shower baths, and blue rugs, and great soft fuzzy bath towels and little white innocent guest towels embroidered with curly H's whose tails writhed at you from all corners.

Orson J. and Mrs. Hubbell had never been in Europe before, and they enjoyed themselves enormously. That is to say, Mrs. Orson J. did, and Orson, seeing her happy, enjoyed himself vicariously. His hand slid in and out of his inexhaustible pocket almost automatically now. And "How much?" was his favourite locution. They went everywhere, did everything. Mary boasted a pretty fair French. Mrs. Hubbell conversed in the various languages of Europe by speaking pidgin English very loud, and omitting all verbs, articles, adverbs, and other cumbersome superfluities. Thus, to the *fille de chambre.*

"Me out now you beds." The red-cheeked one from the provinces understood, in some miraculous way, that Mrs. Hubbell was now going out and that the beds could be made and the rooms tidied.

They reached Nice in February and plunged into its gaieties. "Just think!" exclaimed Mrs. Hubbell rapturously, "only three francs for a facial or a manicure and two for a marcel. It's like finding them."

"If the Mediterranean gets any bluer," said Mary, "I don't think I can stand it, it's so lovely."

Mrs. Hubbell, at tea, expressed a desire to dance. Mary, at tea, desired to dance but didn't express it. Orson J. loathed tea; and the early draying business had somewhat unfitted his sturdy legs for the lighter movements of the dance. But he wanted only their happiness. So he looked about a bit, and asked some questions, and came back.

"Seems there's a lot of young chaps who make a business of dancing with the women-folks who haven't dancing men along. Hotel hires 'em. Funny to us but I guess it's all right, and quite the thing around here. You pay 'em so much a dance, or so much an afternoon. You girls want to try it?"

"I do," said Mrs. Orson J. Hubbell. "It doesn't sound respectable. Then that's what all those thin little chaps are who have been dancing with those pretty American girls. They're sort of ratty looking, aren't they? What do they call 'em? That's a nice-looking one, over there—no, no!—dancing with the girl in grey, I mean. If that's one I'd like to dance with him, Orson. Good land, what would the Winnebago ladies say! What do they call 'em, I wonder."

Mary had been gazing very intently at the nice-looking one over there who was dancing with the girl in grey. She answered her mother's question, still gazing at him. "They call them gigolos," she said, slowly. Then, "Get that one Dad, will you, if you can? You dance with him first, Mother, and then I'll—"

"I can get two," volunteered Orson J.

"No," said Mary Hubbell, sharply.

The nice-looking gigolo seemed to be in great demand, but Orson J. succeeded in capturing him after the third dance. It turned out to be a tango, and though Mrs. Hubbell, pretty well scared, declared that she didn't know it and couldn't dance it, the nice-looking gigolo assured her, through the medium of Mary's interpretation, that Mrs. Hubbell had only to follow his guidance. It was quite simple. He did not seem to look directly at Mary, or at Orson J. or at Mrs. Hubbell, as he spoke. The dance concluded, Mrs. Hubbell came back breathless, but enchanted.

"He has beautiful manners," she said, aloud, in English. "And dance! You feel like a swan when you're dancing with him. Try him, Mary." The gigolo's face, as he bowed before her, was impassive, inscrutable.

But, "Sh!" said Mary.

"Nonsense! Doesn't understand a word."

Mary danced the next dance with him. They danced wordlessly until the dance was half over. Then, abruptly, Mary said in English, "What's your name?"

Close against him she felt a sudden little sharp contraction of the gigolo's diaphragm—the contraction that reacts to surprise or alarm. But he said, in French, *"Pardon?"*

So, "What's your name?" said Mary, in French this time.

The gigolo with the beautiful manners hesitated longer than really beautiful manners should permit. But finally, "Je m'appelle Gédéon Goré." He pronounced it in his most nasal, perfect Paris French. It didn't sound even remotely like Gideon Gory.

"My name's Hubbell," said Mary, in her pretty fair French. "Mary Hubbell. I come from a little town called Winnebago."

The Goré eyebrow expressed polite disinterestedness.

"That's in Wisconsin," continued Mary, "and I love it."

"Naturellement," agreed the gigolo, stiffly.

They finished the dance without further conversation. Mrs. Hubbell had the next dance. Mary the next. They spent the afternoon dancing, until dinner time. Orson J.'s fee, as he handed it to the gigolo, was the kind that mounted grandly into dollars instead of mere francs. The gigolo's face, as he took it, was not more inscrutable than Mary's as she watched him take it.

From that afternoon, throughout the next two weeks, if any girl as thoroughly fine as Mary Hubbell could be said to run after any man, Mary ran after that gigolo. At the same time one could almost have said that he tried to avoid her. Mary took a course of tango lessons, and urged her mother to do the same. Even Orson J. noticed it.

"Look here," he said, in kindly protest. "Aren't you getting pretty thick with this jigger?"

"Sociological study, Dad. I'm all right."

"Yeh, you're all right. But how about him?"

"He's all right, too."

The gigolo resisted Mary's unmaidenly advances, and yet, when he was with her, he seemed sometimes to forget to look sombre and blank and remote. They seemed to have a lot to say to each other. Mary talked about America a good deal. About her home town ... "and big elms and maples and oaks in the yard ... the Fox River valley ... Middle West ... Normal Avenue ... Cass Street ... Fox River paper mills...."

She talked in French and English. The gigolo confessed, one day, to understanding some English, though he seemed to speak none. After that Mary, when very much in earnest, or when enthusiastic, spoke in her native tongue altogether. She claimed an intense interest in European after-war conditions, in reconstruction, in the attitude toward life of those millions of young men who had actually participated in the conflict. She asked questions that might have been considered impertinent, not to say nervy.

"Now you," she said, brutally, "are a person of some education, refinement, and background. Yet you are content to dance around in these—these—well, back home a chap might wash dishes in a cheap restaurant or run an elevator in an east side New York loft building, but he'd never—"

A very faint dull red crept suddenly over the pallor of the gigolo's face. They were sitting out on a bench on the promenade, facing the ocean (in direct defiance on Mary's part of all rules of conduct of respectable girls toward gigolos). Mary Hubbell had said rather brusque things before. But now, for the first time, the young man defended himself faintly.

"For us," he replied in his exquisite French, "it is finished. For us there is nothing. This generation, it is no good. I am no good. They are no good." He waved a hand in a gesture that included the promenaders, the musicians in the cafés, the dancers, the crowds eating and drinking at the little tables lining the walk.

"What rot!" said Mary Hubbell, briskly. "They probably said exactly the same thing in Asia after Alexander had got through with 'em. I suppose there was such dancing and general devilment in Macedonia that every one said the younger generation had gone to the dogs since the war, and the world would never amount to anything again. But it seemed to pick up, didn't it?"

The boy turned and looked at her squarely for the first time, his eyes meeting hers. Mary looked at him. She even swayed toward him a little, her lips parted. There was about her a breathlessness, an expectancy. So they sat for a moment, and between them the air was electric, vibrant. Then, slowly, he relaxed, sat back, slumped a little on the bench. Over his face, that for a moment had been alight with something vital, there crept again the look of defeat, of sombre indifference. At sight of that look Mary Hubbell's jaw set. She leaned forward. She clasped her fine large hands tight. She did not look at the gigolo, but out, across the blue Mediterranean, and beyond it. Her voice was low and a little tremulous and she spoke in English only.

"It isn't finished here—here in Europe. But it's sick. Back home, in America, though, it's alive. Alive! And growing. I wish I could make you understand what it's like there. It's all new, and crude, maybe, and ugly, but it's so darned healthy and sort of clean. I love it. I love every bit of it. I know I sound like a flag-waver but I don't care. I mean it. And I know it's sentimental, but I'm proud of it. The kind of thing I feel about the United States is the kind of thing Mencken sneers at. You don't know who Mencken is. He's a critic who pretends to despise everything because he's really a sentimentalist and afraid somebody'll find it out. I don't say I don't appreciate the beauty of all this Italy and France and England and Germany. But it doesn't get me the way just the mention of a name will get me back home. This trip, for example. Why, last summer four of us—three other girls and I—motored from Wisconsin to California, and we drove every inch of the way ourselves. The Santa Fé Trail! The Ocean-to-Ocean Highway! The Lincoln Highway! The Dixie Highway! The Yellowstone Trail! The very sound of those words gives me a sort of prickly feeling. They mean something so big and vital and new. I get a thrill out of them that I haven't had once over here. Why even this," she threw out a hand that included and dismissed the whole sparkling panorama before her, "this doesn't begin to give the jolt that I got out of Walla Walla, and Butte, and Missoula, and Spokane, and Seattle, and Albuquerque. We drove all day, and ate ham and eggs at some little hotel or lunch-counter at night, and outside the hotel the drummers would be sitting, talking and smoking; and there were Western men, very tanned and tall and lean, in those big two-gallon hats and khaki pants and puttees. And there were sunsets, and sand, and cactus and mountains, and campers and Fords. I can smell the Kansas corn fields and I can see the Iowa farms and the ugly little raw American towns, and the big thin American men, and the grain elevators near the railroad stations, and I know those towns weren't the way towns ought to look. They were ugly and crude and new. Maybe it wasn't all beautiful, but gosh! it was real, and growing, and big and alive! Alive!"

Mary Hubbell was crying. There, on the bench along the promenade in the sunshine at Nice, she was crying.

The boy beside her suddenly rose, uttered a little inarticulate sound, and left her there on the bench in the sunshine. Vanished, completely, in the crowd.

For three days the Orson J. Hubbells did not see their favourite gigolo. If Mary was disturbed she did not look it, though her eye was alert in the throng. During the three days of their gigolo's absence Mrs. Hubbell and Mary availed themselves of the professional services of the Italian gigolo Mazzetti. Mrs. Hubbell said she thought his dancing was, if anything, more nearly perfect than that What's-his-name, but his manner wasn't so nice and she didn't like his eyes. Sort of sneaky. Mary said she thought so, too.

Nevertheless she was undoubtedly affable toward him, and talked (in French) and laughed and even walked with him, apparently in complete ignorance of the fact that these things were not done. Mazzetti spoke frequently of his colleague, Goré, and always in terms of disparagement. A low fellow. A clumsy dancer. One unworthy of Mary's swanlike grace. Unfit to receive Orson J. Hubbell's generous fees.

Late one evening, during the mid-week after-dinner dance, Goré appeared suddenly in the doorway. It was ten o'clock. The Hubbells were dallying with their after-dinner coffee at one of the small tables about the dance floor.

Mary, keen-eyed, saw him first. She beckoned Mazzetti who stood in attendance beside Mrs. Hubbell's chair. She snatched up the wrap that lay at hand and rose. "It's stifling in here. I'm going out on the Promenade for a breath of air. Come on." She plucked at Mazzetti's sleeve and actually propelled him through the crowd and out of the room. She saw Goré's startled eyes follow them.

She even saw him crossing swiftly to where her mother and father sat. Then she vanished into the darkness with Mazzetti. And the Mazzettis put but one interpretation upon a young woman who strolls into the soft darkness of the Promenade with a gigolo.

And Mary Hubbell knew this.

Gédéon Goré stood before Mr. and Mrs. Orson J. Hubbell. "Where is your daughter?" he demanded, in French.

"Oh, howdy-do," chirped Mrs. Hubbell. "Well, it's Mr. Goré! We missed you. I hope you haven't been sick."

"Where is your daughter?" demanded Gédéon Goré, in French. "Where is Mary?"

Mrs. Hubbell caught the word Mary. "Oh, Mary. Why, she's gone out for a walk with Mr. Mazzetti."

"Good God!" said Gédéon Goré, in perfectly plain English. And vanished.

Orson J. Hubbell sat a moment, thinking. Then, "Why, say, he talked English. That young French fella talked English."

The young French fella, hatless, was skimming down the Promenade des Anglais, looking intently ahead, and behind, and to the side, and all around in the darkness. He seemed to be following a certain trail, however. At one side of the great wide walk, facing the ocean, was a canopied bandstand. In its dim shadow, he discerned a wisp of white.

He made for it, swiftly, silently. Mazzetti's voice low, eager, insistent. Mazzetti's voice hoarse, ugly, importunate. The figure in white rose. Goré stood before the two. The girl took a step toward him, but Mazzetti took two steps and snarled like a villain in a movie, if a villain in a movie could be heard to snarl.

"Get out of here!" said Mazzetti, in French, to Goré. "You pig! Swine! To intrude when I talk with a lady. You are finished. Now she belongs to me."

"The hell she does!" said Giddy Gory in perfectly plain American and swung for Mazzetti with his bad right arm. Mazzetti, after the fashion of his kind, let fly in most unsportsmanlike fashion with his feet, kicking at Giddy's stomach and trying to bite with his small sharp yellow teeth. And then Giddy's left, that had learned some neat tricks of boxing in the days of the Gory greatness, landed fairly on the Mazzetti nose. And with a howl of pain and rage and terror the Mazzetti, a hand clapped to that bleeding feature, fled in the darkness.

And, "O, Giddy!" said Mary, "I thought you'd never come."

"Mary. Mary Hubbell. Did you know all the time? You did, didn't you? You think I'm a bum, don't you? Don't you?"

Her hand on his shoulder. "Giddy, I've been stuck on you since I was nine years old, in Winnebago. I kept track of you all through the war, though I never once saw you. Then I lost you. Giddy, when I was a kid I used to look at you from the sidewalk through the hedge of the house on Cass. Honestly. Honestly, Giddy."

"But look at me now. Why, Mary, I'm—I'm no good. Why, I don't see how you ever knew—"

"It takes more than a new Greek nose and French clothes and a bum arm to fool me, Gid. Do you know, there were a lot of photographs of you left up in the attic of the Cass Street house when we bought it. I know them all by heart, Giddy. By heart.... Come on home, Giddy. Let's go home."

NOT A DAY OVER TWENTY-ONE

Aɴʏ one old enough to read this is old enough to remember that favourite heroine of fiction who used to start her day by rising from her couch, flinging wide her casement, leaning out and breathing deep the perfumed morning air. You will recall, too, the pure white rose clambering at the side of the casement, all jewelled with the dew of dawn. This the lady plucked carolling. Daily she plucked it. A hardy perennial if ever there was one. Subsequently, pressing it to her lips, she flung it into the garden below, where stood her lover (likewise an early riser).

Romantic proceeding this, but unhygienic when you consider that her rush for the closed casement was doubtless due to the fact that her bedroom, hermetically sealed during the night, must have grown pretty stuffy by morning. Her complexion was probably bad.

No such idyllic course marked the matin of our heroine. Her day's beginning differed from the above in practically every detail. Thus:

A—When Harrietta rose from her couch (cream enamel, full-sized bed with double hair mattress and box springs) she closed her casement with a bang, having slept in a gale that swept her two-room-and-kitchenette apartment on the eleventh floor in Fifty-sixth Street.

B—She never leaned out except, perhaps, to flap a dust rag, because lean as she might, defying the laws of gravity and the house superintendent, she could have viewed nothing more than roofs and sky and chimneys where already roofs and sky and chimneys filled the eye (unless you consider that by screwing around and flattening one ear and the side of your jaw against the window jamb you could almost get a glimpse of distant green prominently mentioned in the agent's ad as "unexcelled view of Park").

C—The morning air wasn't perfumed for purposes of breathing deep, being New York morning air, richly laden with the smell of warm asphalt, smoke, gas, and, when the wind was right, the glue factory on the Jersey shore across the river.

D—She didn't pluck a rose, carolling, because even if, by some magic Burbankian process, Jack's bean-stalk had been made rose-bearing it would have been hard put to it to reach this skyscraper home.

E—If she had flung it, it probably would have ended its eleven-story flight in the hand cart of Messinger's butcher boy, who usually made his first Fifty-sixth Street delivery at about that time.

F—The white rose would not have been jewelled and sparkling with the dews of dawn, anyway, as at Harrietta's rising hour (between 10.30 and 11.30 A. M.) the New York City dews, if any, have left for the day.

Spartans who rise regularly at the chaste hour of seven will now regard Harrietta with disapproval. These should be told that Harrietta never got to bed before twelve-thirty nor to sleep before two-thirty, which, on an eight-hour sleep count, should even things up somewhat in their minds. They must know, too, that in one corner of her white-and-blue bathroom reposed a pair of wooden dumb-bells, their ankles neatly crossed. She used them daily. Also she bathed, massaged, exercised, took facial and electric treatments; worked like a slave; lived like an athlete in training in order to preserve her hair, skin, teeth, and figure; almost never ate what she wanted nor as much as she liked.

That earlier lady of the closed casement and the white rose probably never even heard of a dentifrice or a cold shower.

The result of Harrietta's rigours was that now, at thirty-seven, she could pass for twenty-seven on Fifth Avenue at five o'clock (flesh-pink, single-mesh face veil); twenty-five at a small dinner (rose-coloured shades over the candles), and twenty-two, easily, behind the amber footlights.

You will have guessed that Harrietta, the Heroine, is none other than Harrietta Fuller, deftest of comediennes, whom you have seen in one or all of those slim little plays in which she has made a name but no money to speak of, being handicapped for the American stage by her intelligence and her humour sense, and, as she would tell you, by her very name itself.

"Harrietta Fuller! Don't you see what I mean?" she would say. "In the first place, it's hard to remember. And it lacks force. Or maybe rhythm. It doesn't clink. It sort of humps in the middle. A name should flow. Take a name like Barrymore—or Bernhardt—or Duse—you can't forget them. Oh, I'm not comparing myself to them. Don't be funny. I just mean—why, take Harrietta alone. It's deadly. A Thackeray miss, all black silk mitts and white cotton stockings. Long ago, in the beginning, I thought of shortening it. But Harriet Fuller sounds like a schoolteacher, doesn't it? And Hattie Fuller makes me think, somehow, of a burlesque actress. You know. 'Hattie Fuller and Her Bouncing Belles.'"

At thirty-seven Harrietta Fuller had been fifteen years on the stage. She had little money, a small stanch following, an exquisite technique, and her fur coat was beginning to look gnawed around the edges. People even said maddeningly: "Harrietta Fuller? I saw her when I was a kid, years ago. Why, she must be le'see—ten—twelve—why, she must be going on pretty close to forty."

A worshipper would defend her. "You're crazy! I saw her last month when she was playing in Cincinnati, and she doesn't look a day over twenty-one. That's a cute play she's in—There and Back. Not much to it, but she's so kind and natural. Made me think of Jen a little."

That was part of Harrietta's art—making people think of Jen. Watching her, they would whisper: "Look! Isn't that Jen all over? The way she sits there and looks up at him while she's sewing."

Harrietta Fuller could take lines that were stilted and shoddy and speak them in a way to make them sound natural and distinctive and real. She was a clear blonde, but her speaking voice had in it a contralto note that usually accompanies brunette colouring.

It surprised and gratified you, that tone, as does mellow wine when you have expected cider. She could walk on to one of those stage library sets that reek of the storehouse and the property carpenter, seat herself, take up a book or a piece of handiwork, and instantly the absurd room became a human, livable place. She had a knack of sitting, not as an actress ordinarily seats herself in a drawing room—feet carefully strained to show the high arch, body posed to form a "line"—but easily, as a woman sits in her own house. If you saw her in the supper scene of My Mistake, you will remember how she twisted her feet about the rungs of the straight little chair in which she sat. Her back was toward the audience throughout the scene, according to stage directions, yet she managed to convey embarrassment, fright, terror, determination, decision in the agonized twisting of those expressive feet.

Authors generally claimed these bits of business as having originated with them. For that matter, she was a favourite with playwrights, as well she might be, considering the vitality which she injected into their hackneyed situations. Every little while some young writer, fired by an inflection in her voice or a nuance in her comedy, would rush back stage to tell her that she never had had a part worthy of her, and that he would now come to her rescue. Sometimes he kept his word, and Harrietta, six months later, would look up from the manuscript to say: "This is delightful! It's what I've been looking for for years. The deftness of the comedy. And that little scene with the gardener!"

But always, after the managers had finished suggesting bits that would brighten it up, and changes that would put it over with the Western buyers, Harrietta would regard the mutilated manuscript sorrowingly. "But I can't play this now, you know. It isn't the same part at all. It's—forgive me—vulgar."

Then some little red-haired ingénue would get it, and it would run a solid year on Broadway and two seasons on the road, and in all that time Harrietta would have played six months, perhaps, in three different plays, in all of which she would score what is known as a "personal success." A personal success usually means bad business at the box office.

Now this is immensely significant. In the advertisements of the play in which Harrietta Fuller might be appearing you never read:

HARRIETTA FULLER

In

Thus and So

No. It was always:

THUS AND SO

With

Harrietta Fuller

Between those two prepositions lies a whole theatrical world of difference. The "In" means stardom; the "With" that the play is considered more important than the cast.

Don't feel sorry for Harrietta Fuller. Thousands of women have envied her; thousands of men admired, and several have loved her devotedly, including her father, the Rev. H. John Scoville (deceased). The H. stands for Harry. She was named for him, of course. When he entered the church he was advised to drop his first name and use his second as being more fitting in his position. But the outward change did not affect his inner self. He remained more Harry than John to the last. It was from him Harrietta got her acting sense, her humour, her intelligence, and her bad luck.

When Harry Scoville was eighteen he wanted to go on the stage. At twenty he entered the ministry. It was the natural outlet for his suppressed talents. In his day and family and environment young men did not go on the stage. The Scovilles were Illinois pioneers and lived in Evanston, and Mrs. Scoville (Harrietta's grandmother, you understand, though Harrietta had not yet appeared) had a good deal to say as to whether coleslaw or cucumber pickles should be served at the Presbyterian church suppers, along with the veal loaf and the scalloped oysters. And when she decided on coleslaw, coleslaw it was. A firm tread had Mother Scoville, a light hand with pastry, and a will that was adamant. She it was who misdirected Harry's gifts toward the pulpit instead of the stage. He never forgave her for it, though he made a great success of his calling and she died unsuspecting his rancour. The women of his congregation shivered deliciously when the Rev. H. John Scoville stood on his tiptoes at the apex of some fiery period and hurled the force of his eloquence at them. He, the minister, was unconsciously dramatizing himself as a minister.

The dramatic method had not then come into use in the pulpit. His method of delivery was more restrained than that of the old-time revivalist; less analytical and detached than that of the present-day religious lecturer.

Presbyterian Evanston wending its way home to Sunday roast and ice cream would say: "Wasn't Reverend Scoville powerful to-day! My!" They never guessed how Reverend Scoville had had to restrain himself from delivering Mark Antony's address to the Romans. He often did it in his study when his gentle wife thought he was rehearsing next Sunday's sermon.

As he grew older he overcame these boyish weaknesses, but he never got over his feeling for the stage. There were certain ill-natured gossips who claimed to have recognized the fine, upright figure and the mobile face with hair greying at the temples as having occupied a seat in the third row of the balcony in the old Grand Opera House during the run of Erminie. The elders put it down as spite talk and declared that, personally, they didn't believe a word of it. The Rev. H. John did rather startle them when he discarded the ministerial black broadcloth for a natty Oxford suit of almost business cut. He was a pioneer in this among the clergy. The congregation soon became accustomed to it; in time, boasted of it as marking their progressiveness.

He had a neat ankle, had the Reverend Scoville, in fine black lisle; a merry eye; a rather grim look about the mouth, as has a man whose life is a secret disappointment. His little daughter worshipped him. He called her Harry. When Harrietta was eleven she was reading Lever and Dickens and Dumas, while other little girls were absorbed in the

Elsie Series and The Wide, Wide World. Her father used to deliver his sermons to her in private rehearsal, and her eager mobile face reflected his every written mood.

"Oh, Rev!" she cried one day (it is to be regretted, but that is what she always called him). "Oh, Rev, you should have been an actor!"

He looked at her queerly. "What makes you think so?"

"You're too thrilling for a minister." She searched about in her agile mind for fuller means of making her thought clear. "It's like when Mother cooks rose geranium leaves in her grape jell. She says they gives it a finer flavour, but they don't really. You can't taste them for the grapes, so they're just wasted when they're so darling and perfumy and just right in the garden." Her face was pink with earnestness.

"D'you see what I mean, Rev?"

"Yes, I think I see, Harry."

Then she surprised him. "I'm going on the stage," she said, "and be a great actress when I'm grown up."

His heart gave a leap and a lurch. "Why do you say that?"

"Because I want to. And because you didn't. It'll be as if you had been an actor instead of a minister—only it'll be me."

A bewildering enough statement to any one but the one who made it and the one to whom it was made. She was trying to say that here was the law of compensation working. But she didn't know this. She had never heard of the law of compensation.

Her gentle mother fought her decision with all the savagery of the gentle.

"You'll have to run away, Harry," her father said, sadly. And at twenty-two Harrietta ran. Her objective was New York. Her father did not burden her with advice. He credited her with the intelligence she possessed, but he did overlook her emotionalism, which was where he made his mistake. Just before she left he said: "Now listen, Harry. You're a good-looking girl, and young. You'll keep your looks for a long time. You're not the kind of blonde who'll get wishy-washy or fat. You've got quite a good deal of brunette in you. It crops out in your voice. It'll help preserve your looks. Don't marry the first man who asks you or the first man who says he'll die if you don't. You've got lots of time."

That kind of advice is a good thing for the young. Two weeks later Harrietta married a man she had met on the train between Evanston and New York. His name was Lawrence Fuller, and Harrietta had gone to school with him in Evanston. She had lost track of him later. She remembered, vaguely, people had said he had gone to New York and was pretty wild. Young as she was and inexperienced, there still was something about his face that warned her. It was pathological, but she knew nothing of pathology. He talked of her and looked at her and spoke, masterfully and yet shyly, of being with her in New York. Harrietta loved the way his hair sprang away from his brow and temples in a clean line. She shoved the thought of his chin out of her mind. His hands touched her a good deal—her shoulder, her knee, her wrist—but so lightly that she couldn't resent it even if she had wanted to. When they did this, queer little stinging flashes darted through her veins. He said he would die if she did not marry him.

They had two frightful years together and eight years apart before he died, horribly, in the sanatorium whose enormous fees she paid weekly. They had regularly swallowed her earnings at a gulp.

Naturally a life like this develops the comedy sense. You can't play tragedy while you're living it. Harrietta served her probation in stock, road companies, one-night stands before she achieved Broadway. In five years her deft comedy method had become distinctive; in ten it was unique. Yet success—as the stage measures it in size of following and dollars of salary—had never been hers.

Harrietta knew she wasn't a success. She saw actresses younger, older, less adroit, lacking her charm, minus her beauty, featured, starred, heralded. Perhaps she gave her audiences credit for more intelligence than they possessed, and they, unconsciously, resented this. Perhaps if she had read the Elsie Series at eleven, instead of Dickens, she might have been willing to play in that million-dollar success called Gossip. It was offered her. The lead was one of those saccharine parts, vulgar, false, and slyly carnal. She didn't in the least object to it on the ground of immorality, but the bad writing bothered her. There was, for example, a line in which she was supposed to beat her breast and say: "He's my mate! He's my man! And I'm his woman!! I love him, I tell you I—*love him!*"

"People don't talk like that," she told the author, in a quiet aside, during rehearsal. "Especially women. They couldn't. They use quite commonplace idiom when they're excited."

"Thanks," said the author, elaborately polite. "That's the big scene in the play. It'll be a knockout."

When Harrietta tried to speak these lines in rehearsal she began to giggle and ended in throwing up the ridiculous part. They gave it to that little Frankie Langdon, and the playwright's prophecy came true. The breast-beating scene was a knockout. It ran for two years in New York alone. Langdon's sables, chinchillas, ermines, and jewels were always sticking out from the pages of *Vanity Fair* and *Vogue*. When she took curtain calls, Langdon stood with her legs far apart, boyishly, and tossed her head and looked up from beneath her lowered lids and acted surprised and sort of gasped like a fish and bit her lip and mumbled to herself as if overcome. The audience said wasn't she a shy, young, bewildered darling!

A hard little rip if ever there was one—Langdon—and as shy as a man-eating crocodile.

This sort of sham made Harrietta sick. She, whose very art was that of pretending, hated pretense, affectation, "coy stuff." This was, perhaps, unfortunate. Your Fatigued Financier prefers the comedy form in which a spade is not only called a spade but a slab of iron for digging up dirt. Harrietta never even pretended to have a cough on an opening night so that the critics, should the play prove a failure, might say: "Harrietta Fuller, though handicapped by a severe cold, still gave her usual brilliant and finished performance in a part not quite worthy of her talents." No. The plaintive smothered cough, the quick turn aside, the heaving shoulder, the wispy handkerchief were clumsy tools beneath her notice.

There often were long periods of idleness when her soul sickened and her purse grew lean. Long hot summers in New York when awnings, window boxes geranium filled, drinks iced and acidulous, and Ken's motor car for cooling drives to the beaches failed to soothe the terror in her. Thirty ... thirty-two ... thirty-four ... thirty-six....

She refused to say it. She refused to think of it. She put the number out of her mind and slammed the door on it—on that hideous number beginning with f. At such times she was given to contemplation of her own photographs—and was reassured. Her intelligence told her that retouching varnish, pumice stone, hard pencil, and etching knife had all gone into the photographer's version of this clear-eyed, fresh-lipped blooming creature gazing back at her so limpidly. But, then, who didn't need a lot of retouching? Even the youngest of them.

All this. Yet she loved it. The very routine of it appealed to her orderly nature: a routine that, were it widely known, would shatter all those ideas about the large, loose life of the actress. Harrietta Fuller liked to know that at such and such an hour she would be in her dressing room; at such and such an hour on the stage; precisely at another hour she would again be in her dressing room preparing to go home. Then the stage would be darkened. They would be putting the scenery away. She would be crossing the bare stage on her way home. Then she would be home, undressing, getting ready for bed, reading. She liked a cup of clear broth at night, or a drink of hot cocoa. It soothed and rested her. Besides, one is hungry after two and a half hours of high-tensioned, nerve-exhausting work. She was in bed usually by twelve-thirty.

"But you can't fall asleep like a dewy babe in my kind of job," she used to explain. "People wonder why actresses lie in bed until noon, or nearly. They have to, to get as much sleep as a stenographer or a clerk or a book-keeper. At midnight I'm all keyed up and over-stimulated, and as wide awake as an all-night taxi driver. It takes two solid hours of reading to send me bye-bye."

The world did not interest itself in that phase of Harrietta's life. Neither did it find fascination in her domestic side. Harrietta did a good deal of tidying and dusting and redding up in her own two-room apartment, so high and bright and spotless. She liked to cook, too, and was expert at it. Not for her those fake pictures of actresses and opera stars in chiffon tea gowns and satin slippers and diamond chains cooking "their favourite dish of spaghetti and creamed mushrooms," and staring out at you bright-eyed and palpably unable to tell the difference between salt and paprika. Harrietta liked the ticking of a clock in a quiet room; oven smells; concocting new egg dishes; washing out lacy things in warm soapsuds. A throw-back, probably, to her grandmother Scoville.

The worst feature of a person like Harrietta is, as you already have discovered with some impatience, that one goes on and on, talking about her. And the listener at last breaks out with: "This is all very interesting, but I feel as if I know her now. What then?"

Then the thing to do is to go serenely on telling, for example, how the young thing in Harrietta Fuller's company invariably came up to her at the first rehearsal and said tremulously: "Miss Fuller, I—you won't mind—I just want to tell you how proud I am to be one of your company. Playing with you. You've been my ideal ever since I was a little g—" then, warned by a certain icy mask slipping slowly over the brightness of Harrietta's features—"ever so long, but I never even hoped—"

These young things always learned an amazing lot from watching the deft, sure strokes of Harrietta's craftsmanship. She was kind to them, too. Encouraged them. Never hogged a scene that belonged to them. Never cut their lines. Never patronized them. They usually played ingénue parts, and their big line was that uttered on coming into a room looking for Harrietta. It was: "Ah, *there* you are!"

How can you really know Harrietta unless you realize the deference with which she was treated in her own little sphere? If the world at large did not acclaim her, there was no lack of appreciation on the part of her fellow workers. They knew artistry when they saw it. Though she had never attained stardom, she still had the distinction that usually comes only to a star back stage. Unless she actually was playing in support of a first-magnitude star, her dressing room was marked "A." Other members of the company did not drop into her dressing room except by invitation. That room was neat to the point of primness. A square of white coarse sheeting was spread on the floor, under the chair before her dressing table, to gather up dust and powder. It was regularly shaken or changed. There were always flowers—often a single fine rose in a slender vase. On her dressing table, in a corner, you were likely to find three or four volumes—perhaps The Amenities of Book-Collecting; something or other of Max Beerbohm's; a book of verse (not Amy Lowell's).

These were not props designed to impress the dramatic critic who might drop in for one of those personal little theatrical calls to be used in next Sunday's "Chats in the Wings." They were there because Harrietta liked them and read them between acts. She had a pretty wit of her own. The critics liked to talk with her. Even George Jean Hathem, whose favourite pastime was to mangle the American stage with his pen and hold its bleeding, gaping fragments up for the edification of Budapest, Petrograd, Vienna, London, Berlin, Paris, and Stevens Point, Wis., said that five minutes of Harrietta Fuller's conversation was worth a lifetime of New York stage dialogue. For that matter I think that Mr. Beerbohm himself would not have found a talk with her altogether dull or profitless.

The leading man generally made love to her in an expert, unaggressive way. A good many men had tried to make love to her at one time or another. They didn't get on very well. Harrietta never went to late suppers. Some of them complained: "When you try to make love to her she laughs at you!" She wasn't really laughing at them. She was laughing at what she knew about life. Occasionally men now married, and living dully content in the prim suburban smugness of Pelham or New Rochelle, boasted of past friendship with her, wagging their heads doggishly. "Little Fuller! I used to know her well."

They lied.

Not that she didn't count among her friends many men. She dined with them and they with her. They were writers and critics, lawyers and doctors, engineers and painters. Actors almost never. They sent her books and flowers; valued her opinion, delighted in her conversation, wished she wouldn't sometimes look at them so quizzically. And if they didn't always comprehend her wit, they never failed to appreciate the contour of her face, where the thoughtful brow was contradicted by the lovely little nose, and both were drowned in the twin wells of the wide-apart, misleadingly limpid eyes that lay ensnaringly between.

"Your eyes!" these gentlemen sometimes stammered, "the lashes are reflected in them like ferns edging a pool."

"Yes. The mascara's good for them. You'd think all that black sticky stuff I have put on, would hurt them, but it really makes them grow, I believe. Sometimes I even use a burnt match, and yet it—"

"Damn your burnt matches! I'm talking about your lashes."

"So am I." She would open her eyes wide in surprise, and the lashes could almost be said to wave at him tantalizingly, like fairy fans. (He probably wished he could have thought of that.)

Ken never talked to her about her lashes. Ken thought she was the most beauteous, witty, intelligent woman in the world, but he had never told her so, and she found herself wishing he would. Ken was forty-one and Knew About Etchings. He knew about a lot of other things, too. Difficult, complex things like Harrietta Fuller, for example. He had to do with some intricate machine or other that was vital to printing, and he was perfecting something connected with it or connecting something needed for its perfection that would revolutionize the thing the machine now did (whatever it was). Harrietta refused to call him an inventor. She said it sounded so impecunious. They had known each other for six years. When she didn't feel like talking he didn't say: "What's the matter?" He never told her that women had no business monkeying with stocks or asked her what they called that stuff her dress was made of, or telephoned before noon. Twice a year he asked her to marry him, presenting excellent reasons. His name was Carrigan. You'd like him.

"When I marry," Harrietta would announce, "which will be never, it will be the only son of a rich iron king from Duluth, Minnesota. And I'll go there to live in an eighteen-room mansion and pluck roses for the breakfast room."

"There are few roses in Duluth," said Ken, "to speak of. And no breakfast rooms. You breakfast in the dining room, and in the winter you wear flannel underwear and galoshes."

"California, then. And he can be the son of a fruit king. I'm not narrow."

Harrietta was thirty-seven and a half when there came upon her a great fear. It had been a wretchedly bad season. Two failures. The rent on her two-room apartment in Fifty-sixth Street jumped from one hundred and twenty-five, which she could afford, to two hundred a month, which she couldn't. Mary—Irish Mary—her personal maid, left her in January. Personal maids are one of the superstitions of the theatrical profession, and an actress of standing is supposed to go hungry rather than maidless.

"Why don't you fire Irish Mary?" Ken had asked Harrietta during a period of stringency.

"I can't afford to."

Ken understood, but you may not. Harrietta would have made it clear. "Any actress who earns more than a hundred a week is supposed to have a maid in her dressing room. No one knows why, but it's true. I remember in The Small-Town Girl I wore the same gingham dress throughout three acts, but I was paying Mary twenty a week just the same. If I hadn't some one in the company would have told some one in another company that Harrietta Fuller was broke. It would have seeped through the director to the manager, and next time they offered me a part they'd cut my salary. It's absurd, but there it is. A vicious circle."

Irish Mary's reason for leaving Harrietta was a good one. It would have to be, for she was of that almost extinct species, the devoted retainer. Irish Mary wasn't the kind of maid one usually encounters back stage. No dapper, slim, black-and-white pert miss, with a wisp of apron and a knowledgeous eye. An ample, big-hipped, broad-bosomed woman with an apron like a drop curtain and a needle knack that kept Harrietta mended, be-ribboned, beruffled, and exquisite from her garters to her coat hangers. She had been around the theatre for twenty-five years, and her thick, deft fingers had served a long line of illustrious ladies—Corinne Foster, Gertrude Bennett, Lucille Varney. She knew all the shades of grease paint from Flesh to Sallow Old Age, and if you gained an ounce she warned you.

Her last name was Lesom, but nobody remembered it until she brought forward a daughter of fifteen with the request that she be given a job; anything—walk-on, extra, chorus. Lyddy, she called her. The girl seldom spoke. She was extremely stupid, but a marvellous mimic, and pretty beyond belief; fragile, and yet with something common about her even in her fragility. Her wrists had a certain flat angularity that bespoke a peasant ancestry, but she had a singular freshness and youthful bloom. The line of her side face from the eye socket to the chin was a delicious thing that curved with the grace of a wing. The high cheek-bone sloped down so that the outline was heart-shaped. There were little indentations at the corners of her mouth. She had eyes singularly clear, like a child's, and a voice so nasal, so strident, so dreadful that when she parted her pretty lips and spoke, the sound shocked you like a peacock's raucous screech.

Harrietta had managed to get a bit for her here, a bit for her there, until by the time she was eighteen she was giving a fairly creditable performance in practically speechless parts. It was dangerous to trust her even with an "Ah, there you are!" line. The audience, startled, was so likely to laugh.

At about this point she vanished, bound for Hollywood and the movies. "She's the little fool, just," said Irish Mary. "What'll she be wantin' with the movies, then, an' her mother connected with the theayter for years an' all, and her you might say brought up in it?"

But she hadn't been out there a year before the world knew her as Lydia Lissome. Starting as an extra girl earning twenty-five a week or less, she had managed, somehow, to get the part of Betty in the screen version of The Magician, probably because she struck the director as being the type; or perhaps her gift of mimicry had something to do with it, and the youth glow that was in her face. At any rate, when the picture was finished and released, no one was more surprised than Lyddy at the result. They offered her three thousand a week on a three-year contract. She wired her mother, but Irish Mary wired back: "I don't believe a word of it hold out for five am coming." She left for the Coast. Incidentally, she got the five for Lyddy. Lyddy signed her name to the contract—Lydia Lissome—in a hand that would have done discredit to an eleven-year-old.

Harrietta told Ken about it, not without some bitterness: "Which only proves one can't be too careful about picking one's parents. If my father had been a hod carrier instead of a minister of the Gospel and a darling old dreamer, I'd be earning five thousand a week, too."

They were dining together in Harrietta's little sitting room so high up and quiet and bright with its cream enamel and its log fire. Almost one entire wall of that room was window, facing south, and framing such an Arabian Nights panorama as only a New York eleventh-story window, facing south, can offer.

Ken lifted his right eyebrow, which was a way he had when being quizzical. "What would you do with five thousand a week, just supposing?"

"I'd do all the vulgar things that other people do who have five thousand a week."

"You wouldn't enjoy them. You don't care for small dogs or paradise aigrettes or Italian villas in Connecticut or diamond-studded cigarette holders or plush limousines or butlers." He glanced comprehensively about the little room—at the baby grand whose top was pleasantly littered with photographs and bonbon dishes and flower vases; at the smart little fire snapping in the grate; at the cheerful reds and blues and ochres and sombre blues and purples and greens of the books in the open bookshelves; at the squat clock on the mantelshelf; at the gorgeous splashes of black and gold glimpsed through the many-paned window. "You've got everything you really want right here"—his gesture seemed, somehow, to include himself—"if you only knew it."

"You talk," snapped Harrietta, "as the Rev. H. John Scoville used to." She had never said a thing like that before. "I'm sick of what they call being true to my art. I'm tired of having last year's suit relined, even if it is smart enough to be good this year. I'm sick of having the critics call me an intelligent comedienne who is unfortunate in her choice of plays. Some day"—a little flash of fright was there—"I'll pick up the *Times* and see myself referred to as 'that sterling actress.' Then I'll know I'm through."

"You!"

"Tell me I'm young, Ken. Tell me I'm young and beautiful and bewitching."

"You're young and beautiful and bewitching."

"Ugh! And yet they say the Irish have the golden tongues."

Two months later Harrietta had an offer to go into pictures. It wasn't her first, but it undeniably was the best. The sum offered per week was what she might usually expect to get per month in a successful stage play. To accept the offer meant the Coast. She found herself having a test picture taken and trying to believe the director who said it was good; found herself expatiating on the brightness, quietness, and general desirability of the eleventh-floor apartment in Fifty-sixth Street to an acquaintance who was seeking a six months' city haven for the summer.

"She'll probably ruin my enamel dressing table with toilet water and ring my piano top with wet glasses and spatter grease on the kitchenette wall. But I'll be earning a million," Harrietta announced, recklessly, "or thereabouts. Why should I care?"

She did care, though, as a naturally neat and thrifty woman cares for her household goods which have, through years of care of them and association with them, become her household gods. The clock on the mantel wasn't a clock, but a plump friend with a white smiling face and a soothing tongue; the low, ample davenport wasn't a davenport only, but a soft bosom that pillowed her; that which lay spread shimmering beneath her window was not New York alone—it was her View. To a woman like this, letting her apartment furnished is like farming out her child to strangers.

She had told her lessee about her laundress and her cleaning woman and how to handle the balky faucet that controlled the shower. She had said good-bye to Ken entirely surrounded by his books, magazines, fruit, and flowers. She was occupying a Pullman drawing room paid for by the free-handed filmers. She was crossing farm lands, plains, desert. She was wondering if all those pink sweaters and white flannel trousers outside the Hollywood Hotel were there for the same reason that she was. She was surveying a rather warm little room shaded by a dense tree whose name she did not know. She was thinking it felt a lot like her old trouping days, when her telephone tinkled and a voice announced Mrs. Lissome. Lissome? Lesam. Irish Mary, of course. Harrietta's maid, engaged for the trip, had failed her at the last moment. Now her glance rested on the two massive trunks and the litter of smart, glittering bags that strewed the room. A relieved look crept into her eyes. A knock at the door. A resplendent figure was revealed at its opening. The look in Harrietta's eyes vanished.

Irish Mary looked like the mother of a girl who was earning five thousand a week. She was marcelled, silk-clad, rustling, gold-meshed, and, oh, how real in spite of it all as she beamed upon the dazzled Harrietta.

"Out with ye!" trumpeted this figure, brushing aside Harrietta's proffered chair. "There'll be no stayin' here for you. You're coming along with me, then, bag *and* baggage." She glanced sharply about. "Where's your maid, dearie?"

"Disappointed me at the last minute. I'll have to get someone—"

"We've plenty. You're coming up to our place."

"But, Mary, I can't. I couldn't. I'm tired. This room—"

"A hole. Wait till you see The Place. Gardens and breakfast rooms and statues and fountains and them Jap boys runnin' up and down like mice. We rented it for a year from that Goya Ciro. She's gone back East. How she ever made good in pictures I don't know, and her face like a hot-water bag for expression. Lyddy's going to build next year. They're drawin' up the plans now. The Place'll be nothin' compared to it when it's finished. Put on your hat. The boys'll see to your stuff here."

"I can't. I couldn't. You're awfully kind, Mary dear—"

Mary dear was at the telephone. "Mrs. Lissome. That's who. Send up that Jap boy for the bags."

Mrs. Lissome's name and Mrs. Lissome's commands apparently carried heavily in Hollywood. A uniformed Jap appeared immediately as though summoned by a genie. The bags seemed to spring to him, so quickly was he enveloped by their glittering surfaces. He was off with the burdens, invisible except for his gnomelike face and his sturdy bow legs in their footman's boots.

"I can't," said Harrietta, feebly, for the last time. It was her introduction to the topsy-turvy world into which she had come. She felt herself propelled down the stairs by Irish Mary, who wasn't Irish Mary any more, but a Force whose orders were obeyed. In the curved drive outside the Hollywood Hotel the little Jap was stowing the last of the bags into the great blue car whose length from nose to tail seemed to span the hotel frontage. At the wheel, rigid, sat a replica of the footman.

Irish Mary with a Japanese chauffeur. Irish Mary with a Japanese footman. Irish Mary with a great glittering car that was as commodious as the average theatre dressing room.

"Get in, dearie. Lyddy's using the big car to-day. They're out on location. Shootin' the last of Devils and Men."

Harrietta was saying to herself: "Don't be a nasty snob, Harry. This is a different world. Think of the rotten time Alice would have had in Wonderland if she hadn't been broad-minded. Take it as it comes."

Irish Mary was talking as they sped along through the hot white Hollywood sunshine.... "Stay right with us as long as you like, dearie, but if after you're workin' you want a place of your own, I know of just the thing you can rent furnished, and a Jap gardener and house man and cook right on the places besides—"

"But I'm not signed for five thousand a week, like Lydia," put in Harrietta.

"I know what you're signed for. 'Twas me put 'em up to it, an' who else! 'Easy money,' I says, 'an' why shouldn't she be gettin' some of it?' Lyddy spoke to Gans about it. What Lyddy says goes. She's a good girl, Lyddy is, an' would you believe the money an' all hasn't gone to her brains, though what with workin' like a horse an' me to steady her, an' shrewder than the lawyers themself, if I do say it, she ain't had much chance. And here's The Place."

And here was The Place. Sundials, rose gardens, gravel paths, dwarf trees, giant trees, fountains, swimming pools, tennis courts, goldfish, statues, verandas, sleeping porches, awnings, bird baths, pergolas.

Inside more Japs. Maids. Rooms furnished like the interior of movie sets that Harrietta remembered having seen. A bedroom, sitting room, dressing room, and bath all her own in one wing of the great white palace, only one of thousands of great white palaces scattered through the

77

hills of Hollywood. The closet for dresses, silk-lined and scented, could have swallowed whole her New York bedroom.

"Lay down," said Irish Mary, "an' get easy. Lyddy won't be home till six if she's early, an' she'll prob'bly be in bed by nine now they're rushin' the end of the picture, an' she's got to be on the lot made up by nine or sooner."

"Nine—in the morning!"

"Well, sure! You soon get used to it. They've got to get all the daylight they can, an' times the fog's low earlier, or they'd likely start at seven or eight. You look a little beat, dearie. Lay down. I'll have you unpacked while we're eatin'."

But Harrietta did not lie down. She went to the window. Below a small army of pigmy gardeners were doing expert things to flower beds and bushes that already seemed almost shamelessly prolific. Harrietta thought, suddenly, of her green-painted flower boxes outside the eleventh-story south window in the New York flat. Outside her window here a great scarlet hibiscus stuck its tongue out at her. Harrietta stuck her tongue out at it, childishly, and turned away. She liked a certain reticence in flowers, as in everything else. She sat down at the desk, took up a sheet of lavender and gold paper and the great lavender plumed pen. The note she wrote to Ken was the kind of note that only Ken would understand, unless you've got into the way of reading it once a year or so, too:

> *Ken, dear, I almost wish I hadn't gone down that rabbit hole, and yet—and yet—it's rather curious, you know, this sort of life.*

Two weeks later, when she had begun to get used to her new work, her new life, the strange hours, people, jargon, she wrote him another cryptic note:

> *Alice—"Well, in our country you'd generally get to somewhere else—if you ran very fast for a long time, as I've been doing."*
>
> *Red Queen—"Here it takes all the running you can do to keep in the same place."*

In those two weeks things had happened rather breathlessly. Harrietta had moved from the splendours of The Place to her own rose-embowered bungalow. Here, had she wanted to do any casement work with a white rose, like that earlier heroine, she could easily have managed it had not the early morning been so feverishly occupied in reaching the lot in time to be made up by nine. She soon learned the jargon. "The lot" meant the studio in which she was working, and its environs. "We're going to shoot you this morning," meant that she would be needed in to-day's scenes. Often she was in bed by eight at night, so tired that she could not sleep. She wondered what the picture was about. She couldn't make head or tail of it.

They were filming J. N. Gardner's novel, Romance of Arcady, but they had renamed it Let's Get a Husband. The heroine in the novel was the young wife of twenty-seven who had been married five years. This was Harrietta's part. In the book there had been a young girl, too—a saccharine miss of seventeen who was the minor love interest. This was Lydia Lissome's part. Slowly it dawned on Harrietta that things had been nightmarishly tampered with in the film version, and that the change in name was the least of the indignities to which the novel had been subjected.

It took Harrietta some time to realize this because they were not taking the book scenes in their sequence. They took them according to light, convenience, location. Indoor scenes were taken in one group, so that the end of the story might often be the first to be filmed.

For a week Harrietta was dressed, made up, and ready for work at nine o'clock, and for a week she wasn't used in a single scene. The hours of waiting made her frantic. The sun was white hot. Her little dressing room was stifling. She hated her face with its dead-white mask and blue-lidded eyes. When, finally, her time came she found that after being dressed and ready from nine until five-thirty daily she was required, at 4:56 on the sixth day, to cross the set, open a door, stop, turn, appear to be listening, and recross the set to meet someone entering from the opposite side. This scene, trivial as it appeared, was rehearsed seven times before the director was satisfied with it.

The person for whom she had paused, turned, and crossed was Lydia Lissome. And Lydia Lissome, it soon became evident, had the lead in this film. In the process of changing from novel to scenario, the Young Wife had become a rather middle-aged wife, and the Flapper of seventeen had become the heroine. And Harrietta Fuller, erstwhile actress of youthful comedy parts for the stage, found herself moving about in black velvet and pearls and a large plumed fan as a background for the white ruffles and golden curls and sunny scenes in which Lydia Lissome held the camera's eye.

For years Harrietta Fuller's entrance during a rehearsal always had created a little stir among the company. This one rose to give her a seat; that one made her a compliment; Sam Klein, the veteran director, patted her cheek and said: "You're going to like this part, Miss Fuller. And they're going to eat it up. *You* see." The author bent over her in mingled nervousness and deference and admiration. The Young Thing who was to play the ingénue part said shyly: "Oh, Miss Fuller, may I tell you how happy I am to be playing with you? You've been my ideal, etc."

And now Harrietta Fuller, in black velvet, was the least important person on the lot. No one was rude to her. Everyone was most kind, in fact. Kind! To Harrietta Fuller! She found that her face felt stiff and expressionless after long hours of waiting, waiting, and an elderly woman who was playing a minor part showed her how to overcome this by stretching her face, feature for feature, as a dancer goes through limbering exercises in the wings. The woman had been a trouper in the old days of one-night stands. Just before she stepped in front of the camera you saw her drawing down her face grotesquely, stretching her mouth to form an oval, dropping her jaw, twisting her lips to the right, to the left, rolling her eyes round and round. It was a perfect lesson in facial calisthenics, and Harrietta was thankful for it. Harrietta was interested in such things—interested in them, and grateful for what they taught her.

She told herself that she didn't mind the stir that Lydia Lissome made when she was driven up in the morning in her great blue limousine with the two Japs sitting so straight and immobile in front, like twin Nipponese gods. But she did. She told herself she didn't mind when the director said: "Miss Fuller, if you'll just watch Miss Lissome work. She has perfect picture tempo." But she did. The director was the new-fashioned kind, who spoke softly, rehearsed you almost privately, never bawled through a megaphone. A slim young man in a white shirt and flannel trousers and a pair of Harvard-looking glasses. Everybody was young. That was it! Not thirty, or thirty-two, or thirty-four, or thirty-seven, but young. Terribly, horribly, actually young. That was it.

Harrietta Fuller was too honest not to face this fact squarely. When she went to a Thursday-night dance at the Hollywood Hotel she found herself in a ballroom full of slim, pliant, corsetless young things of eighteen, nineteen, twenty. The men, with marcelled hair and slim feet and sunburnt faces, were mere boys. As juveniles on the stage they might have been earning seventy-five or one hundred or one hundred and fifty dollars a week. Here they owned estates, motor cars in fleets, power boats; had secretaries, valets, trainers. Their technique was perfect and simple. They knew their work. When they kissed a girl, or entered a room, or gazed after a woman, or killed a man in the presence of a woman (while working) they took off their hats. Turned slowly, and took off their hats. They were mannerly, too, outside working hours. They treated Harrietta with boyish politeness—when they noticed her at all.

"Oh, won't you have this chair, Miss Fuller? I didn't notice you were standing."

They didn't notice she was standing!

"What are you doing, Miss—ah—Fuller? Yes, you did say Fuller. Names—Are you doing a dowager bit?"

"Dowager bit?"

"I see. You're new to the game, aren't you? I saw you working to-day. We always speak of these black-velvet parts as dowager bits. Just excuse me. I see a friend of mine—" The friend of mine would be a willow wand with golden curls, and what Harrietta rather waspishly called a Gunga Din costume. She referred to that Kipling description in which:

> The uniform 'e wore
> Was nothin' much before,
> An' rather less than 'arf o' that be'ind.

"They're wearing them that way here in Hollywood," she wrote Ken. She wrote Ken a good many things. But there were, too, a good many things she did not write him.

At the end of the week she would look at her check—and take small comfort. "You've got everything you really want right here," Ken had said, "if you only knew it."

If only she had known it.

Well, she knew it now. Now, frightened, bewildered, resentful. Thirty-seven. Why, thirty-seven was old in Hollywood. Not middle-aged, or getting on, or well preserved, but old. Even Lydia Lissome, at twenty, always made them put one thickness of chiffon over the camera's lens before she would let them take the close-ups. Harrietta thought of that camera now as a cruel Cyclops from whose hungry eye nothing escaped—wrinkles, crow's-feet—nothing.

They had been working two months on the picture. It was almost finished. Midsummer. Harrietta's little bungalow garden was ablaze with roses, dahlias, poppies, asters, strange voluptuous flowers whose names she did not know. The roses, plucked and placed in water, fell apart, petal by petal, two hours afterward. From her veranda she saw the Sierra Madre range and the foothills. She thought of her "unexcelled view of Park" which could be had by flattening one ear and the side of your face against the window jamb.

The sun came up, hard and bright and white, day after day. Hard and white and hot and dry. "Like a woman," Harrietta thought, "who wears a red satin gown all the time. You'd wish she'd put on gingham just once, for a change." She told herself that she was parched for a walk up Riverside Drive in a misty summer rain, the water sloshing in her shoes.

"Happy, my ducky?" Irish Mary would say, beaming upon her.

"Perfectly," from Harrietta.

"It's time, too. Real money you're pullin' down here. And a paradise if ever there was one."

"I notice, though, that as soon as they've completed a picture they take the Overland back to New York and make dates with each other for lunch at the Claridge, like matinée girls."

Irish Mary flapped a negligent palm. "Ah, well, change is what we all want, now and then." She looked at Harrietta sharply. "You're not wantin' to go back, are ye?"

"N-no," faltered Harrietta. Then, brazenly, hotly: "Yes, yes!" ending, miserably, with: "But my contract. Six months."

"You can break it, if you're fool enough, when they've finished this picture, though why you should want to—" Irish Mary looked as belligerent as her kindly Celtic face could manage.

But it was not until the last week of the filming of Let's get a Husband that Harrietta came to her and said passionately: "I do! I do!"

"Do what?" Irish Mary asked, blankly.

"Do want to break my contract. You said I could after this picture."

"Sure you can. They hired you because I put Lyddy up to askin' them to. I'd thought you'd be pleased for the big money an' all. There's no pleasin' some."

"It isn't that. You don't understand. To-day—"

"Well, what's happened to-day that's so turrible, then?"

But how could Harrietta tell her? "To-day—" she began again, faltered, stopped. To-day, you must know, this had happened: It was the Big Scene of the film. Lydia Lissome, in black lace nightgown and ermine negligee, her hair in marcel waves, had just been "shot" for it.

"Now then, Miss Fuller," said young Garvey, the director, "you come into the garden, see? You've noticed Joyce go out through the French window and you suspect she's gone to meet Talbot. We show just a flash of you looking out of the drawing-room windows into the garden. Then you just glance over your shoulder to where your husband is sitting in the library, reading, and you slip away, see? Then we jump to where you find them in the garden. Wait a minute"—He consulted the sheaf of typewritten sheets in his hand—"yeh—here it says: 'Joyce is keeping her tryst under the great oak in the garden with her lover.' Yeh. Wait a minute ... 'tryst under tree with'—well, you come quickly forward—down to about here—and you say: 'Ah, *there* you are!'"

Harrietta looked at him for a long, long minute. Her lips were parted. Her breath came quickly. She spoke: "I say—*what?*"

"You say: 'Ah, *there* you are.'"

"Never!" said Harrietta Fuller, and brought her closed fist down on her open palm for emphasis. "Never!"

✴

It was August when she again was crossing desert, plains, and farmlands. It was the tail-end of a dusty, hot, humid August in New York when Ken stood at the station, waiting. As he came forward, raising one arm, her own arm shot forward in quick protest, even while her glad eyes held his.

"Don't take it off!"

"What off?"

"Your hat. Don't take it off. Kiss me—but leave your hat on."

She clutched his arm. She looked up at him. They were in the taxi bound for Fifty-sixth Street. "She moved? She's out? She's gone? You told her I'd pay her anything—a bonus—" Then, as he nodded, she leaned back, relaxed. Something in her face prompted him.

"You're young and beautiful and bewitching," said Ken.

"Keep on saying it," pleaded Harrietta. "Make a chant of it." ...

Sam Klein, the veteran, was the first to greet her when she entered the theatre at that first September rehearsal. The company was waiting for her. She wasn't late. She had just pleasantly escaped being unpunctual. She came in, cool, slim, electric. Then she hesitated. For the fraction of a second she hesitated. Then Sam Klein greeted her: "Company's waiting, Miss Fuller, if you're ready." And the leading man came forward, a flower in his buttonhole, carefully tailored and slightly yellow as a leading man of forty should be at 10:30 A. M. "How wonderful you're looking, Harrietta," he said.

Sam Klein took her aside. "You're going to make the hit of your career in this part, Miss Fuller. Yessir, dear, the hit of your career. You mark my words."

"Don't you think," stammered Harrietta—"don't you think it will take someone—someone—younger—to play the part?"

83

"Younger than what?"

"Than I."

Sam Klein stared. Then he laughed. "Younger than you! Say, listen, do you want to get the Gerry Society after me?"

And as he turned away a Young Thing with worshipful eyes crept up to Harrietta's side and said tremulously: "Oh, Miss Fuller, this is my first chance on Broadway, and may I tell you how happy I am to be playing with you? You've been my ideal ever since I was a—for a long, long time."

HOME GIRL

WILSON avenue, Chicago, is not merely an avenue but a district; not only a district but a state of mind; not a state of mind alone but a condition of morals. For that matter, it is none of these things so much as a mode of existence. If you know your Chicago—which you probably don't—(*sotto voce* murmur, Heaven forbid!)—you are aware that, long ago, Wilson Avenue proper crept slyly around the corner and achieved a clandestine alliance with big glittering Sheridan Road; which escapade changed the demure thoroughfare into Wilson Avenue improper.

When one says "A Wilson Avenue girl," the mind—that is, the Chicago mind—pictures immediately a slim, daring, scented, exotic creature dressed in next week's fashions; wise-eyed; doll-faced; rapacious. When chiffon stockings are worn Wilson Avenue's hosiery is but a film over the flesh. Aigrettes and mink coats are its winter uniform. A feverish district this, all plate glass windows and delicatessen dinners and one-room-and-kitchenette apartments, where light housekeepers take their housekeeping too lightly.

At six o'clock you are likely to see Wilson Avenue scurrying about in its mink coat and its French heels and its crepe frock, assembling its haphazard dinner. Wilson Avenue food, as displayed in the ready-cooked shops, resembles in a startling degree the Wilson Avenue ladies themselves: highly coloured, artificial, chemically treated, tempting to the eye, but unnutritious. In and out of the food emporia these dart, buying dabs of this and bits of that. Chromatic viands. Vivid scarlet, orange, yellow, green. A strip of pimento here. A mound of mayonnaise there. A green pepper stuffed with such burden of deceit as no honest green pepper ever was meant to hold. Two eggs. A quarter-pound of your best creamery butter. An infinitesimal bottle of cream. "*And* what else?" says the plump woman in the white bib-apron, behind the counter. "*And* what else?" Nothing. I guess that'll be all. Mink coats prefer to dine out.

As a cripple displays his wounds and sores, proudly, so Wilson Avenue throws open its one-room front door with a grandiloquent gesture as it boasts, "Two hundred and fifty a month!" Shylock, purchasing a paper-thin slice of pinky ham in Wilson Avenue, would know his own early Venetian transaction to have been pure philanthropy.

It took Raymond and Cora Atwater twelve years to reach this Wilson Avenue, though they carried it with them all the way. They had begun their married life in this locality before it had become a definite district. Twelve years ago the neighbourhood had shown no signs of mushrooming into its present opulence. Twelve years ago Raymond, twenty-eight, and Cora, twenty-four, had taken a six-room flat at Racine and Sunnyside. Six rooms. Modern. Light. Rental, $28.50 per month.

"But I guess I can manage it, all right," Raymond had said. "That isn't so terrible—for six rooms."

Cora's full under lip had drawn itself into a surprisingly thin straight line. Later, Raymond came to recognize the meaning of that labial warning. "We don't need all those rooms. It's just that much more work."

"I don't want you doing your own work. Not unless you want to. At first, maybe, it'd be sort of fun for you. But after a while you'll want a girl to help. That'll take the maid's room off the kitchen."

"Well, supposing? That leaves an extra room, anyway."

A look came into Raymond's face. "Maybe we'll need that, too—later. Later on." He actually could have been said to blush, then, like a boy. There was much of the boy in Raymond at twenty-eight.

Cora did not blush.

Raymond had married Cora because he loved her; and because she was what is known as a "home girl." From the first, business girls—those alert, pert, confident little sparrows of office and shop and the street at lunch hour—rather terrified him. They gave you as good as you sent. They were always ready with their own nickel for carfare. You never knew whether they were laughing at you or not. There was a little girl named Calhoun in the binoculars (Raymond's first Chicago job was with the Erwin H. Nagel Optical Company on Wabash). The Calhoun girl was smart. She wore those plain white waists. Tailored, Raymond thought they called them. They made her skin look fresh and clear and sort of downy-blooming like the peaches that grew in his own Michigan state back home. Or perhaps only girls with clear fresh skins could wear those plain white waist things. Raymond had heard that girls thought and schemed about things that were becoming to them, and then stuck to those things. He wondered how the Calhoun girl might look in a fluffy waist. But she never wore one down to work. When business was dull in the motor and sun-glasses (which was where he held forth) Raymond would stroll over to Laura Calhoun's counter and talk. He would talk about the Invention. He had no one else to talk to about it. No one he could trust, or who understood.

The Calhoun girl, polishing the great black eyes of a pair of field glasses, would look up brightly to say, "Well, how's the Invention coming on?" Then he would tell her.

The Invention had to do with spectacles. Not only that, if you are a wearer of spectacles of any kind, it has to do with you. For now, twelve years later, you could not well do without it. The little contraption that keeps the side-piece from biting into your ears—that's Raymond's.

Knowing, as we do, that Raymond's wife is named Cora we know that the Calhoun girl of the fresh clear skin, the tailored white shirt-waists, and the friendly interest in the Invention, lost out. The reason for that was Raymond's youth, and Raymond's vanity, and Raymond's unsophistication, together with Lucy Calhoun's own honesty and efficiency. These last qualities would handicap any girl in love, no matter how clear her skin or white her shirtwaist.

Of course, when Raymond talked to her about the Invention she should have looked adoringly into his eyes and said, "How perfectly *wonderful!* I don't see how you think of such things."

What she said, after studying its detail thoughtfully for a moment, was: "Yeh, but look. If this little tiny wire had a spring underneath—just a little bit of spring—it'd take all the pressure off when you wear a hat. Now women's hats are worn so much lower over their ears, d'you see? That'd keep it from pressing. Men's hats, too, for that matter."

She was right. Grudgingly, slowly, he admitted it. Not only that, he carried out her idea and perfected the spectacle contrivance as you know it to-day. Without her suggestion it would have had a serious flaw. He knew he ought to be grateful. He told himself that he was grateful. But in reality he was resentful. She was a smart girl, but—well—a fella didn't feel comfortable going with a girl that knew more than he did. He took her to the theatre—it was before the motion picture had attained its present-day virulence. She enjoyed it. So did he. Perhaps they might have repeated the little festivity and the white shirtwaist might have triumphed in the end. But that same week Raymond met Cora.

Though he had come to Chicago from Michigan almost a year before, he knew few people. The Erwin H. Nagel Company kept him busy by day. The Invention occupied him at night. He read, too, books on optometry. Don't think that he was a Rollo. He wasn't. But he was naturally somewhat shy, and further handicapped by an unusually tall lean frame which he handled awkwardly. If you had a good look at his eyes you forgot his shyness, his leanness, his awkwardness, his height. They were the keynote of his gentle, studious, kindly, humorous nature. But Chicago, Illinois, is too busy looking to see anything. Eyes are something you see with, not into.

Two of the boys at Nagel's had an engagement for the evening with two girls who were friends. On the afternoon of that day one of the boys went home at four with a well-developed case of grippe. The other approached Raymond with his plea.

"Say, Atwater, help me out, will you? I can't reach my girl because she's downtown somewheres for the afternoon with Cora. That's her girl friend. And me and Harvey was to meet 'em for dinner, see? And a show. I'm in a hole. Help me out, will you? Go along and fuss Cora. She's a nice girl. Pretty, too, Cora is. Will you, Ray? Huh?"

Ray went. By nine-thirty that evening he had told Cora about the Invention. And Cora had turned sidewise in her seat next to him at the theatre and had looked up at him adoringly, awe-struck. "Why, how perfectly *wonderful!* I don't see how you think of such things."

"Oh, that's nothing. I got a lot of ideas. Things I'm going to work out. Say, I won't always be plugging down at Nagel's, believe me. I got a lot of ideas."

"Really! Why, you're an inventor, aren't you! Like Edison and those. My, it must be wonderful to think of things out of your head. Things that nobody's ever thought of before."

Ray glowed. He felt comfortable, and soothed, and relaxed and stimulated. And too large for his clothes. "Oh, I don't know. I just think of things. That's all there is to it. That's nothing."

"Oh, isn't it! No, I guess not. I've never been out with a real inventor before ... I bet you think I'm a silly little thing."

He protested, stoutly. "I should say not." A thought struck him. "Do you do anything? Work downtown somewheres, or anything?"

She shook her head. Her lips pouted. Her eyebrows made pained twin crescents. "No. I don't do anything. I was afraid you'd ask that." She looked down at her hands—her white, soft hands with little dimples at the finger-bases. "I'm just a home girl. That's all. A home girl.

Now you *will* think I'm a silly stupid thing." She flashed a glance at him, liquid-eyed, appealing.

He was surprised (she wasn't) to find his hand closed tight and hard over her soft dimpled one. He was terror-stricken (she wasn't) to hear his voice saying, "I think you're wonderful. I think you're the most wonderful girl I ever saw, that's what." He crushed her hand and she winced a little. "Home girl."

Cora's name suited her to a marvel. Her hair was black and her colouring a natural pink and white, which she abetted expertly. Cora did not wear plain white tailored waists. She wore thin, fluffy, transparent things that drew your eyes and fired your imagination. Raymond began to call her Coral in his thoughts. Then, one evening, it slipped out. Coral. She liked it. He denied himself all luxuries and most necessities and bought her a strand of beads of that name, presenting them to her stammeringly, clumsily, tenderly. Tender pink and cream, they were, like her cheeks, he thought.

"Oh, Ray, for me! How darling! You naughty boy!... But I'd rather have had those clear white ones, without any colouring. They're more stylish. Do you mind?"

When he told Laura Calhoun she said, "I hope you'll be very happy. She's a lucky girl. Tell me about her, will you?"

Would he! His home girl!

When he had finished she said, quietly, "Oh, yes."

And so Raymond and Cora were married and went to live in six-room elegance at Sunnyside and Racine. The flat was furnished sumptuously in Mission and those red and brown soft leather cushions with Indian heads stamped on them. There was a wooden rack on the wall with six monks' heads in coloured plaster, very life-like, stuck on it. This was a pipe-rack, though Raymond did not smoke a pipe. He liked a mild cigar. Then there was a print of Gustave Richter's "Queen Louise" coming down that broad marble stair, one hand at her breast, her great girlish eyes looking out at you from the misty folds of her scarf. What a lot of the world she has seen from her stairway! The shelf that ran around the dining room wall on a level with your head was filled with steins in such shapes and colours as would have curdled their contents—if they had ever had any contents.

They planned to read a good deal, evenings. Improve their minds. It was Ray's idea, but Cora seconded it heartily. This was before their marriage.

"Now, take history alone," Ray argued: "American history. Why, you can read a year and hardly know the half of it. That's the trouble. People don't know the history of their own country. And it's interesting, too, let me tell you. Darned interesting. Better'n novels, if folks only knew it."

"My, yes," Cora agreed. "And French. We could take up French, evenings. I've always wanted to study French. They say if you know French you can travel anywhere. It's all in the accent; and goodness knows I'm quick at picking up things like that."

"Yeh," Ray had said, a little hollowly, "yeh, French. Sure."

But, somehow, these literary evenings never did materialize. It may have been a matter of getting the books. You could borrow them from the public library, but that made you feel so hurried. History was something you wanted to take your time over. Then, too, the books you wanted never were in. You could buy them. But buying books like that! Cora showed her first real display of temper. Why, they came in sets and cost as much as twelve or fifteen dollars. Just for books! The literary evenings degenerated into Ray's thorough scanning of the evening paper, followed by Cora's skimming of the crumpled sheets that carried the department store ads, the society column, and the theatrical news. Raymond began to use the sixth room—the unused bedroom—as a workshop. He had perfected the spectacle contrivance and had made the mistake of selling his rights to it. He got a good sum for it.

"But I'll never do that again," he said, grimly. "Somebody'll make a fortune on that thing." He had unwisely told Cora of this transaction. She never forgave him for it. On the day he received the money for it he had brought her home a fur set of baum marten. He thought the stripe in it beautiful. There was a neckpiece known as a stole, and a large muff.

"Oh, honey!" Cora had cried. "Aren't you *fun*-ny!" She often said that, always with the same accent. "Aren't you *fun*-ny!"

"What's the matter?"

"Why didn't you let me pick it out? They're wearing Persian lamb sets."

"Oh. Well, maybe the feller'll change it. It's all paid for, but maybe he'll change it."

"Do you mind? It may cost a little bit more. You don't mind my changing it though, do you?"

"No. No-o-o-o! Not a bit."

They had never furnished the unused bedroom as a bedroom. When they moved out of the flat at Racine and Sunnyside into one of those new four-room apartments on Glengyle the movers found only a long rough work-table and a green-shaded lamp in that sixth room. Ray's delicate tools and implements were hard put to it to find a resting place in the new four-room apartment. Sometimes Ray worked in the bath-room. He grew rather to like the white-tiled place, with its look of a laboratory. But then, he didn't have as much time to work at home as he formerly had had. They went out more evenings.

The new four-room flat rented at sixty dollars. "Seems the less room you have the more you pay," Ray observed.

"There's no comparison. Look at the neighbourhood! And the living room's twice as big."

It didn't seem to be. Perhaps this was due to its furnishings. The Mission pieces had gone to the second-hand dealer. Ray was assistant manager of the optical department at Nagel's now and he was getting royalties on a new smoked glass device. There were large over-stuffed chairs in the new living room, and a seven-foot davenport, and orien-tal rugs, and lamps and lamps and lamps. The silk lampshade confla-gration had just begun to smoulder in the American household. The dining room had one of those built-in Chicago buffets. It sparkled with cut glass. There was a large punch bowl in the centre, in which Cora usually kept receipts, old bills, moth balls, buttons, and the tar-nished silver top to a syrup jug that she always meant to have repaired. Queen Louise was banished to the bedroom where she surveyed a world of cretonne.

Cora was a splendid cook. She had almost a genius for flavour-ing. Roast or cheese soufflé or green apple pie—your sense of taste never experienced that disappointment which comes of too little salt, too much sugar, a lack of shortening. Expert as she was at it, Cora didn't like to cook. That is, she didn't like to cook day after day. She rather liked doing an occasional meal and producing it in a sort of red-cheeked triumph. When she did this it was an epicurean thing, savoury, hot, satisfying. But as a day-after-day programme Cora would not hear of it. She had banished the maid. Four rooms could not ac-commodate her. A woman came in twice a week to wash and iron and clean. Often Cora did not get up for breakfast and Ray got his at one of the little lunch rooms that were springing up all over that section of the North Side. Eleven o'clock usually found Cora at the manicure's, or the dressmaker's, or shopping, or telephoning luncheon arrangements with one of the Crowd. Ray and Cora were going out a good deal with the Crowd. Young married people like themselves, living royally just a little beyond their income. The women were well-dressed, vivacious, somewhat shrill. They liked stories that were a little off-colour. "Blue," one of the men called these stories. He was in the theatrical business.

The men were, for the most part, a rather drab-looking lot. Colourless, good-natured, open-handed. Almost imperceptibly the Crowd began to use Ray as a target for a certain raillery. It wasn't particularly ill-natured, and Ray did not resent it.

"Oh, come on, Ray! Don't be a wet blanket.... Lookit him! I bet he's thinking about those smoked glasses again. Eh, Atwater? He's in a daze about that new rim that won't show on the glasses. Come out of it! First thing you know you'll lose your little Cora."

There was little danger of that. Though Cora flirted mildly with the husbands of the other girls in the Crowd (they all did) she was true to Ray.

Ray was always talking of building a little place of their own. People were beginning to move farther and farther north, into the suburbs.

"Little place of your own," Ray would say, "that's the only way to live. Then you're not paying it all out in rent to the other feller. Little place of your own. That's the right idear."

But as the years went by, and Ray earned more and more money, he and Cora seemed to be getting farther and farther away from the right idear. In the $28.50 apartment Cora's morning marketing had been an orderly daily proceeding. Meat, vegetables, fruit, dry groceries. But now the maidless four-room apartment took on, in spite of its cumbersome furnishings, a certain air of impermanence.

"Ray, honey, I haven't a scrap in the house. I didn't get home until almost six. Those darned old street cars. I hate 'em. Do you mind going over Jo Bauer's to eat? I won't go, because Myrtle served a regular spread at four. I couldn't eat a thing. D'you mind?"

"Why, no." He would get into his coat again and go out into the bleak November wind-swept street to Bauer's restaurant.

Cora was always home when Raymond got there at six. She prided herself on this. She would say, primly, to her friends, "I make a point of being there when Ray gets home. Even if I have to cut a round of bridge. If a woman can't be there when a man gets home from work I'd like to know what she's good for, anyway."

The girls in the Crowd said she was spoiling Raymond. She told Ray this. "They think I'm old-fashioned. Well, maybe I am. But I guess I never pretended to be anything but a home girl."

"That's right," Ray would answer. "Say, that's the way you caught me. With that home-girl stuff."

"Caught you!" The thin straight line of the mouth. "If you think for one minute—"

"Oh, now, dear. You know what I mean, sweetheart. Why, say, I never could see any girl until I met you. You know that."

He was as honestly in love with her as he had been nine years before. Perhaps he did not feel now, as then, that she had conferred a favour upon him in marrying him. Or if he did he must have known that he had made fair return for such favour.

Cora had a Hudson seal coat now, with a great kolinsky collar. Her vivid face bloomed rosily in this soft frame. Cora was getting a little heavier. Not stout, but heavier, somehow. She tried, futilely, to reduce. She would starve herself at home for days, only to gain back the vanished pounds at one afternoon's orgy of whipped-cream salad, and coffee, and sweets at the apartment of some girl in the Crowd. Dancing had come in and the Crowd had taken it up vociferously. Raymond was not very good at it. He had not filled out with the years. He still was lean and tall and awkward. The girls in the crowd tried to avoid dancing with him. That often left Cora partnerless unless she wanted to dance again and again with Raymond.

"How can you expect the boys to ask me to dance when you don't dance with their wives! Good heavens, if they can learn, you can. And for pity's sake *don't count!* You're so *fun*-ny!"

He tried painstakingly to heed her advice, but his long legs made a sorry business of it. He heard one of the girls refer to him as "that giraffe." He had put his foot through an absurd wisp of tulle that she insisted on calling a train.

They were spending a good deal of money now, but Ray jousted the landlord, the victualler, the furrier, the milliner, the hosiery maker, valiantly and still came off the victor. He did not have as much time as he would have liked to work on the new invention. The invisible rim. It was calculated so to blend with the glass of the lens as to be, in appearance, one with it, while it still protected the eyeglass from breakage. "Fortune in it, girlie," he would say, happily, to Cora. "Million dollars, that's all."

He had been working on the invisible rim for five years. Familiarity with it had bred contempt in Cora. Once, in a temper, "Invisible is right," she had said, slangily.

They had occupied the four-room apartment for five years. Cora declared it was getting beyond her. "You can't get any decent help. The washwoman acts as if she was doing me a favour coming from eight to four, for four dollars and eighty-five cents. And yesterday she said she couldn't come to clean any more on Saturdays. I'm sick and tired of it."

Raymond shook a sympathetic head. "Same way down at the store. Seems everything's that way now. You can't get help and you can't get goods. You ought to hear our customers. Yesterday I thought I'd go clear out of my nut, trying to pacify them."

Cora inserted the entering wedge, deftly. "Goodness knows I love my home. But the way things are now ..."

"Yeh," Ray said, absently. When he spoke like that Cora knew that the invisible rim was revolving in his mind. In another moment he would be off to the little cabinet in the bathroom where he kept his tools and instruments.

She widened the opening. "I noticed as I passed to-day that those new one-room kitchenette apartments on Sheridan will be ready for occupancy October first." He was going toward the door. "They say they're wonderful."

"Who wants to live in one room, anyway?"

"It's really two rooms—and the kitchenette. There's the living room—perfectly darling—and a sort of combination breakfast room and kitchen. The breakfast room is partitioned off with sort of cupboards so that it's really another room. And so handy!"

"How'd you know?"

"I went in—just to look at them—with one of the girls."

Until then he had been unconscious of her guile. But now, suddenly, struck by a hideous suspicion—"Say, looka here. If you think—"

"Well, it doesn't hurt to look at 'em, does it!"

A week later. "Those kitchenette apartments on Sheridan are almost all gone. One of the girls was looking at one on the sixth floor. There's a view of the lake. The kitchen's the sweetest thing. All white enamel. And the breakfast room thing is done in Italian."

"What d'you mean—done in Italian?"

"Why—uh—Italian period furniture, you know. Dark and rich. The living room's the same. Desk, and table, and lamps."

"Oh, they're furnished?"

"Complete. Down to the kettle covers and the linen and all. The work there would just be play. All the comforts of a home, with none of the terrible aggravations."

"Say, look here, Coral, we don't want to go to work and live in any one room. You wouldn't be happy. Why, we'd feel cooped up. No room to stretch.... Why, say, how about the beds? If there isn't a bedroom how about the beds? Don't people sleep in those places?"

"There are Murphy beds, silly."

"Murphy? Who's he?"

"Oh, goodness, I don't know! The man who invented 'em, I suppose. Murphy."

Raymond grinned in anticipation of his own forthcoming joke. "I should think they'd call 'em Morphy beds." Then, at her blank stare. "You know—short for Morpheus, god of sleep. Learned about him at high school."

Cora still looked blank. Cora hardly ever understood Ray's jokes, or laughed at them. He would turn, chuckling, to find her face a blank. Not even bewildered, or puzzled, or questioning. Blank. Unheeding. Disinterested as a slate.

Three days later Cora developed an acute pain in her side. She said it was nothing. Just worn out with the work, and the worry and the aggravation, that's all. It'll be all right.

Ray went with her to look at the Sheridan Road apartment. It was one hundred and fifty dollars. "Phew!"

"But look at what you save? Gas. Light. Maid service. Laundry. It's really cheaper in the end."

Cora was amazingly familiar with all the advantages and features of the sixth-floor apartment. "The sun all morning." She had all the agent's patter. "Harvey-Dickson ventilated double-spring mattresses. Dressing room off the bathroom. No, it isn't a closet. Here's the closet. Range, refrigerator, combination sink and laundry tub. Living room's all panelled in ivory. Shower in the bathroom. Buffet kitchen. Breakfast room has folding-leaf Italian table. Look at the chairs. Aren't they darlings! Built-in book shelves—"

"Book shelves?"

"Oh, well, we can use them for fancy china and ornaments. Or—oh, look!—you could keep your stuff there. Tools and all. Then the bathroom wouldn't be mussy all the time."

"Beds?"

"Right here. Isn't that wonderful. Would you ever know it was there? You can work it with one hand. Look."

"Do you really like it, Coral?"

"I love it. It's heavenly."

He stood in the centre of the absurd living room, a tall, lank, awkward figure, a little stooped now. His face was beginning to be furrowed with lines—deep lines that yet were softening, and not unlovely. He made you think, somehow, as he stood there, one hand on his own coat lapel, of Saint-Gaudens' figure of Lincoln, there in the park, facing the Drive. Kindly, thoughtful, harried.

They moved in October first.

The over-stuffed furniture of the four-room apartment was sold. Cora kept a few of her own things—a rug or two, some china, silver, bric-à-brac, lamps. Queen Louise was now permanently dethroned. Cora said her own things—"pieces"—would spoil the effect of the living room. All Italian.

"No wonder the Italians sit outdoors all the time, on the steps and in the street"—more of Ray's dull humour. He surveyed the heavy gloomy pieces, so out of place in the tiny room. One of the chairs was black velvet. It was the only really comfortable chair in the room but Ray never sat in it. It reminded him, vaguely, of a coffin. The corridors of the apartment house were long, narrow, and white-walled. You traversed these like a convict, speaking to no one, and entered your own cubicle. A toy dwelling for toy people. But Ray was a man-size man. When he was working downtown his mind did not take temporary refuge in the thought of the feverish little apartment to which he was to return at night. It wasn't a place to come back to, except for sleep. A roost. Bedding for the night. As permanent-seeming as a hay-mow.

Cora, too, gave him a strange feeling of impermanence. He realized one day, with a shock, that he hardly ever saw her with her hat off. When he came in at six or six-thirty Cora would be busy at the tiny sink, or the toy stove, her hat on, a cigarette dangling limply from her mouth. Ray did not object to women smoking. That is, he had no moral objection. But he didn't think it became them. But Cora said a cigarette rested and stimulated her. "Doctors say all nervous women should smoke," she said. "Soothes them." But Cora, cooking in the little kitchen, squinting into a kettle's depths through a film of cigarette smoke, outraged his sense of fitness. It was incongruous, offensive. The time, and occupation, and environment, together with the limply dangling cigarette, gave her an incredibly rowdy look.

When they ate at home they had steak or chops, and, perhaps, a chocolate éclair for dessert; and a salad. Raymond began to eat mental meals. He would catch himself thinking of breaded veal chops, done slowly, simmeringly, in butter, so that they came out a golden brown on a parsley-decked platter. With this mashed potatoes with brown butter and onions that have just escaped burning; creamed spinach with egg grated over the top; a rice pudding, baked in the oven, and served with a tart crown of grape jell. He sometimes would order these things in a restaurant at noon, or on the frequent evenings when they dined out. But they never tasted as he had thought they would.

They dined out more and more as spring drew on and the warm weather set in. The neighbourhood now was aglitter with eating places of all sorts and degrees, from the humble automat to the proud plush of the Sheridan Plaza dining room. There were tea-rooms, cafeterias, Hungarian cafés, chop suey restaurants. At the table d'hôte places you got a soup, followed by a lukewarm plateful of meat, vegetables, salad. The meat tasted of the vegetables, the vegetables tasted of the meat, and the salad tasted of both. Before ordering Ray would sit down and peer about at the food on the near-by tables as one does in a dining car when the digestive fluids have dried in your mouth at the first whiff through the doorway. It was on one of these evenings that he noticed Cora's hat.

"What do you wear a hat for all the time?" he asked, testily.

"Hat?"

"Seems to me I haven't seen you without a hat in a month. Gone bald, or something?" He was often cross like this lately. Grumpy, Cora called it. Hats were one of Cora's weaknesses. She had a great variety of them. These added to Ray's feeling of restlessness and impermanence. Sometimes she wore a hat that came down over her head, covering her forehead and her eyes, almost. The hair he used to love to touch was concealed. Sometimes he dined with an ingénue in a poke bonnet; sometimes with a senorita in black turban and black lace veil, mysterious and provocative; sometimes with a demure miss in a wistful little turned-down brim. It was like living with a stranger who was always about to leave.

When they ate at home, which was rarely, Ray tried, at first, to dawdle over his coffee and his mild cigar, as he liked to do. But you couldn't dawdle at a small, inadequate table that folded its flaps and shrank into a corner the minute you left it. Everything in the apartment folded, or flapped, or doubled, or shot in, or shot out, or concealed something else, or pretended to be something it was not. It was very irritating. Ray took his cigar and his evening paper and wandered uneasily into the Italian living room, doubling his lean length into one of his queer, angular hard chairs.

Cora would appear in the doorway, hatted. "Ready?"

"Huh? Where you going?"

"Oh, Ray, aren't you *fun*-ny! You know this is the Crowd's poker night at Lil's."

The Crowd began to say that old Ray was going queer. Honestly, didja hear him last week? Talking about the instability of the home, and the home being the foundation of the state, and the country crumbling? Cora's face was a sight! I wouldn't have wanted to be in his boots when she got him home. What's got into him, anyway?

Cora was a Wilson Avenue girl now. You saw her in and out of the shops of the district, expensively dressed. She was almost thirty-six. Her legs, beneath the absurdly short skirt of the day, were slim and shapely in their chiffon hose, but her upper figure was now a little prominent. The scant, brief skirt fore-shortened her; gave her a stork-like appearance; a combination of girlishness and matronliness not pleasing.

There were times when Ray rebelled. A peace-loving man, and gentle. But a man. "I don't want to go out to eat. My God, I'm tired! I want to eat at home."

"Honey, dear, I haven't a thing in the house. Not a scrap."

"I'll go out and get something, then. What d'you want?"

"Get whatever looks good to you. I don't want a thing. We had tea after the matinée. That's what made me so late. I'm always nagging the girls to go home. It's getting so they tease me about it."

He would go foraging amongst the delicatessen shops of the neighbourhood. He saw other men, like himself, scurrying about with moist paper packets and bags and bundles, in and out of Leviton's, in and out of the Sunlight Bakery. A bit of ham. Some cabbage salad in a wooden boat. A tiny broiler, lying on its back, its feet neatly trussed, its skin crackly and tempting-looking, its white meat showing beneath the brown. But when he cut into it at home it tasted like sawdust and gutta-percha. *"And* what else?" said the plump woman in the white bib-apron behind the counter. *"And* what else?"

In the new apartment you rather prided yourself on not knowing your next-door neighbours. The paper-thin walls permitted you to hear them living the most intimate details of their lives. You heard them laughing, talking, weeping, singing, scolding, caressing. You didn't know them. You did not even see them. When you met in the halls or elevators you did not speak. Then, after they had lived in the new apartment about a year Cora met the woman in 618 and Raymond met the woman in 620, within the same week. The Atwaters lived in 619.

There was some confusion in the delivery of a package. The woman in 618 pressed the Atwaters' electric button for the first time in their year's residence there.

A plump woman, 618; blonde; in black. You felt that her flesh was expertly restrained in tight pink satin brassières and long-hipped corsets and many straps.

"I hate to trouble you, but did you get a package for Mrs. Hoyt? It's from Field's."

It was five-thirty. Cora had her hat on. She did not ask the woman to come in. "I'll see. I ordered some things from Field's to-day, too. I haven't opened them yet. Perhaps yours ... I'll look."

The package with Mrs. Hoyt's name on it was there. "Well, thanks so much. It's some georgette crepe. I'm making myself one those new two-tone slip-over negligees. Field's had a sale. Only one sixty-nine a yard."

Cora was interested. She sewed rather well when she was in the mood. "Are they hard to make?"

"Oh, land, no! No trick to it at all. They just hang from the shoulder, see? Like a slip-over. And then your cord comes round—"

She stepped in. She undid the box and shook out the vivid folds of the filmy stuff, vivid green and lavender. "You wouldn't think they'd go well together but they do. Makes a perfectly stunning negligee."

Cora fingered the stuff. "I'd get some. Only I don't know if I could cut the—"

"I'll show you. Glad to." She was very friendly. Cora noticed she used expensive perfume. Her hair was beautifully marcelled. The woman folded up the material and was off, smiling. "Just let me know when you get it. I've got a lemon cream pie in the oven and I've got to run." She called back over her shoulder. "Mrs. Hoyt."

Cora nodded and smiled. "Mine's Atwater." She saw that the woman's simple-seeming black dress was one she had seen in a Michigan Avenue shop, and had coveted. Its price had been beyond her purse.

Cora mentioned the meeting to Ray when he came home. "She seems real nice. She's going to show me how to cut out a new negligee."

"What'd you say her name was?" She told him. He shrugged. "Well, I'll say this: she must be some swell cook. Whenever I go by that door at dinner time my mouth just waters. One night last week there was something must have been baked spare-ribs and sauerkraut. I almost broke in the door."

The woman in 618 did seem to cook a great deal. That is, when she cooked. She explained that Mr. Hoyt was on the road a lot of the time and when he was home she liked to fuss for him. This when she was helping Cora cut out the georgette negligee.

"I'd get coral colour if I was you, honey. With your hair and all," Mrs. Hoyt had advised her.

"Why, that's my name! That is, it's what Ray calls me. My name's really Cora." They were quite good friends now.

It was that same week that Raymond met the woman in 620. He had left the apartment half an hour later than usual (he had a heavy cold, and had not slept) and encountered the man and woman just coming out of 620.

"And guess who it was!" he exclaimed to Cora that evening. "It was a girl who used to work at Nagel's, in the binoculars, years ago, when I started there. Calhoun, her name was. Laura Calhoun. Smart little girl, she was. She's married now. And guess what! She gets a big salary fitting glasses for women at the Bazaar. She learned to be an optician. Smart girl."

Cora bridled, virtuously. "Well, I think she'd better stay home and take care of that child of hers. I should think she'd let her husband earn the living. That child is all soul alone when she comes home from school. I hear her practising. I asked Mrs. Hoyt about her. She say's she's seen her. A pindling scrawny little thing, about ten years old. She leaves her alone all day."

Ray encountered the Calhoun girl again, shortly after that, in the way encounters repeat themselves, once they have started.

"She didn't say much but I guess her husband is a nit-wit. Funny how a smart girl like that always marries one of these sap-heads that can't earn a living. She said she was working because she wanted her child to have the advantages she'd missed. That's the way she put it."

One heard the long-legged, melancholy child next door practising at the piano daily at four. Cora said it drove her crazy. But then, Cora was rarely home at four. "Well," she said now, virtuously, "I don't know what she calls advantages. The way she neglects that kid. Look at her! I guess if she had a little more mother and a little less education it'd be better for her."

"Guess that's right," Ray agreed.

It was in September that Cora began to talk about the mink coat. A combination anniversary and Christmas gift. December would mark their twelfth anniversary. A mink coat.

Raymond remembered that his mother had had a mink coat, back there in Michigan, years ago. She always had taken it out in November and put it away in moth balls and tar paper in March. She had done this for years and years. It was a cheerful yellow mink, with a slightly darker marking running through it, and there had been little mink tails all around the bottom edge of it. It had spread comfortably at the waist. Women had had hips in those days. With it his mother had carried a mink muff; a small yellow-brown cylinder just big enough for her two hands. It had been her outdoor uniform, winter after winter, for as many years as he could remember of his boyhood. When she had died the mink coat had gone to his sister Carrie, he remembered.

A mink coat. The very words called up in his mind sharp winter days; the pungent moth-bally smell of his mother's fur-coated bosom when she had kissed him good-bye that day he left for Chicago; comfort; womanliness. A mink coat.

"How much could you get one for? A mink coat."

Cora hesitated a moment. "Oh—I guess you could get a pretty good one for three thousand."

"You're crazy," said Ray, unemotionally. He was not angry. He was amused.

But Cora was persistent. Her coat was a sight. She had to have something. She never had had a real fur coat.

"How about your Hudson seal?"

"Hudson seal! Did you ever see any seals in the Hudson! Fake fur. I've never had a really decent piece of fur in my life. Always some mangy make-believe. All the girls in the Crowd are getting new coats this year. The woman next door—Mrs. Hoyt—is talking of getting one. She says Mr. Hoyt—"

"Say, who are these Hoyts, anyway?"

Ray came home early one day to find the door to 618 open. He glanced in, involuntarily. A man sat in the living room—a large, rather red-faced man, in his shirt-sleeves, relaxed, comfortable, at ease. From the open door came the most tantalizing and appetizing smells of candied sweet potatoes, a browning roast, steaming vegetables.

Mrs. Hoyt had run in to bring a slice of fresh-baked chocolate cake to Cora. She often brought in dishes of exquisitely prepared food thus, but Raymond had never before encountered her. Cora introduced them. Mrs. Hoyt smiled, nervously, and said she must run away and tend to her dinner. And went. Ray looked after her. He strode into the kitchenette where Cora stood, hatted, at the sink.

"Say, looka here, Cora. You got to quit seeing that woman, see?"

"What woman?"

"One calls herself Mrs. Hoyt. That woman. Mrs. Hoyt! Ha!"

"Why, Ray, what in the world are you talking about! Aren't you *fun*-ny!"

"Yeh; well, you cut her out. I won't have you running around with a woman like that. Mrs. Hoyt! Mrs. Fiddlesticks!"

They had a really serious quarrel about it. When the smoke of battle cleared away Raymond had paid the first instalment on a three thousand dollar mink coat. And, "If we could sub-lease," Cora said, "I think it would be wonderful to move to the Shoreham. Lil and Harry are going there in January. You know yourself this place isn't half respectable."

Raymond had stared. "Shoreham! Why, it's a hotel. Regular hotel."

"Yes," placidly. "That's what's so nice about it. No messing around in a miserable little kitchenette. You can have your meals sent up. Or you can go down to the dining room. Lil says it's wonderful. And if you order for one up in your room the portions are big enough for two. It's really economy, in the end."

"Nix," said Ray. "No hotel in mine. A little house of our own. That's the right idea. Build."

"But nobody's building now. Materials are so high. It'll cost you ten times as much as it would if you waited a few—a little while. And no help. No maids coming over, hardly. I think you might consider me a little. We could live at the Shoreham a while, anyway. By that time things will be better, and we'd have money saved up and then we might talk of building. Goodness knows I love my home as well as any woman—"

They looked at the Shoreham rooms on the afternoon of their anniversary. They were having the Crowd to dinner, downtown, that evening. Cora thought the Shoreham rooms beautiful, though she took care not to let the room-clerk know she thought so. Ray, always a silent, inarticulate man, was so wordless that Cora took him to task for it in a sibilant aside.

"Ray, for heaven's, sake say something. You stand there! I don't know what the man'll think."

"A hell of a lot I care what he thinks." Ray was looking about the garish room—plush chairs, heavy carpets, brocade hangings, shining table-top, silly desk.

"Two hundred and seventy-five a month," the clerk was saying. "With the yearly lease, of course. Otherwise it's three twenty-five." He seemed quite indifferent.

Ray said nothing. "We'll let you know," said Cora.

The man walked to the door. "I can't hold it for you, you know. Our apartments are practically gone. I've a party who practically has closed for this suite already. I'd have to know."

Cora looked at Ray. He said nothing. He seemed not to have heard. His face was gaunt and haggard. "We'll let you know—to-morrow," Cora said. Her full under lip made a straight thin line.

When they came out it was snowing. A sudden flurry. It was already dark. "Oh, dear," said Cora. "My hat!" Ray summoned one of the hotel taxis. He helped Cora into it. He put money into the driver's hand.

"You go on, Cora. I'm going to walk."

"Walk! Why! But it's snowing. And you'll have to dress for dinner."

"I've got a little headache. I thought I'd walk. I'll be home. I'll be home."

He slammed the door then, and turned away. He began to walk in the opposite direction from that which led toward the apartment house. The snow felt cool and grateful on his face. It stung his cheeks. Hard and swift and white it came, blinding him. A blizzard off the lake. He plunged through it, head down, hands jammed into his pockets.

So. A home girl. Home girl. God, it was funny. She was a selfish, idle, silly, vicious woman. She was nothing. Nothing. It came over him in a sudden blinding crashing blaze of light. The woman in 618 who wasn't married to her man, and who cooked and planned to make him comfortable; the woman in 620 who blindly left her home and her child every day in order to give that child the thing she called advantages— either of these was better than his woman. Honester. Helping someone. Trying to, anyway. Doing a better job than she was.

He plunged across the street, blindly, choking a little with the bitterness that had him by the throat.

Hey! Watcha!—A shout rising to a scream.

A bump. Numbness. Silence. Nothingness.

✤

"Well, anyway, Cora," said the girls in the Crowd, "you certainly were a wonderful wife to him. You can always comfort yourself with that thought. My! the way you always ran home so's to be there before he got in."

"I know it," said Cora, mournfully. "I always was a home girl. Why, we always had planned we should have a little home of our own some day. He always said that was the right idear—idea."

Lil wiped her eyes. "What are you going to do about your new mink coat, Cora?"

Cora brushed her hair away from her forehead with a slow, sad gesture. "Oh, I don't know. I've hardly thought of such trifling things. The woman next door said she might buy it. Hoyt, her name is. Of course I couldn't get what we paid for it, though I've hardly had it on. But money'll count with me now. Ray never did finish that invisible rim he was working on all those years. Wasting his time. Poor Ray.... I thought if she took it, I'd get a caracul, with a black fox collar. After I bought it I heard mink wasn't so good anyway, this year. Everything's black. Of course, I'd never have said anything to Raymond about it. I'd just have worn it. I wouldn't have hurt Ray for the world."

AIN'T NATURE WONDERFUL!

When a child grows to boyhood, and a boy to manhood under the soul-searing blight of a given name like Florian, one of two things must follow. He will degenerate into a weakling, crushed beneath the inevitable diminutive—Flossie; or he will build up painfully, inch by inch, a barrier against the name's corroding action. He will boast of his biceps, flexing them the while. He will brag about cold baths. He will prate of chest measurements; regard golf with contempt; and speak of the West as God's country.

Florian Sykes was five feet three and a half, and he liked to quote those red-blooded virile poems about the big open spaces out where the West begins. The biggest open space in his experience was Madison Square, New York; and Eighth Avenue spelled the Far West for him. When Florian spoke or thought of great heights it was never in terms of nature, such as mountains, but in artificial ones, like skyscrapers. Yet his job depended on what he called the great outdoors.

The call of the wild, by the time it had filtered into his city abode, was only a feeble cheep. But he answered it daily from his rooms to the store in the morning, from the store to his rooms in the evening. It must have been fully ten blocks each way. There are twenty New York blocks to the mile. He threw out his legs a good deal when he walked and came down with his feet rather flat, and he stooped ever so little with the easy slouch that came in with the one-button sack suit. It's the walk you see used by English actors of the what-what school who come over here to play gentlemanly juveniles.

Down at Inverness & Heath's they called him Nature's Rival, but that was mostly jealousy, with a strong dash of resentment. Two of the men in his department had been Maine guides, and another boasted that he knew the Rockies as he knew the palm of his hand. But Florian, whose trail-finding had all been done in the subway shuttle, and who thought that butter sauce with parsley was a trout's natural element, had been promoted above their heads half a dozen times until now he lorded it over the fifth floor.

Not one of you, unless bedridden from birth, but has felt the influence of the firm of Inverness & Heath. You may never have seen the great establishment itself, rising story on story just off New York's main shopping thoroughfare. But you have felt the call of their catalogue. Surely at one time or another, they have supplied you with tents or talcum; with sleeping-bags or skis or skates; with rubber boots, or resin or reels. On their fourth floor you can be hatted for Palm Beach or booted for Skagway. On the third, outfitted for St. Moritz or San Antonio. But the fifth floor is the pride of the store. There is the camper's dream realized. There you will find man's most ingenious devices for softening Mother Nature's flinty bosom. Mosquito-proof tents; pails that will not leak; fleece-lined sleeping-bags; cooking outfits made up of pots and pans of every size, each shaped to disappear mysteriously into the next, like a conjurer's outfit, the whole swallowed up by a magic leather case.

Here Florian reigned. If you were a regular Inverness & Heath customer you learned to ask for him as soon as the elevator tossed you up to his domain. He met you with what is known in the business efficiency guides as the strong personality greeting. It consisted in clasping your hand with a grip that drove your ring into the bone, looking you straight in the eye, registering alert magnetic force, and pronouncing your name very distinctly. Like this: hand-clasp firm—straight in the eye—"How do you do, Mr. Outertown. Haven't seen you since last June. How was the trip?" He didn't mean to be a liar. And yet he lied daily and magnificently for years, to the world and himself. When, for example, in the course of purchasing rods, flies, tents, canoes, saddles, boots, or sleeping-bags of him, you spoke of the delights of your contemplated vacation, he would say, "That's the life. I'm a Western man, myself.... God's country!" He said it with a deep breath, and an exhalation, as one who pants to be free of the city's noisome fumes. You felt he must have been born with an equipment of chaps, quirts, spurs, and sombrero. You see him flinging himself on a horse and clattering off with a flirt of hoofs as they do it in the movies. His very manner sketched in a background of plains, mountains, six-shooters, and cacti.

The truth of it was Florian Sykes had been born in Kenosha, Wisconsin. At the age of three he had been brought to New York by a pair of inexpert and migratory parents. Their reasons for migrating need not concern us. They must, indeed, have been bad reasons. For Florian, at thirteen, a spindle-legged errand-boy in over-size knickers, a cold sore on his lip, and shoes chronically in need of resoling, had started to work for the great sporting goods store of Inverness & Heath.

Now, at twenty-nine, he was head of the fifth floor. The cold sore had vanished permanently under a régime of health-food, dumb-bells, and icy plunges. The shoes were bench-made and flawless. If the legs still were somewhat spindling their correctly creased casings hid the fact.

There's little doubt that if Florian had been named Bill, and if the calves of his legs had bulged, and if, in his youth, he had gone to work for a wholesale grocer, he would never have forged for himself a coat of mail whose links were pretense and whose bolts were sham. He probably would have been frankly content with the sight of an occasional ball-game out at the Polo Grounds, and the newspaper bulletins of a prizefight by rounds. But here he was at the base that supplied America's outdoor equipment. He who outfitted mountaineers must speak knowingly of glaciers, chasms, crevices, and peaks. He who advised canoeists must assume wisdom of paddles, rapids, currents, and portages. He whose sleeping hours were spangled with the clang of the street cars must counsel such hardy ones as were preparing cheerfully to seek rest rolled in blankets before a camp-fire's dying embers. And so, slowly, year by year, in his rise from errand to stock boy, from stock boy to clerk, from clerk to assistant manager, thence to his present official position, he had built about himself a tissue of in-nocent lies. He actually believed them himself.

Sometimes a customer who in June had come in to purchase his vacation supplies with the city pallor upon him, returned in September, brown, hard, energized, to thank Florian for the comfort of the outfit supplied him.

"I just want to tell you, Sykes, that that was a great little outfit you sold me. Yessir! Not a thing too much, and not a thing too little, either. Remember how I kicked about that air mattress? Well, say, it saved my life! I slept like a baby every night. And the trip! You've been there, haven't you?"

Florian would smile and nod his head. His grateful customer would clap him on the shoulder. "Some pebble, that mountain!"

"Get to the top?" Florian would ask.

"Well, we didn't do the peak. That is, not right to the top. Started to a couple of times, but the girls got tired, and we didn't want to leave 'em alone. Pretty stiff climb, let me tell you, young feller."

"You should have made the top."

"Been up, have you?"

"A dozen times."

"Oh, well, that's your business, you might say. Next time, maybe, we'll do it. The missus says she wants to go back there every year."

Florian would shake his head. "Oh, you don't want to do that. Have you been out to Glacier? Have you done the Yellowstone on horseback? Ever been down the Grand Canyon?"

"Why—no—but—"

"You've got a few thrills coming to you then."

The sunburned traveller would flush mahogany. "That's all right for you to say. But I'm no chamois. But it was a great trip, just the same. I want to thank you."

Then, for example, Florian's clothes. He had adopted that careful looseness—that ease of fit—that skilful sloppiness—which is the last word in masculine sartorial smartness. In talking he dropped his final g's and said "sportin'" and "mountain climbin'" and "shootin'." From June until September he wore those Norfolk things with bow ties, and his shirt patterns were restrained to the point of austerity. A signet ring with a large scrolled monogram on the third finger of his right hand was his only ornament, and he had worn a wrist watch long before the War. He had never seen a mountain. The ocean meant Coney Island. He breakfasted at Child's. He spent two hours over the Sunday papers. He was a Tittlebat Titmouse without the whiskers. And Myra loved him.

If Florian had not pretended to be something he wasn't; and if he had not professed an enthusiastic knowledge of things of which he was ignorant, he would, in the natural course of events, have loved Myra quickly in return. In fact, he would have admitted that he had loved her first, and desperately. And there would have been no story entitled, "Ain't Nature Wonderful!"

Myra worked in the women's and misses', third floor, and she didn't care a thing about the big outdoors or the great open spaces. She didn't even pretend to—at first. A clear-eyed, white-throated, capable young woman, almost poignantly pretty. You sensed it was the kind of loveliness that fades a bit with marriage. In its place come two sturdy babies to carry on the torch of beauty. You sensed, too, that Myra would keep their noses wiped, their knees scrubbed, and their buttons buttoned and that, between a fresh blouse for herself and fresh rompers for them, the blouse would always lose.

She hated discomfort, did Myra, as does one who has always had too much of it. After you have stood all day, from 8:30 A. M. to 5:30 P. M., selling sweaters, riding togs, golf clothes, and trotteurs to athletic Dianas whose lines are more lathe than lithe, you can't work up much enthusiasm about exercising for the pure joy of it. Myra had never used a tennis-racket in her life, but daily she outfitted for the sport bronzed young ladies who packed a nasty back-hand wallop in their right. She wore (and was justly proud of) a 4-A shoe, and took a good deal of comfort in the fact as she sold 7-Cs at $22.50 a pair to behemothian damsels who possessed money in proportion to Myra's beauty. Myra was the only girl in her section who never tried to dress in imitation of the moneyed ones whom she served. The other girls were wont to wear severely tailored shirts, mannish ties, stocks, flat-heeled shoes, rough tweed skirts. Not so Myra. That delicate cup-like hollow at the base of her white throat was fittingly framed in a ruffle of frilly georgette. She did her hair in soft undulations that flowed away from forehead and temple, and she powdered her nose a hundred times a day. Her little shoes were high-heeled and her hands were miraculously white, and if you prefer Rosalind to Viola you'd better quit her now.

"Anybody who wants to wear those cross-country clothes is welcome to them," she said. "I'm a girl and I'm satisfied to be. I don't see why I should wear a hard-boiled shirt and a necktie any more than a man should wear a pink georgette trimmed with filet. By the end of the week, when I've spent six solid days selling men's clothes to women, I feel's if I'd die happy if I could take a milk bath and put on white satin and pearls and a train six yards long from the shoulders—*you* know."

Not the least of Myra's charm was a certain unexpected and pleasing humour. It was as though, on opening a chocolate box, you were to find it contained caviar.

Of course by now you know that Myra is the girl you used to see smiling out at you from the Inverness & Heath catalogue entitled Sportswomen's Apparel. The head of her department had soon discovered that Myra, posing for illustrations to be used in the spring booklet, raised that pamphlet's selling power about 100 per cent. Sunburned misses, with wind-ravaged complexions, gazing at the picture of Myra, cool, slim, luscious-looking, saw themselves as they would fain be—and bought the Knollwood sweater depicted—in silk or wool—putty, maize, navy, rose, copen, or white—$35. Myra posed in paddock coat and breeches—she who had never been nearer a horse than the distance between sidewalk and road. She smiled at you over her shoulder radiant in a white tricot Palm Beach suit, who thought palms grew in jardinières only. On page 17 she was revealed in the boyish impudence of our Aiken Polo Habit, complete, $90. She was ravishing in her golf clothes, her small feet in sturdy, flat-heeled boots planted far apart, and only the most carping would have commented on the utter impossibility of her stance. Then there was the Killiecrankie Travel Tog (background of assorted mountains) made of Scotch tweed (she would never come nearer Scotland than oatmeal for breakfast) only $140. To say nothing of motor clothes, woodland suits, trap-shooting costumes, Yellowstone Park outfits, hunting habits. She wore brogues, and boots, and skating shoes, and puttees and tennis ties; sou'westers, leather topcoats, Jersey silks, military capes. You saw her fishing, hunting, boating, riding, golfing, snow-shoeing, swimming. She was equally lovely in khaki with woollen stockings, or in a habit of white linen and the shiniest of riding-boots. And as she peeled off the one to put on the next she remarked wearily, "A kimono and felt slippers and my hair down my back will look pretty good to me to-night, after this."

You see, Myra and Florian really had so much in common that if he had been honest with himself the course of their love would have run too smooth to be true. But Florian, in his effort to register as a two-fisted, hard-riding, nature-taming male, made such a success of it that for a long time he deceived even Myra who loved him. And during that time she, too, lied in her frantic effort to match her step with his. When he talked of riding and swimming; of long, hard mountain hikes; of impenetrable woods, she looked at him with sparkling eyes. (She didn't need to throw much effort into that, nature having supplied her with the ground materials.) When, on their rare Sundays together, he suggested a long tramp up the Palisades she agreed enthusiastically, though she hated it. Not only that, she went, loathing it. The stones hurt her feet. Her slender ankles ached. The sun burned her delicate skin. The wind pierced her thin coat. Florian strode along with the exaggerated step of the short man who bitterly resents his lack of stature. Every now and then he stood still, and breathed deeply, and said, "Glorious!" And Myra looked at his straight back, and his clear-cut profile, and his well-dressed legs and said, "Isn't it!" and wished he would kiss her. But he never did.

In between times he bemoaned his miserable two weeks' vacation which made impossible the sort of thing he said he craved—a long, hard, rough trip into a mountain interior. The Rockies, preferably, in their jaggedest portions.

"That's the kind of thing that makes a fellow over. Roughing it. You forget about the city. In the saddle all day—nothing but sky and mountains. God's big open spaces! That's the life!"

Myra trudged along, painfully. "But isn't it awfully uncomfortable? You know. Cold? And tents? I don't think I'd like—"

"I wouldn't give a cent for a person who was so soft they couldn't stand roughing it a little. That's the trouble with you Easterners. Soft! No red blood. Too many street cars, and high buildings, and restaurants. Chop down a few trees and fry your own bacon, and make your own camp, and saddle your own horses—that's what I call living. I'm going back to it some day, see if I don't."

Myra looked down at her own delicate wrists, with the blue veins so exquisitely etched against the white flesh. A little look of terror and hopelessness came into her eyes.

"I—I couldn't chop down a tree," she said. She was panting a little in keeping up with him, for he was walking very fast. "I'd be afraid to saddle a horse. You have to stand right next to them, don't you? Most girls can't chop—"

Florian smiled a little superior smile. "Miss Jessie Heath can." Myra looked up at him, quickly. "She's a wonder! She was in yesterday," he went on. "Spent all of two hours up in my department, looking things over. There's nothing she can't do. She won a blue ribbon at the Horse Show in February. Saddle. She's climbed every peak that amounts to anything in Europe. Did the Alps when she was a little girl. This summer she's going to do the Rockies, because things are so mussed up in Europe, she says. I'm selecting the outfit for the party. Gad, what a trip!" He sighed, deeply.

Myra was silent. She was not ungenerous toward women, as are so many pretty girls. But she was human, after all, and she did love this Florian, and Jessie Heath was old man Heath's daughter. Whenever she came into the store she created a little furore among the clerks. Myra could not resist a tiny flash of claws.

"She's flat, like a man. And she wears 7-1/2-C. And her face looks as if it had been rubbed with a scouring brick."

"She's a goddess!" said Florian, striding along. Myra laughed, a little high hysterical laugh. Then she bit her lip, and then she was silent for a long time. He was silent, too, until suddenly he heard a little sound that made him turn quickly to look at her stumbling along at his side. And she was crying.

"Why—what's the matter! What's!—"

"I'm tired," sobbed Myra, and sank in a little limp heap on a conve-nient rock. "I'm tired. I want to go home."

"Why"—he was plainly bewildered—"why didn't you tell me you were tired!"

"I'm telling you now."

They took the nearest ferry across the river, and the Subway home. At the entrance to the noisy, crowded flat in which she lived Myra turned to face him. She was through with pretense. She was tired of make-believe. She felt a certain relief in the thought of what she had to say. She faced him squarely.

"I've lived in the city all my life and I'm crazy about it. I love it. I like to walk in the park a little maybe, Sundays, but I hate tramping like we did this afternoon, and you might as well know it. I wouldn't chop down a tree, not if I was freezing to death, and I'd hate to have to sleep in a tent, so there! I hate sunburn, and freckles, and ants in the pie, and blisters on my feet, and getting wet, and flat-heeled shoes, and I never saddled a horse. I'd be afraid to. And what's more, I don't believe you do, either."

"Don't believe I do what?" asked Florian in a stunned kind of voice.

But Myra had turned and left him. And as he stood there, aghast, bewildered, resentful, clear and fair in the back of his mind, against all the turmoil of thoughts that seethed there, was the picture of her white, slim, exquisite throat with a little delicate pulse beating in it as she cried out her rebellion. He wished—or some one inside him that he could not control wished—that he could put his fingers there on her throat, gently.

It was very warm that evening, for May. And as he sat by the window in his pajamas, just before going to bed, he thought about Myra, and he thought about himself. But when he thought about himself he slammed the door on what he saw. Florian's rooms were in Lexington Avenue in the old brownstone district that used to be the home of white-headed millionaires with gold-headed canes, who, on dying, left their millions to an Alger newsboy who had once helped them across the street. Mil-lionaires, gold-headed canes, and newsboys had long vanished, and the old brownstone fronts were rooming houses now, interspersed with deli-catessens, interior decorators, and dressmaking establishments. Florian was fond of boasting when he came down to the store in the morning, after a hot, muggy July night, "My place is like a summer resort. Breeze just sweeps through it. I have to have the covers on."

Sometimes Mrs. Pet, his landlady, made him a pitcher of lemonade and brought it up to him, and he sipped it, looking out over the city, soothed by its roar, fascinated by its glow and brilliance. Mrs. Pet said it was a pleasure to have him around, he was so neat.

Florian was neat. Not only neat, but methodical. He had the same breakfast every week-day morning at Child's; half a grapefruit, one three-minute egg, coffee, rolls. On Sunday morning he had bacon and eggs. It was almost automatic. Speaking of automatics, he never took his meals at one of those modern mechanical feeders. Though at Child's he never really beheld the waitress with his seeing eye, he liked to have her slap his dishes down before him with a genial crash. A gentleman has his little foibles, and being waited on at meal-time was one of his. Occasionally, to prove to himself that he wasn't one of those fogies who get in a rut, he ordered wheat cakes with maple syrup for breakfast. They always disagreed with him.

She was a wise young woman, Myra.

Perhaps Florian, as he sat by his window that Sunday night of Myra's outburst, thought on these things. But he would not admit to himself whither his thinking led. And presently he turned back the spread, neatly, and turned out the light, and opened the window a little wider, and felt of his chin, as men do, though the next shave is eight hours distant, and slept, and did not dream of white throats as he had secretly hoped he would.

And next morning, at eleven, a very wonderful thing began to happen. Next morning, at eleven, Miss Jessie Heath loped (well, it can't be helped. That describes it exactly) into the broad aisles of the fifth floor. She had been coming in a great deal, lately. The Western trip, no doubt.

Descriptions of people are clumsy things, at best, and stop one's story. But Jessie Heath must have her paragraph. A half-dozen lines ought to do it. Well—she was the kind of girl who always goes around with a couple of Airedales, and in woollen stockings, low shoes and mannish shirts, and shell-rimmed glasses, and you felt she wore Ferris waists. Her hair was that ashen blonde with no glint of gold in it. You knew it would become grey in middle age with no definite period of transition. She never buttoned her heavy welted gloves but wore them back over her hand, like a cuff, very English. You felt there must be a riding crop concealed about her somewhere. Perhaps up her spine.

As has been said, there was always a little flurry when she came into the big store that had made millions for her father. It would be nonsense to suppose that Jessie Heath ever deliberately set out to attract a man who was an employee in that store. But it is pleasant and soothing to be admired, and to have a fine pair of eyes look fine things into one's own (shell-rimmed) ones. And, after all, the Jessie Heaths of this world are walked with, and golfed with, and ridden with, and tennised with, and told that they're wonderful pals. But it's the Myras that are made love to. So now, when Florian Sykes looked at her, and flushed a little, and said, "I suppose there are a lot of lucky ones going along with you on this trip, Miss—Jessie," she flushed, too, and flicked her boot with her riding crop—No, no! I forgot. She didn't have a riding crop. Well, anyway she gave the effect of flicking her boot with her riding crop, and said:

"Would you like to go?"

"Would I like to go—!" He choked over it. Then he sighed, and smiled rather wistfully. "That's needlessly cruel of you, Miss Jessie."

"Maybe it's not so cruel as you think," Jessie Heath answered. "Did you make out that list?"

"I spent practically all of yesterday on it." Which we know was a lie because, look, wasn't he with Myra?

They went over the list together. Fishing tackle, tents, pocket-flashes, puttees, ponchos, chocolate, quirts, slickers, matches, medicine-case, sweaters, cooking utensils, blankets. It grew longer, and longer. Their heads came close together over it. And they trailed from department to department, laughing and talking together. And the two Maine ex-guides and the clerk who boasted he knew the Rockies like the palm of his hand, said to one another, "Get on to Nature's Rival trying to make a hit with Jessie."

Meanwhile Jessie was saying, "Of course you know the Rockies, being a Western man, and all."

Florian smiled rather deprecatingly. "Queer part of it is I don't know the Rockies so well—" with an emphasis on the word Rockies that led one to think his more noteworthy feats of altitude had been accomplished about the Alps, the Pyrenees, the Andes, and the lesser Appalachians.

"But you've climbed them, haven't you?"

He burned his bridges behind him. "Only the—ah—eastern slopes."

"Oh, that's all right, then. We're going to do the west. It'll be wonderful having you—"

"Me!"

"Nothing. Let's go on with the list. M-m-m—where were we? Oh, yes. Now trout flies. Which do you honestly think best for mountain trout? The Silver Doctor or the Gray Hackle or the Yellow Professor? U'm?"

Inspiration comes to us at such times. It could have been nothing less that prompted him to say, "Well—doesn't that depend a lot on the weather and the depth of the—ahem!—water?"

"Yes, of course. How silly of me. We'll take a lot of all kinds, and then we'll be safe."

He breathed again and smiled. He had a winning smile, Florian. Jessie Heath smiled in return and they stood there, the two of them, lips parted, eyes holding eyes.

"My God!" said the man who boasted he knew the Rockies like the palm of his own hand, "it looks as if he'd landed her, the stiff."

Certainly it looked as if he had. For next morning old Heath, red-faced, genial-looking (and not so genial as he looked) approached the head of the fifth floor and said, "How long you been with us, Sykes?"

"Well, I came here as errand boy at thirteen. That's ten—twelve—fifteen—just about sixteen years next June. Yes, sir."

"How'd Jessie—how'd my daughter get the idea you were from the West, and a regular mountain goat, and a peak-climber and all that?"

He did look a little uncomfortable then, but it was too late for withdrawal. "I am from the West, you know."

"Have you had any long vacations since you've been with us?"

"No, sir. You see, in the summer, of course—our busy season. I never can get away then. So I've taken my two weeks in the fall."

Old Heath's eyes narrowed musingly. "Well, you couldn't have done all this mountain climbing before you were thirteen. And Jessie says—" He paused, rather blankly. "You say you do know the Rockies, though, eh?"

Florian drew himself up a little. "As well as I know any mountain."

"Oh, well, then, that's all right. Seems Jessie thinks you'd be a fine fellow to have along on this trip. I can't go myself. I hate this mountain climbing, anyway. Too darned hard work. But it's all right for young folks. Well, now, what do you say? Want to go? You've earned a vacation, after sixteen years. There's about eight in Jessie's crowd. Not counting guides. What do you say? Like to go?"

For a dazed moment Florian stared at him. "Why, yessir. Yes, sir, I'd—I'd like to go—very much." And he coughed to hide his joy and terror.

And two weeks later he went.

The thing swept the store like a flame. In an hour everyone knew it from the shipping-room to the roof-restaurant. Myra saw him the day he left. She was game, that girl.

"I hope you're going to have a beautiful time, Mr. Sykes."

"Thanks, Myra." He could afford to be lenient with her, poor little girl.

She ventured a final wretched word or two. "It's—it's wonderful of Mr. Heath and—Miss Heath—isn't it?" She was rubbing salt into her own wound and taking a fierce sort of joy in it.

"Wonderful! Say, they're a couple of God's green footstools, that's what they are!" He was a little mixed, but very much in earnest. "A couple of God's green footstools." And he went.

He went, and Myra watched him go, and except for a little swelling gulp in her white throat you'd never have known she'd been hit. He was going with Jessie Heath. Now, Myra had no illusions about those things. Old man Heath's wife, now dead, had been a girl with no money and no looks, and yet he had married her. If Jessie Heath happened to take a fancy to Florian, why—

Myra's little world stood still, and in it were small voices, far away, asking for 6-1/2-B; and have you it in brown, and other unimportant things like that.

Ten minutes after the train had started Florian Sykes knew he shouldn't have come. He had suspected it before. He kept saying to himself, over and over: "You've always wanted a mountain trip, and now you're going to have it. You're a lucky guy, that's what you are. A lucky guy." But in his heart he knew he was lying.

In the first place, they were all so glib with their altitudes, and their packs, and their trails, and their horses and their camps. It was a rather mixed and raggle-taggle group that Miss Jessie Heath had gathered about her for this expedition to the West. They ranged all the way from a little fluffy witless golden-haired girl they all called Mud, for some obscure reason, and who had been Miss Heath's room-mate at college, surprisingly enough, to a lady of stern and rock-bound countenance who looked like a stage chaperon made up for the part. She was Miss Heath's companion in lieu of Mrs. Heath, deceased. In between there were a couple of men of Florian's age; two youngsters of twenty-one or two who talked of Harvard and asked Florian what his university had been; an old girl whose name Florian never did learn; and two others of Jessie Heath's age and general style. Florian found himself as bewildered by their talk and views as though they had been jabbering a foreign language. Every now and then, though, one of them would turn to him for a bit of technical advice. If it happened to concern equipment Florian could answer it readily enough. Ten years on the fifth floor had taught him many things. But if the knowledge sought happened to be of things geographical or of nature, he floundered, struggled, sank. And it took them just about half a day to learn this. The trip out takes four, from New York.

At first they asked him things to see him suffer. But they tired of that, after a bit. It was too easy. Queerly enough, Jessie Heath, mountain-wise though she was, believed in him almost to the end. But that only made the next three weeks the bitterer for Florian Sykes. For when it came to leaping from peak to peak Jessie turned out to be the young gazelle. And she liked to have Florian with her. On the trail she was a mosquito afoot, a jockey ahorseback. A thousand times, in those three weeks of torture, he would fix his eye on a tree ten feet away, up the steep trail. And to himself he would say, "I'll struggle, somehow, as far as that tree, and then die under it." And he would stagger another ten feet, his heart pounding in the unaccustomed altitude, his lungs bursting, his lips parted, his breath coming sobbingly, his eyes starting from his head. Leaping lightly ahead of him, around the bend, was Jessie, always. She had a way of calling to the laggard—hallooing, I believe it's supposed to be. And she expected an answer. An answer! When your lungs were bursting through your chest and your heart was crowding your tonsils. When he reached her it was always to find her perched on a seemingly inaccessible rock, demanding that he join her to admire the view. Before three days had gone by the sound of that halloo with its breeziness and breath-control and power, made him sick all over. Sometimes she sang, going up the trail. He could not have croaked a note if failure to do it had meant instant death. The Harvard hellions (it is his own term) were indefatigable, simian, pitiless. At nine thousand feet they aimed at ten. At ten they would have nothing less than twelve. At twelve thousand they were all for making another drive for it and having lunch at an altitude of thirteen thousand five hundred. As he toiled painfully along hundreds of feet behind them, Florian used to take a hideous pleasure in fancying how, on reaching the ever-distant top, the Harvard hellions would be missing. And after searching and hallooing he would peer over the edge (13,500 feet, at the very least, surely) and there, at the bottom, would discern their mangled forms, distorted, crushed, and quite, quite dead.

"Yoo-o-o—hoo-oo-oo-oo!" Jessie, up the trail. His rosy dream would vanish.

He learned why seasoned mountain climbers make nothing of the ascent. He learned, in bitterness and unshed tears, that it is the descent that breaks the heart and shatters the already broken frame. That down-climb with your toes crashing through your boots at every step; with your knee-brakes refusing to work, your thighs creaking, your joints spavined. The views were wonderful. But, oh, the price he paid! The air was intoxicating. But what, he asked himself, was wine to a dead man! Miserable little cockney that he was he told himself a hundred times a day that if he ever survived this he'd never look at another view again, unless from the Woolworth Tower, on a calm day. He thought of New York as a traveller, dying of thirst in the desert, thinks of the lush green oasis. New York in July! Dear New York in July, its furs in storage, its collar unstarched, its coat unbuttoned; even its doormen and chauffeurs almost human. Would he ever see it again? And then, as if in answer to his question, there befell an incident so harrowing, so nerve-shattering, as almost to make a negative answer seem inevitable.

Florian got lost.

It was the third week of the trip. Florian had answered Jessie's eleven thousandth question about things of which he was quite, quite ignorant. His brain felt queer and tight, as though something were about to snap.

They were to climb the Peak next day. All that day they had been approaching it. Florian looked at it. And he hated it. It was like a colossal forbidding finger pointing upward, upward, taunting him, menacing him. He wished that some huge cataclysm of nature would occur, swallowing up this hideous mass of pitiless rock.

Jessie Heath's none too classic nose had peeled long ere this and her neck was like a choice cut of underdone beefsteak. Florian told himself that there was something almost indecent about a girl who cared so little about her skin, and hair, and eyes, and hands. He actually hated her sturdy legs in their boots or puttees—those tireless, pitiless legs, always twinkling ahead of him, up the trail.

On the fateful day he was tired. He had often been tired to the point of desperation during the past three weeks. But this was different. Every step was torture. Every breath was pain. Jessie was a few hundred feet up the trail, as always, and hallooing to him every dozen paces. The Harvard hellions were doing the chamois ahead of her. The rest of the party were toiling along behind. One guide was just ahead. Another, leading two horses, bringing up the rear. Suddenly, desperately, Florian knew he must rest. He would fling himself on a bed of moss by the side of the trail, in the shade, near a stunted, wind-tortured timber-line pine, and let the whole procession pass him, and then catch up with them before they disappeared.

He stepped to the side of the narrow trail, almost indiscernible at this height, flung himself down with a little groan of relief, and shut his sun-seared eyes. The voices of the others came to him. There was little conversation. He heard Jessie's accursed halloo. Then the soft thud of the pack-horses' hoofs, the creak of the saddles. He must get up and follow now. In a minute. In a minute. In a m—

He must have slept there for two hours. When he awoke the light had changed and the air was chill. He sat up, bewildered. He rose. He looked about, called, hallooed, shouted, did all the futile frenzied things that a city man does who is lost in the mountains, and, knowing he is lost, is panic-stricken. The trail, of course! He looked for it, and there was no trail, to his town-wise eyes. He ran hither and thither, and back to hither again. He went forward, seemingly, and found himself back whence he started. He looked for cairns, for tree-blazes, for any one of the signs of which he had learned in the last three weeks. He found none. He called again, shrilly. A terror seized him. Terror of those grim, menacing, towering mountain masses. He ran round and round and round; darted backward and forward; called; stumbled; fell, and subsided, beaten.

He had a tiny box of matches with him, but little else. He had found the trail difficult enough without being pack-burdened. Food? He bethought himself of a little blue tin box in his coat pocket. He took it out and looked at it. Its very name struck terror to his heart.

U. S. Emergency Ration. It was printed on the box. Just below that he made out:

Powdered sugar
Chocolate
Cocoa butter
Malted milk
Egg Albumin
Casein.
Not to be opened except on command of officer.

My God! He had come to this! He looked at it, wide-eyed. He was very hungry. The ration, in its blue tin, like a box of shaving talcum, had been handed to each of the party in a chorus of shouting and laughter. And now it was to save his life. He managed to pry open the box, and ate some of its contents, slowly. It was not agreeable.

Dusk was coming on. There were mountain lions, he knew that. Those rocks and crevices were peopled with all sorts of stealthy, snarling, slinking, four-footed creatures. He would build a fire. They were afraid of the flames, he had read somewhere, and would not come near. Perhaps the others would see the light, and come back to find him. Curse them! Why hadn't they come before now!

It was dusk by the time he had his fire built. He had crouched over it for a half-hour, blowing it, coaxing it, wheedling it. There were few twigs or sticks at this height. He was very cold. His heavy sweater was in the pack on the horse's back. Finally he was rewarded with a feeble flicker, a tiny tongue of flame. He rose from his knees and passed his hand over his forehead with a gesture of utter weariness and despair. And then he stared, transfixed. For on the plateau above him rose a great shaft of fire. The kind of fire that only Pete, the most expert among guides, could build. And as he stared there burst out at him from behind trees, rocks, crevices, a whole horde of imps shrieking with fiendish laughter.

"Ho, ho," laughed Jessie.

And "Ha, ha!" howled the Harvard hellions.

"Thought you were lost, didn'tcha?"

"Gosh, you looked funny!"

"Your face!—"

Florian stared at them. He did not smile. He went quietly over to his tiny camp-fire and stamped it out, neatly, as he had been taught to do. He took his can of emergency ration (not to be opened except on command of officer) and hurled it far, far down the mountainside. Jessie Heath laughed, contemptuously. And Florian, looking at her, didn't care. Didn't care. Didn't care.

The nightmare was over in August. Over, that is, for Florian. The rest were to do another four weeks of it, farther into the interior. Florian sickened at the thought of it. When he bade them farewell he was so glad to be free of them that he almost loved them. When he found himself actually on the little jerkwater train that was to connect him with the main line he patted the dusty red plush seat, gratefully, as one would stroke a faithful beast. When he came into the Grand Central station he would have stooped and kissed the steps of the marble staircase if his porter had not been on the point of vanishing with his bags. That night on reaching home he stayed in the bathtub for an hour, just lying there in the warm, soothing liquid, only moving to dapple his fingers now and then as a lazy fish moves a languid fin. God's country! This was it.

"My, it's nice to have you back again, Mr. Sykes," said Mrs. Pet.

"Is your big two-room suite on the next floor vacant?" said Florian, cryptically.

Mrs. Pet stared a little, wonderingly. "Yes, that's vacant since the Ostranders left, in July. Why do you ask, Mr. Sykes?"

"Nothing," Florian answered, airily. "Not a thing. Just asked."

His train had come in at nine. It was eleven now, but he was restless, and a little hungry, and very much exhilarated. "You certainly look grand," Mrs. Pet had exclaimed, admiringly. "And my, how you're sunburned!"

He left the Lexington Avenue house, now, and strolled over to the near-by white-tiled restaurant. There, in the window, was the white-capped one, flapping pancakes. Florian could have kissed him. He sat down. A waitress approached him.

"I don't know," mused Florian. "I'm sort of hungry, but I don't just—"

"The pork and beans are elegant to-night," suggested the girl.

And "Pork and beans! NO!" thundered Florian.

The girl drew herself up icily. "I ain't deef. You don't need to yell."

Florian looked up at her contritely, and smiled his winning smile. "I'm sorry. I didn't mean—I—I never want to see beans again as long as I live!"

He was down at the store early, early next morning. His practised eye swept the department for possible slackness, for changes, for needed adjustments. The two Maine ex-guides and the chap who knew the Rockies like the palm of his hand welcomed him with Judas-like slaps on the shoulder. "Like it?" they asked him. And, "God's country—the West," he answered, mechanically. After that he ignored them. At nine he ran down the two flights of stairs to the third floor. He did not wait for the elevator.

For a moment he could not find her and his heart sank. She might be away on a vacation. Then he spied her in a corner half-hidden by a rack of covert coats. She was hanging them up. The floor was empty of customers thus early. He strode over to her. She turned. Into her eyes there leaped a look which she quickly veiled as had been taught her by a thousand thousand female ancestors.

"I got your postals," she said.

Florian said nothing.

"My, you're brown!"

Florian said nothing.

"Did you—have a good time?"

Florian said nothing.

"What—what—" Her hand went to her throat, where his eyes were fastened.

Then Florian spoke. "How white your throat is!" he said. "How white your throat is!"

Myra stepped out, then, from among the covert coats on the rack. Her head was lifted high on the creamy column that supported it. She had her pride, had Myra.

"It's no whiter than it was a month ago, that I can see."

"I know it." His tone was humble, with a little pleading note in it. "I know a lot of things that I didn't know a month ago, Myra."

THE SUDDEN SIXTIES

H<small>ANNAH</small> Winter was sixty all of a sudden, as women of sixty are. Just yesterday—or the day before, at most—she had been a bride of twenty in a wine-coloured silk wedding gown, very stiff and rich. And now here she was, all of a sudden, sixty.

The actual anniversary that marked her threescore had had nothing to do with it. She had passed that day painlessly enough—happily, in fact. But now, here she was, all of a sudden, consciously, bewilderingly, sixty. This is the way it happened!

She was rushing along Peacock Alley to meet her daughter Marcia. Any one who knows Chicago knows that smoke-blackened pile, the Congress Hotel; and any one who knows the Congress Hotel has walked down that glittering white marble crypt called Peacock Alley. It is neither so glittering nor so white, nor, for that matter, so prone to preen itself as it was in the hotel's palmy '90s. But it still serves as a convenient short cut on a day when Chicago's lake wind makes Michigan Boulevard a hazard, and thus Hannah Winter was using it. She was to have met Marcia at the Michigan Boulevard entrance at two, sharp. And here it was 2.07. When Marcia said two, there she was at two, waiting, lips slightly compressed. When you came clattering up, breathless, at 2.07, she said nothing in reproach. But within the following half hour bits of her conversation, if pieced together, would have summed up something like this:

"I had to get the children off in time and give them their lunch first because it's wash day and Lutie's busy with the woman and won't do a single extra thing; and all my marketing for to-day and to-morrow because to-morrow's Memorial Day and they close at noon; and stop at the real estate agent's on Fifty-third to see them about the wall paper before

I came down. I didn't even have time to swallow a cup of tea. And yet I was here at two. You haven't a thing to do. Not a blessed thing, living at a hotel. It does seem to me ..."

So then here it was 2.07, and Hannah Winter, rather panicky, was rushing along Peacock Alley, dodging loungers, and bell-boys, and travelling salesmen and visiting provincials and the inevitable red-faced delegates with satin badges. In her hurry and nervous apprehension she looked, as she scuttled down the narrow passage, very much like the Rabbit who was late for the Duchess's dinner. Her rubber-heeled oxfords were pounding down hard on the white marble pavement. Suddenly she saw coming swiftly toward her a woman who seemed strangely familiar—a well-dressed woman, harassed looking, a tense frown between her eyes, and her eyes staring so that they protruded a little, as one who runs ahead of herself in her haste. Hannah had just time to note, in a flash, that the woman's smart hat was slightly askew and that, though she walked very fast, her trim ankles showed the inflexibility of age, when she saw that the woman was not going to get out of her way. Hannah Winter swerved quickly to avoid a collision. So did the other woman. Next instant Hannah Winter brought up with a crash against her own image in that long and tricky mirror which forms a broad full-length panel set in the marble wall at the north end of Peacock Alley. Passersby and the loungers on near-by red plush seats came running, but she was unhurt except for a forehead bump that remained black-and-blue for two weeks or more. The bump did not bother her, nor did the slightly amused concern of those who had come to her assistance. She stood there, her hat still askew, staring at this woman—this woman with her stiff ankles, her slightly protruding eyes, her nervous frown, her hat a little sideways—this stranger—this murderess who had just slain, ruthlessly and forever, a sallow, lively, high-spirited girl of twenty in a wine-coloured silk wedding gown.

Don't think that Hannah Winter, at sixty, had tried to ape sixteen. She was not one of those grisly sexagenarians who think that, by wearing pink, they can combat the ochre of age. Not at all. In dress, conduct, mode of living she was as an intelligent and modern woman of sixty should be. The youth of her was in that intangible thing called, sentimentally, the spirit. It had survived forty years of buffeting, and disappointment, and sacrifice and hard work. Inside this woman who wore well-tailored black and small close hats and clean white wash gloves (even in Chicago) was the girl, Hannah Winter, still curious about this adventure known as living; still capable of bearing its disappointments or enjoying its surprises. Still capable, even, of being surprised. And all this is often the case, all unsuspected by the Marcias until the Marcias are, themselves, suddenly sixty. When it is too late to say to the Hannah Winters, "Now I understand."

We know that Hannah Winter had been married in wine-coloured silk, very stiff and grand. So stiff and rich that the dress would have stood alone if Hannah had ever thought of subjecting her wedding gown to such indignity. It was the sort of silk of which it is said that they don't make such silk now. It was cut square at the neck and trimmed with passementerie and fringe brought crosswise from breast to skirt hem. It's in the old photograph and, curiously enough, while Marcia thinks it's comic, Joan, her nine-year-old daughter, agrees with her grandmother in thinking it very lovely. And so, in its quaintness and stiffness and bravery, it is. Only you've got to have imagination.

While wine-coloured silk wouldn't have done for a church wedding it was quite all right at home; and Hannah Winter's had been a home wedding (the Winters lived in one of the old three-story red-bricks that may still be seen, in crumbling desuetude, over on Rush Street) so that wine-coloured silk for a twenty-year-old bride was quite in the mode.

It is misleading, perhaps, to go on calling her Hannah Winter, for she married Hermie Slocum and became, according to law, Mrs. Hermie Slocum, but remained, somehow, Hannah Winter in spite of law and clergy, though with no such intent on her part. She had never even heard of Lucy Stone. It wasn't merely that her Chicago girlhood friends still spoke of her as Hannah Winter. Hannah Winter suited her—belonged to her and was characteristic. Mrs. Hermie Slocum sort of melted and ran down off her. Hermie was the sort of man who, christened Herman, is called Hermie. That all those who had known her before her marriage still spoke of her as Hannah Winter forty years later was merely another triumph of the strong over the weak.

At twenty Hannah Winter had been a rather sallow, lively, fun-loving girl, not pretty, but animated; and forceful, even then. The Winters were middle-class, respected, moderately well-to-do Chicago citizens— or had been moderately well-to-do before the fire of '71. Horace Winter had been caught in the financial funk that followed this disaster and the Rush Street household, almost ten years later, was rather put to it to supply the wine-coloured silk and the supplementary gowns, linens, and bedding. In those days you married at twenty if a decent chance to marry at twenty presented itself. And Hermie Slocum seemed a decent chance, undoubtedly. A middle-class, respected, moderately well-to-do person himself, Hermie, with ten thousand dollars saved at thirty-five and just about to invest it in business in the thriving city of Indianapolis. A solid young man, Horace Winter said. Not much given to talk. That indicated depth and thinking. Thrifty and far-sighted, as witness the good ten thousand in cash. Kind. Old enough, with his additional fifteen years, to balance the lively Hannah who was considered rather flighty and too prone to find fun in things that others considered serious. A good thing she never quite lost that fault. Hannah resolutely and dutifully put out of her head (or nearly) all vagrant thoughts of Clint Darrow with the crisp black hair and the surprising blue eyes thereto, and the hat worn rakishly a little on one side, and the slender cane and the pointed shoes. A whipper-snapper, according to Horace Winter. Not a solid business man like Hermie Slocum. Hannah did not look upon herself as a human sacrifice. She was genuinely fond of Hermie. She was fond of her father, too; the rather harassed and hen-pecked Horace Winter; and of her mother, the voluble and quick-tongued and generous Bertha Winter, who was so often to be seen going down the street, shawl and bonnet-strings flying, when she should have been at home minding her household. Much of the minding had fallen to Hannah.

And so they were married, and went to the thriving city of Indianapolis to live, and Hannah Winter was so busy with her new household goods, and the linens, and the wine-coloured silk and its less magnificent satellites, that it was almost a fortnight before she realized fully that this solid young man, Hermie Slocum, was not only solid but immovable; not merely thrifty, but stingy; not alone taciturn but quite conversationless. His silences had not proceeded from the unplumbed depths of his knowledge. He merely had nothing to say. She learned, too, that the ten thousand dollars, soon dispelled, had been made for him by an energetic and shrewd business partner with whom he had quarrelled and from whom he had separated a few months before.

There never was another lump sum of ten thousand of Hermie Slocum's earning.

Well. Forty years ago, having made the worst of it you made the best of it. No going home to mother. The word "incompatibility" had not come into wide-spread use. Incompatibility was a thing to hide, not to flaunt. The years that followed were dramatic or commonplace, depending on one's sense of values. Certainly those years were like the married years of many another young woman of that unplastic day. Hannah Winter had her job cut out for her and she finished it well, and alone. No reproaches. Little complaint. Criticism she made in plenty, being the daughter of a voluble mother; and she never gave up hope of stiffening the spine of the invertebrate Hermie.

The ten thousand went in driblets. There never was anything dashing or romantic about Hermie Slocum's failures. The household never felt actual want, nor anything so picturesque as poverty. Hannah saw to that.

You should have read her letters back home to Chicago—to her mother and father back home on Rush Street, in Chicago; and to her girlhood friends, Sarah Clapp, Vinie Harden, and Julia Pierce. They were letters that, for stiff-lipped pride and brazen boasting, were of a piece with those written by Sentimental Tommy's mother when things were going worst with her.

"My wine-coloured silk is almost worn out," she wrote. "I'm thinking of making it over into a tea-gown with one of those new cream pongee panels down the front. Hermie says he's tired of seeing me in it, evenings. He wants me to get a blue but I tell him I'm too black for blue. Aren't men stupid about clothes! Though I pretend to Hermie that I think his taste is excellent, even when he brings me home one of those expensive beaded mantles I detest."

Bald, bare-faced, brave lying.

The two children arrived with mathematical promptness—first Horace, named after his grandfather Winter, of course; then Martha, named after no one in particular, but so called because Hermie Slocum insisted, stubbornly, that Martha was a good name for a girl. Martha herself fixed all that by the simple process of signing herself Marcia in her twelfth year and forever after. Marcia was a throw-back to her grandmother Winter—quick-tongued, restless, volatile. The boy was an admirable mixture of the best qualities of his father and mother; slow-going, like Hermie Slocum, but arriving surely at his goal, like his mother. With something of her driving force mixed with anything his father had of gentleness. A fine boy, and uninteresting. It was Hannah Winter's boast that Horace never caused her a moment's sorrow or uneasiness in all his life; and so Marcia, the troublous, was naturally her pride and idol.

As Hermie's business slid gently downhill Hannah tried with all her strength to stop it. She had a shrewd latent business sense and this she vainly tried to instil in her husband. The children, stirring in their sleep in the bedroom adjoining that of their parents, would realize, vaguely, that she was urging him to try something to which he was opposed. They would grunt and whimper a little, and perhaps remonstrate sleep-ily at being thus disturbed, and then drop off to sleep again to the sound of her desperate murmurs. For she was desperate. She was resolved not to go to her people for help. And it seemed inevitable if Hermie did not heed her. She saw that he was unsuited for business of the mercantile sort; urged him to take up the selling of insurance, just then getting such a strong and wide hold on the country.

In the end he did take it up, and would have made a failure of that, too, if it had not been for Hannah. It was Hannah who made friends for him, sought out prospective clients for him, led social conversation into business channels whenever chance presented itself. She had the boy and girl to think of and plan for. When Hermie objected to this or that luxury for them as being stuff and nonsense Hannah would say, not without a touch of bitterness, "I want them to have every advantage I can give them. I want them to have all the advantages I never had when I was young."

"They'll never thank you for it."

"I don't want them to."

Adam and Eve doubtless had the same argument about the bringing up of Cain and Abel. And Adam probably said, after Cain's shocking crime, "Well, what did I tell you! Was I right or was I wrong? Who spoiled him in the first place!"

They had been married seventeen years when Hermie Slocum, fifty-two, died of pneumonia following a heavy cold. The thirty-seven-year-old widow was horrified (but not much surprised) to find that the insurance solicitor had allowed two of his own policies to lapse. The company was kind, but businesslike. The insurance amounted, in all, to about nine thousand dollars. Trust Hermie for never quite equalling that ten again.

They offered her the agency left vacant by her husband, after her first two intelligent talks with them.

"No," she said, "not here. I'm going back to Chicago to sell insurance. Everybody knows me there. My father was an old settler in Chicago. There'll be my friends, and their husbands, and their sons. Besides, the children will have advantages there. I'm going back to Chicago."

She went. Horace and Bertha Winter had died five years before, within less than a year of each other. The old Rush Street house had been sold. The neighbourhood was falling into decay. The widow and her two children took a little flat on the south side. Widowed, one might with equanimity admit stress of circumstance. It was only when one had a husband that it was disgraceful to show him to the world as a bad provider.

"I suppose we lived too well," Hannah said when her old friends expressed concern at her plight. "Hermie was too generous. But I don't mind working. It keeps me young."

And so, truly, it did. She sold not only insurance but coal, a thing which rather shocked her south side friends. She took orders for tons of this and tons of that, making a neat commission thereby. She had a desk in the office of a big insurance company on Dearborn, near Monroe, and there you saw her every morning at ten in her neat sailor hat and her neat tailored suit. Four hours of work lay behind that ten o'clock appearance. The children were off to school a little after eight. But there was the ordering to do; cleaning; sewing; preserving, mending. A woman came in for a few hours every day but there was no room for a resident helper. At night there were a hundred tasks. She helped the boy and girl with their home lessons, as well, being naturally quick at mathematics. The boy Horace had early expressed the wish to be an engineer and Hannah contemplated sending him to the University of Wisconsin because she had heard that there the engineering courses were particularly fine. Not only that, she actually sent him.

Marcia showed no special talent. She was quick, clever, pretty, and usually more deeply engaged in some school-girl love affair than Hannah Winter approved. She would be an early bride, one could see that. No career for Marcia, though she sketched rather well, sewed cleverly, played the piano a little, sang just a bit, could trim a hat or turn a dress, danced the steps of the day. She could even cook a commendable dinner. Hannah saw to that. She saw to it, as well, that the boy and the girl went to the theatre occasionally; heard a concert at rare intervals. There was little money for luxuries. Sometimes Marcia said, thoughtlessly, "Mother, why do you wear those stiff plain things all the time?"

Hannah, who had her own notion of humour, would reply, "The better to clothe you, my dear."

Her girlhood friends she saw seldom. Two of them had married. One was a spinster of forty. They had all moved to the south side during the period of popularity briefly enjoyed by that section in the late '90s. Hannah had no time for their afternoon affairs. At night she was too tired or too busy for outside diversions. When they met her they said, "Hannah Winter, you don't grow a day older. How do you do it!"

"Hard work."

"A person never sees you. Why don't you take an afternoon off some time? Or come in some evening? Henry was saying only yesterday that he enjoyed his talk with you so much, and that you were smarter than any man insurance agent. He said you sold him I don't know how many thousand dollars' worth before he knew it. Now I suppose I'll have to go without a new fur coat this winter."

Hannah smiled agreeably. "Well, Julia, it's better for you to do without a new fur coat this winter than for me to do without any."

The Clint Darrow of her girlhood dreams, grown rather paunchy and mottled now, and with the curling black hair but a sparse grizzled fringe, had belied Horace Winter's contemptuous opinion. He was a moneyed man now, with an extravagant wife, but no children. Hannah underwrote him for a handsome sum, received his heavy compliments with a deft detachment, heard his complaints about his extravagant wife with a sympathetic expression, but no comment—and that night spent the ten minutes before she dropped off to sleep in pondering the impenetrable mysteries of the institution called marriage. She had married the solid Hermie, and he had turned out to be quicksand. She had not married the whipper-snapper Clint, and now he was one of the rich city's rich men. Had she married him against her parents' wishes would Clint Darrow now be complaining of her extravagance, perhaps, to some woman he had known in his youth? She laughed a little, to herself, there in the dark.

"What in the world are you giggling about, Mother?" called Marcia, who slept in the bedroom near by. Hannah occupied the davenport couch in the sitting room. There had been some argument about that. But Hannah had said she preferred it; and the boy and girl finally ceased to object. Horace in the back bedroom, Marcia in the front bedroom, Hannah in the sitting room. She made many mistakes like that. So, then, "What in the world are you giggling about, Mother?"

"Only a game," answered Hannah, "that some people were playing to-day."

"A new game?"

"Oh, my, no!" said Hannah, and laughed again. "It's old as the world."

Hannah was forty-seven when Marcia married. Marcia married well. Not brilliantly, of course, but well. Edward was with the firm of Gaige & Hoe, Importers. He had stock in the company and an excellent salary, with prospects. With Horace away at the engineering school Hannah's achievement of Marcia's trousseau was an almost superhuman feat. But it was a trousseau complete. As they selected the monogrammed linens, the hand-made lingerie, the satin-covered down quilts, the smart frocks, Hannah thought, quite without bitterness, of the wine-coloured silk. Marcia was married in white. She was blonde, with a fine fair skin, in her father's likeness, and she made a picture-book bride. She and Ed took a nice little six-room apartment on Hyde Park Boulevard, near the Park and the lake. There was some talk of Hannah's coming to live with them but she soon put that right.

"No," she had said, at once. "None of that. No flat was ever built that was big enough for two families."

"But you're not a family, Mother. You're us."

Hannah, though, was wiser than that.

She went up to Madison for Horace's commencement. He was very proud of his youthful looking, well-dressed, intelligent mother. He introduced her, with pride, to the fellows. But there was more than pride in his tone when he brought up Louise. Hannah knew then, at once. Horace had said that he would start to pay back his mother for his university training with the money earned from his very first job. But now he and Hannah had a talk. Hannah hid her own pangs—quite natural pangs of jealousy and something very like resentment.

"There aren't many Louises," said Hannah. "And waiting doesn't do, somehow. You're an early marrier, Horace. The steady, dependable kind. I'd be a pretty poor sort of mother, wouldn't I, if—" etc.

Horace's first job took him out to South America. He was jubilant, excited, remorseful, eager, downcast, all at once. He and Louise were married a month before the time set for leaving and she went with him. It was a job for a young and hardy and adventurous. On the day they left, Hannah felt, for the first time in her life, bereaved, widowed, cheated.

There followed, then, ten years of hard work and rigid economy. She lived in good boarding houses, and hated them. She hated them so much that, toward the end, she failed even to find amusement in the inevitable wall pictures of plump, partially draped ladies lounging on couches and being tickled in their sleep by overfed cupids in mid-air. She saved and scrimped with an eye to the time when she would no longer work. She made some shrewd and well-advised investments. At the end of these ten years she found herself possessed of a considerable sum whose investment brought her a sufficient income, with careful management.

Life had tricked Hannah Winter, but it had not beaten her. And there, commonplace or dramatic, depending on one's viewpoint, you have the first sixty years of Hannah Winter's existence.

This is the curious thing about them. Though heavy, these years had flown. The working, the planning, the hoping, had sped them by, somehow. True, things that never used to tire her tired her now, and she acknowledged it. She was older, of course. But she never thought of herself as old. Perhaps she did not allow herself to think thus. She had married, brought children into the world, made their future sure—or as sure as is humanly possible. And yet she never said, "My work is done. My life is over." About the future she was still as eager as a girl. She was a grandmother. Marcia and Ed had two children, Joan, nine, and Peter, seven (strong simple names were the mode just then).

Perhaps you know that hotel on the lake front built during the World's Fair days? A roomy, rambling, smoke-blackened, comfortable old structure, ringed with verandas, its shabby facade shabbier by contrast with the beds of tulips or geraniums or canna that jewel its lawn. There Hannah Winter went to live. It was within five minutes' walk of Marcia's apartment. Rather expensive, but as homelike as a hotel could be and housing many old-time Chicago friends.

She had one room, rather small, with a bit of the lake to be seen from one window. The grim, old-fashioned hotel furniture she lightened and supplemented with some of her own things. There was a day bed—a narrow and spindling affair for a woman of her height and comfortable plumpness. In the daytime this couch was decked out with taffeta pillows in rose and blue, with silk fruit and flowers on them, and gold braid. There were two silk-shaded lamps, a shelf of books, the photographs of the children in flat silver frames, a leather writing set on the desk, curtains of pale tan English casement cloth at the windows. A cheerful enough little room.

There were many elderly widows like herself living in the hotel on slender, but sufficient, incomes. They were well-dressed women in trim suits or crepes, and Field's special walking oxfords; and small smart hats. They did a little cooking in their rooms—not much, they hastened to tell you. Their breakfasts only—a cup of coffee and a roll or a slice of toast, done on a little electric grill, the coffee above, the toast below. The hotel dining room was almost free of women in the morning. There were only the men, intent on their papers, and their eggs and the 8.40 I. C. train. It was like a men's club, except, perhaps, for an occasional business woman successful enough or indolent enough to do away with the cooking of the surreptitious matutinal egg in her own room. Sometimes, if they were to lunch at home, they carried in a bit of cold ham, or cheese, rolls, butter, or small dry groceries concealed in muffs or handbags. They even had diminutive iceboxes in closets. The hotel, perforce, shut its eyes to this sort of thing. Even permitted the distribution of tiny cubes of ice by the hotel porter. It was a harmless kind of cheating. Their good dinners they ate in the hotel dining room when not invited to dine with married sons or daughters or friends.

At ten or eleven in the morning you saw them issue forth, or you saw "little" manicures going in. One spoke of these as "little" not because of their size, which was normal, but in definition of their prices. There were "little" dressmakers as well, and "little" tailors. In special session they confided to one another the names or addresses of any of these who happened to be especially deft, or cheap, or modish.

"I've found a little tailor over on Fifty-fifth. I don't want you to tell any one else about him. He's wonderful. He's making me a suit that looks exactly like the model Hexter's got this year and guess what he's charging!" The guess was, of course, always a triumph for the discoverer of the little tailor.

The great lake dimpled or roared not twenty feet away. The park offered shade and quiet. The broad veranda invited one with its ample armchairs. You would have thought that peace and comfort had come at last to this shrewd, knowledgeous, hard-worked woman of sixty. She was handsomer than she had been at twenty or thirty. The white powdering her black hair softened her face, lightened her sallow skin, gave a finer lustre to her dark eyes. She used a good powder and had an occasional facial massage. Her figure, though full, was erect, firm, neat. Around her throat she wore an inch-wide band of black velvet that becomingly hid the chords and sagging chin muscles.

Yet now, if ever in her life, Hannah Winter was a slave.

Every morning at eight o'clock Marcia telephoned her mother. The hotel calls cost ten cents, but Marcia's was an unlimited phone. The conversation would start with a formula.

"Hello—Mama?... How are you?"

"Fine."

"Sleep all right?"

"Oh, yes. I never sleep all night through any more."

"Oh, you probably just think you don't.... Are you doing anything special this morning?"

"Well, I—Why?"

"Nothing. I just wondered if you'd mind taking Joan to the dentist's. Her brace came off again this morning at breakfast. I don't see how I can take her because Elsie's giving that luncheon at one, you know, and the man's coming about upholstering that big chair at ten. I'd call up and try to get out of the luncheon, but I've promised, and there's bridge afterward and it's too late now for Elsie to get a fourth. Besides, I did that to her once before and she was furious. Of course, if you can't ... But I thought if you haven't anything to do, really, why—"

Through Hannah Winter's mind would flash the events of the day as she had planned it. She had meant to go downtown shopping that morning. Nothing special. Some business at the bank. Mandel's had advertised a sale of foulards. She hated foulards with their ugly sprawling patterns. A nice, elderly sort of material. Marcia was always urging her to get one. Hannah knew she never would. She liked the shops in their spring vividness. She had a shrewd eye for a bargain. A bite of lunch somewhere; then she had planned to drop in at that lecture at the Woman's Club. It was by the man who wrote "Your Town." He was said to be very lively and insulting. She would be home by five, running in to see the children for a minute before going to her hotel to rest before dinner.

A selfish day, perhaps. But forty years of unselfish ones had paid for it. Well. Shopping with nine-year-old Joan was out of the question. So, too, was the lecture. After the dentist had mended the brace Joan would have to be brought home for her lunch. Peter would be there, too. It was Easter vacation time. Hannah probably would lunch with them, in Marcia's absence, nagging them a little about their spinach and chop and apple sauce. She hated to see the two children at table alone, though Marcia said that was nonsense.

Hannah and Marcia differed about a lot of things. Hannah had fallen into the bad habit of saying, "When you were children I didn't—"

"Yes, but things are different now, please remember, Mother. I want my children to have all the advantages I can give them. I want them to have all the advantages I never had."

If Ed was present at such times he would look up from his paper to say, "The kids'll never thank you for it, Marsh."

"I don't want them to."

There was something strangely familiar about the whole thing as it sounded in Hannah's ears.

The matter of the brace, alone. There was a tiny gap between Joan's two front teeth and, strangely enough, between Peter's as well. It seemed to Hannah that every well-to-do child in Hyde Park had developed this gap between the two incisors and that all the soft pink child mouths in the district parted to display a hideous and disfiguring arrangement of complicated wire and metal. The process of bringing these teeth together was a long and costly one, totalling between six hundred and two thousand dollars, depending on the reluctance with which the parted teeth met, and the financial standing of the teeths' progenitors. Peter's dental process was not to begin for another year. Eight was considered the age. It seemed to be as common as vaccination.

From Hannah: "I don't know what's the matter with children's teeth nowadays. My children's teeth never had to have all this contraption on them. You got your teeth and that was the end of it."

"Perhaps if they'd paid proper attention to them," Marcia would reply, "there wouldn't be so many people going about with disfigured jaws now."

Then there were the dancing lessons. Joan went twice a week, Peter once. Joan danced very well the highly technical steps of the sophisticated dances taught her at the Krisiloff School. Her sturdy little legs were trained at the practice bar. Her baby arms curved obediently above her head or in fixed relation to the curve of her body in the dance. She understood and carried into effect the French technical terms. It was called gymnastic and interpretive dancing. There was about it none of the spontaneity with which a child unconsciously endows impromptu dance steps. But it was graceful and lovely. Hannah thought Joan a second Pavlowa; took vast delight in watching her. Taking Joan and Peter to these dancing classes was one of the duties that often devolved upon her. In the children's early years Marcia had attended a child study class twice a week and Hannah had more or less minded the two in their mother's absence. The incongruity of this had never struck her. Or if it had she had never mentioned it to Marcia. There were a good many things she never mentioned to Marcia. Marcia was undoubtedly a conscientious mother, thinking of her children, planning for her children, hourly: their food, their clothes, their training, their manners, their education. Asparagus; steak; French; health shoes; fingernails; dancing; teeth; hair; curtseys.

"Train all the independence out of 'em," Hannah said sometimes, grimly. Not to Marcia, though. She said it sometimes to her friends Julia Pierce or Sarah Clapp, or even to Vinie Harding, the spinster of sixty, for all three, including the spinster Vinie, who was a great-aunt, seemed to be living much the same life that had fallen to Hannah Winter's lot.

Hyde Park was full of pretty, well-dressed, energetic young mothers who were leaning hard upon the Hannah Winters of their own families. You saw any number of grey-haired, modishly gowned grandmothers trundling go-carts; walking slowly with a moist baby fist in their gentle clasp; seated on park benches before which blue rompers dug in the sand or gravel or tumbled on the grass. The pretty young mothers seemed very busy, too, in another direction. They attended classes, played bridge, marketed, shopped, managed their households. Some of them had gone in for careers. None of them seemed conscious of the frequency with which they said, "Mother, will you take the children from two to five this afternoon?" Or, if they were conscious of it, they regarded it as a natural and normal request. What are grandmothers for?

Hannah Winter loved the feel of the small velvet hands in her own palm. The clear blue-white of their eyes, the softness of their hair, the very feel of their firm, strong bare legs gave her an actual pang of joy. But a half hour—an hour—with them, and she grew restless, irritable. She didn't try to define this feeling.

"You say you love the children. And yet when I ask you to be with them for half a day—"

"I do love them. But they make me nervous."

"I don't see how they can make you nervous if you really care about them."

Joan was Hannah's favourite; resembled her. The boy, Peter, was blond, like his mother. In Joan was repeated the grandmother's sallow skin, dark eyes, vivacity, force. The two, so far apart in years, were united by a strong natural bond of sympathy and alikeness. When they were together on some errand or excursion they had a fine time. If it didn't last too long.

Sometimes the young married women would complain to each other about their mothers. "I don't ask her often, goodness knows. But I think she might offer to take the children one or two afternoons during their vacation, anyway. She hasn't a thing to do. Not a thing."

Among themselves the grandmothers did not say so much. They had gone to a sterner school. But it had come to this: Hannah was afraid to plan her day. So often had she found herself called upon to forego an afternoon at bridge, a morning's shopping, an hour's mending, even, or reading.

She often had dinner at Marcia's, but not as often as she was asked. More and more she longed for and appreciated the orderly quiet and solitude of her own little room. She never analyzed this, nor did Marcia or Ed. It was a craving for relaxation on the part of body and nerves strained throughout almost half a century of intensive living.

Ed and Marcia were always doing charming things for her. Marcia had made the cushions and the silk lampshades for her room. Marcia was always bringing her jellies, and a quarter of a freshly baked cake done in black Lutie's best style. Ed and Marcia insisted periodically on her going with them to the theatre or downtown for dinner, or to one of the gardens where there was music and dancing and dining. This was known as "taking mother out." Hannah Winter didn't enjoy these affairs as much, perhaps, as she should have. She much preferred a mild spree with one of her own cronies. Ed was very careful of her at street crossings and going down steps, and joggled her elbow a good deal. This irked her, though she tried not to show it. She preferred a matinée, or a good picture or a concert with Sarah, or Vinie, or Julia. They could giggle, and nudge and comment like girls together, and did. Indeed, they were girls in all but outward semblance. Among one another they recognized this. Their sense of enjoyment was un-dulled. They liked a double chocolate ice cream soda as well as ever; a new gown; an interesting book. As for people! Why, at sixty the world walked before them, these elderly women, its mind unclothed, all-revealing. This was painful, sometimes, but interesting always. It was one of the penalties—and one of the rewards—of living.

After some such excursion Hannah couldn't very well refuse to take the children to see a Fairbanks film on a Sunday afternoon when Ed and Marcia were spending the half-day at the country club. Marcia was very strict about the children and the films. They were allowed the saccharine Pickford, and of course Fairbanks's gravity-defying feats, and Chaplin's gorgeous grotesqueries. You had to read the titles for Peter. Hannah wasn't as quick at this as were Ed or Marcia, and Peter was sometimes impatient, though politely so.

And so sixty swung round. At sixty Hannah Winter had a suitor. Inwardly she resented him. At sixty Clint Darrow, a widower now and reverent in speech of the departed one whose extravagance he had deplored, came to live at the hotel in three-room grandeur, overlooking the lake. A ruddy, corpulent, paunchy little man, and rakish withal. The hotel widows made much of him. Hannah, holding herself aloof, was often surprised to find her girlhood flame hovering near now, speaking of loneliness, of trips abroad, of a string of pearls unused. There was something virgin about the way Hannah received these advances. Marriage was so far from her thoughts; this kindly, plump little man so entirely outside her plans. He told her his troubles, which should have warned her. She gave him some shrewd advice, which encouraged him. He rather fancied himself as a Lothario. He was secretly distressed about his rotund waist line and, theoretically, never ate a bite of lunch. "I never touch a morsel from breakfast until dinner time." Still you might see him any day at noon at the Congress, or at the Athletic Club, or at one of the restaurants known for its savoury food, busy with one of the richer luncheon dishes and two cups of thick creamy coffee.

Though the entire hotel was watching her Hannah was actually unconscious of Clint Darrow's attentions, or their markedness, until her son-in-law Ed teased her about him one day. "Some gal!" said Ed, and roared with laughter. She resented this indignantly; felt that they regarded her as senile. She looked upon Clint Darrow as a fat old thing, if she looked at him at all; but rather pathetic, too. Hence her kindliness toward him. Now she avoided him. Thus goaded he actually proposed marriage and repeated the items of the European trip, the pearls, and the unused house on Woodlawn Avenue. Hannah, feeling suddenly faint and white, refused him awkwardly. She was almost indignant. She did not speak of it, but the hotel, somehow, knew. Hyde Park knew. The thing leaked out.

"But why?" said Marcia, smiling—giggling, almost. "Why? I think it would have been wonderful for you, Mother!"

Hannah suddenly felt that she need not degrade herself to explain why—she who had once triumphed over her own ordeal of marriage.

Marcia herself was planning a new career. The children were seven and nine—very nearly eight and ten. Marcia said she wanted a chance at self-expression. She announced a course in landscape gardening—"landscape architecture" was the new term.

"Chicago's full of people who are moving to the suburbs and buying big places out north. They don't know a thing about gardens. They don't know a shrub from a tree when they see it. It's a new field for women—in the country, at least—and I'm dying to try it. That youngest Fraser girl makes heaps, and I never thought much of her intelligence. Of course, after I finish and am ready to take commissions, I'll have to be content with small jobs, at first. But later I may get a chance at grounds around public libraries and hospitals and railway stations. And if I can get one really big job at one of those new-rich north shore places I'll be made."

The course required two years and was rather expensive. But Marcia said it would pay, in the end. Besides, now that the war had knocked Ed's business into a cocked hat for the next five years or more, the extra money would come in very handy for the children and herself and the household.

Hannah thought the whole plan nonsense. "I can't see that you're pinched, exactly. You may have to think a minute before you buy fresh strawberries for a meringue in February. But you do buy them." She was remembering her own lean days, when February strawberries would have been as unattainable as though she had dwelt on a desert island.

On the day of the mirror accident in Peacock Alley, Hannah was meeting Marcia downtown for the purpose of helping her select spring outfits for the children. Later, Marcia explained, there would be no time. Her class met every morning except Saturday. Hannah tried to deny the little pang of terror at the prospect of new responsibility that this latest move of Marcia's seemed about to thrust upon her. Marcia wasn't covering her own job, she told herself. Why take another! She had given up an afternoon with Sarah because of this need of Marcia's to-day. Marcia depended upon her mother's shopping judgment more than she admitted. Thinking thus, and conscious of her tardiness (she had napped for ten minutes after lunch) Hannah Winter had met, face to face, with a crash, this strange, strained, rather haggard elderly woman in the mirror.

It was, then, ten minutes later than 2.07 when she finally came up to Marcia waiting, lips compressed, at the Michigan Avenue entrance, as planned.

"I bumped into that mirror—"

"Oh, Mom! I'm sorry. Are you hurt? How in the world?... Such a morning ... wash day ... children their lunch ... marketing ... wall paper ... Fifty-third Street ... two o'clock ..."

Suddenly, "Yes, I know," said Hannah Winter, tartly. "I had to do all those things and more, forty years ago."

Marcia had a list.... Let's see ... Those smocked dresses for Joan would probably be all picked over by this time ... Light-weight underwear for Peter ... Joan's cape ...

Hannah Winter felt herself suddenly remote from all this; done with it; finished years and years ago. What had she to do with smocked dresses, children's underwear, capes? But she went in and out of the shops, up and down the aisles, automatically, gave expert opinion. By five it was over. Hannah felt tired, depressed. She was to have dinner at Marcia's to-night. She longed, now, for her own room. Wished she might go to it and stay there, quietly.

"Marcia, I don't think I'll come to dinner to-night. I'm so tired. I think I'll just go home—"

"But I got the broilers specially for you, and the sweet potatoes candied the way you like them, and a lemon cream pie."

When they reached home they found Joan, listless, on the steps. One of her sudden sore throats. Stomach, probably. A day in bed for her.

By to-morrow she would be quite all right. Hannah Winter wondered why she did not feel more concern. Joan's throats had always thrown her into a greater panic than she had ever felt at her own children's illnesses. To-day she felt apathetic, indifferent.

She helped tuck the rebellious Joan in bed. Joan was spluttering about some plan for to-morrow. And Marcia was saying, "But you can't go to-morrow, Joan. You know you can't, with that throat. Mother will have to stay home with you, too, and give up her plans to go to the country club with Daddy, and it's the last chance she'll have, too, for a long, long time. So you're not the only one to suffer." Hannah Winter said nothing.

They went in to dinner at 6.30. It was a good dinner. Hannah Winter ate little, said little. Inside Hannah Winter a voice—a great, strong voice, shaking with its own earnestness and force—was shouting in rebellion. And over and over it said, to the woman in the mirror at the north end of Peacock Alley: "Three score—and ten to go. That's what it says—'and ten.' And I haven't done a thing I've wanted to do. I'm afraid to do the things I want to do. We all are, because of our sons and daughters. Ten years. I don't want to spend those ten years taking care of my daughter's children. I've taken care of my own. A good job, too. No one helped me. No one helped me. What's the matter with these modern mothers, with their newfangled methods and their efficiency and all? Maybe I'm an unnatural grandmother, but I'm going to tell Marcia the truth. Yes, I am. If she asks me to stay home with Joan and Peter to-morrow, while she and Ed go off to the country club, I'm going to say, 'No!' I'm going to say, 'Listen to me, Ed and Marcia. I don't intend to spend the rest of my life toddling children to the park and playing second assistant nursemaid. I'm too old—or too young. I've only got ten years to go, according to the Bible, and I want to have my fun. I've sown. I want to reap. My teeth are pretty good, and so is my stomach. They're better than yours will be at my age, for all your smart new dentists. So are my heart and my arteries and my liver and my nerves. Well. I don't want luxury. What I want is leisure. I want to do the things I've wanted to do for forty years, and couldn't. I want, if I feel like it, to start to learn French and read Jane Austen and stay in bed till noon. I never could stay in bed till noon, and I know I can't learn now, but I'm going to do it once, if it kills me. I'm too old to bring up a second crop of children, I want to play. It's terrible to realize that you don't learn how to live until you're ready to die; and, then it's too late. I know I sound like a selfish old woman, and I am, and I don't care. I don't care. I want to be selfish. So will you, too, when you're sixty, Martha Slocum. You think you're young. But all of a sudden you'll be sixty, like me. All of a sudden you'll realize—"

"Mother, you're not eating a thing." Ed's kindly voice.

Marcia, flushed of face, pushed her hair back from her forehead with a little frenzied familiar gesture. "Eat! Who could eat with Joan making that insane racket in there! Ed, will you tell her to stop! Can't you speak to her just once! After all, she is your child, too, you know.... Peter, eat your lettuce or you can't have any dessert."

How tired she looked, Hannah Winter thought. Little Martha. Two babies, and she only a baby herself yesterday. How tired she looked.

"I wanna go!" wailed Joan, from her bedroom prison. "I wanna go to-morrow. You promised me. You said I could. I wanna GO!"

"And I say you can't. Mother has to give up her holiday, too, because of you. And yet you don't hear me—"

"You!" shouted the naughty Joan, great-granddaughter of her great-grandmother, and granddaughter of her grandmamma. "*You* don't care. Giving up's easy for you. You're an old lady."

And then Hannah Winter spoke up. "I'll stay with her to-morrow, Marcia. You and Ed go and have a good time."

IF I SHOULD EVER TRAVEL!

The fabric of my faithful love
No power shall dim or ravel
Whilst I stay here,—but oh, my dear,
If I should ever travel!
                    —Millay.

IF you've spent more than one day in Okoochee, Oklahoma, you've had dinner at Pardee's. Someone—a business acquaintance, a friend, a townsman—has said, "Oh, you stopping at the Okmulgee Hotel? WON—derful, isn't it? Nothing finer here to the Coast. I bet you thought you were coming to the wilderness, didn't you? You Easterners! Think we live in tents and eat jerked venison and maize, huh? Never expected, I bet, to see a twelve-story hotel with separate ice-water faucet in every bathroom and a bath to every room. What'd you think of the Peacock grill, h'm?"

"Well—uh"—hesitatingly—"very nice, but why don't you have something native ... Decorations and ... Peacock grill is New York, not Okla—"

"Z'that so! Well, let me tell you you won't find any better food or service in any restaurant, New York or I don't care where. But say, hotel meals are hotel meals. You get tired of 'em. Ever eat at Pardee's, up the street? Say, there's food! If you're going to be here in town any time why'n't you call up there some evening before six—you have to leave 'em know—and get one of Pardee's dinners? Thursday's chicken. And when I say chicken I mean—Well, just try it, that's all.... And for God's sake don't make a mistake and tip Maxine."

Pardee's you find to be a plain box-like two-story frame house in a quiet and commonplace residential district. Plainly—almost scant-ily—furnished as to living room and dining room. The dining room comfortably seats just twenty, but the Pardees "take" eighteen diners— no more. This because Mrs. Pardee has eighteen of everything in silver. And that means eighteen of everything from grapefruit spoons to cheese knives; and finger bowls before and after until you feel like an early Roman. As for Maxine—the friendly warning is superfluous. You would as soon have thought of slipping Hebe a quarter on Olympus—a rather severe-featured Hebe in a white silk blouse ordered through *Vogue*.

All this should have been told in the past tense, because Pardee's is no more. But Okoochee, Oklahoma, is full of paradoxes like Pardee's. Before you understand Maxine Pardee and her mother in the kitchen (dishing up) you have to know Okoochee. And before you know Okoochee you have to know Sam Pardee, missing.

There are all sorts of stories about Okoochee, Oklahoma—and almost every one of them is true. Especially are the fantastic ones true—the incredible ones. The truer they are the more do they make such Arabian knights as Aladdin and Ali Baba appear dull and worthy gentlemen in the retail lamp and oil business, respectively. Ali Baba's exploit in oil, indeed, would have appeared too trivial for recounting if compared with that of any one of a dozen Okoochee oil wizards.

Take the tale of the Barstows alone, though it hasn't the slightest bearing on this story. Thirteen years ago the Barstows had a parched little farm on the outskirts of what is now the near-metropolis of Okoochee, but what was then a straggling village in the Indian Territory. Ma Barstow was a woman of thirty-five who looked sixty; withered by child-bearing; scorched by the sun; beaten by the wind; gnarled with toil; gritty with dust. Ploughing the barren little farm one day Clem Barstow had noticed a strange oily scum. It seeped up through the soil and lay there, heavily. Oil! Weeks of suspense, weeks of disappointment, weeks of hope. Through it all Ma Barstow had washed, scrubbed, cooked as usual, and had looked after the welfare of the Barstow litter. Seventeen years of drudgery dull the imagination. When they struck the great gusher—it's still known as Barstow's Old Faithful—they came running to her with the news. She had been washing a great tubful of harsh greasy clothes— overalls, shirts, drawers. As the men came, shouting, she appeared in the doorway of the crazy wooden lean-to, wiping her hands on her apron.

"Oil!" they shouted, idiotically. "Millions! Biggest gusher yet! It'll mean millions! You're a millionaire!" Then, as she looked at them, dazedly, "What're you going to do, Mis' Barstow, huh? What're you going to do with it?"

Ma Barstow had brought one hand up to push back a straggling wisp of damp hair. Then she looked at that hand as she brought it down— looked at it and it's mate, parboiled, shrunken, big-knuckled from toil. She wiped them both on her apron again, bringing the palms down hard along her flat thighs. "Do?" The miracles that millions might accomplish burst full force on her work-numbed brain. "Do? First off I'm a-going to have the washing done out."

Last week Mrs. Clement Barstow was runner-up in the women's amateur golf tournament played on the Okoochee eighteen-hole course. She wore tweed knickers. The Barstow place on the Edgecombe Road is so honeycombed with sleeping porches, sun dials, swimming pools, bird baths, terraces, sunken gardens, and Italian marble benches that the second assistant Japanese gardener has to show you the way to the tennis courts.

That's Okoochee.

It was inevitable that Sam Pardee should hear of Okoochee; and, hearing of it, drift there. Sam Pardee was drawn to a new town, a boom town, as unerringly as a small boy scents a street fight. Born seventy-five years earlier he would certainly have been one of those intrepid Forty-niners; a fearless canvas-covered fleet crawling painfully across a continent, conquering desert and plain and mountain; starving, thirsting, fighting Indians, eating each other if necessity demanded, with equal dexterity and dispatch. Perhaps a trip like this would have satisfied his wanderlust. Probably not. He was like a child in a berry patch. The fruit just beyond was always the ripest and reddest. The Klondike didn't do it. He was one of the first up the Yukon in that mad rush. He returned minus all the money and equipment with which he had started, including the great toe of his right foot—tribute levied by the frozen North. From boom town to boom town he went. The first stampede always found him there, deep in blue-prints, engineering sheets, prospectuses. But no sooner did the town install a water-works and the First National Bank house itself in a Portland-cement Greek temple with Roman pillars and a mosaic floor than he grew restless and was on the move.

A swashbuckler, Sam Pardee, in tan shoes and a brown derby. An 1890 Villon handicapped by a home-loving wife; an incurable romantic married to a woman who judged as shiftless any housewife possessed of less than two dozen bath towels, twelve tablecloths, eighteen wash cloths, and at least three dozen dish towels, hand-hemmed. Milly Pardee's idea of adventure was testing the recipes illustrated in the How To Use The Cheaper Cuts page in the back of the woman's magazines.

Perversely enough, they had been drawn together by the very attraction of dissimilarity. He had found her feminine home-loving qualities most appealing. His manner of wearing an invisible cloak, sword and buckler, though actually garbed in ready-mades, thrilled her. She had come of a good family; he of, seemingly, no family at all. When the two married, Milly's people went through that ablutionary process known as washing their hands of her. Thus ideally mismated they tried to make the best of it—and failed. At least, Sam Pardee failed. Milly Pardee said, "Goodness knows I tried to be a good wife to him." The plaint of all unappreciated wives since Griselda.

Theirs was a feast-and-famine existence. Sometimes Sam Pardee made sudden thousands. Mrs. Pardee would buy silver, linen, and other household furnishings ranging all the way from a grand piano to a patent washing machine. The piano and the washing machine usually were whisked away within a few weeks or months, at the longest. But she cannily had the linen and silver stamped—stamped unmistakably and irrevocably with a large, flourishing capital P, embellished with floral wreaths. Eventually some of the silver went the way of the piano and washing machine. But Milly Pardee clung stubbornly to a dozen and a half of everything. She seemed to feel that if once she had less than eighteen fish forks the last of the solid ground of family respectability would sink under her feet. For years she carried that silver about wrapped in trunks full of the precious linen, and in old underwear and cotton flannel kimonos and Sam's silk socks and Maxine's discarded baby-clothes. She clung to it desperately, as other women cling to jewels, knowing that when this is gone no more will follow.

When the child was born Milly Pardee wanted to name her Myrtle but her husband had said, suddenly, "No, call her Maxine."

"After whom?" In Mrs. Pardee's code you named a child "after" someone.

He had seen Maxine Elliott in the heyday of her cold, clear, brainless beauty, with her great, slightly protuberant eyes set so far apart, her exquisitely chiselled white nose, and her black black hair. She had thrilled him.

"After my Uncle Max that lives in—uh—Australia."

"I've never heard you talk of any Uncle Max," said Mrs. Pardee, coldly.

But the name had won. How could they know that Maxine would grow up to be a rather bony young woman who preferred these high-collared white silk blouses; and said "eyether."

Maxine had been about twelve when Okoochee beckoned Sam Pardee. They were living in Chicago at the time; had been there for almost three years—that is, Mrs. Pardee and Maxine had been there. Sam was in and out on some mysterious business of his own. His affairs were always spoken of as "deals" or "propositions." And they always, seemingly, required his presence in a city other than that in which they were living—if living can be said to describe the exceedingly impermanent perch to which they clung. They had a four-room flat. Maxine was attending a good school. Mrs. Pardee was using the linen and silver daily. There was a linen closet down the hall, just off the dining room. You could open the door and feast your eyes on orderly piles of neatly laundered towels, sheets, tablecloths, napkins, tea towels. Mrs. Pardee marketed and cooked, contentedly. She was more than a merely good cook; she was an alchemist in food stuffs. Given such raw ingredients as butter, sugar, flour, eggs, she could evolve a structure of pure gold that melted on the tongue. She could take an ocherous old hen, dredge its parts in flour, brown it in fat sizzling with onion at the bottom of an iron kettle, add water, a splash of tomato and a pinch of seasoning, and bear triumphantly to the table a platter heaped with tender fricassee over which a smooth, saddle-brown gravy simmered fragrantly. She ate little herself, as do most expert cooks, and found her reward when Sam or Maxine uttered a choked and appreciative "Mmm!"

In the midst of creature comforts such as these Sam Pardee said, one evening, "Oil."

Mrs. Pardee passed it, but not without remonstrance. "It's the same identical French dressing you had last night, Sam. I mixed enough for twice. And you didn't add any oil last night."

Sam Pardee came out of his abstraction long enough to emit a roar of laughter and an unsatisfactory explanation. "I was thinking of oil in wells, not in cruets. Millions of barrels of oil, not a spoonful. Crude, not olive."

She saw her child, her peace, her linen closet threatened. "Sam Pardee, you don't mean—"

"Oklahoma. That's what I meant by oil. It's oozing with it."

Real terror leaped into Milly Pardee's eyes. "Not Oklahoma. Sam, I couldn't stand—" Suddenly she stiffened with resolve. Maxine's report card had boasted three stars that week. Oklahoma! Why, there probably were no schools at all in Oklahoma. "I won't bring my child up in Oklahoma. Indians, that's what! Scalped in our beds."

Above Sam Pardee's roar sounded Maxine's excited treble. "Oo, Oklahoma! I'd love it."

Her mother turned on her, almost fiercely. "You wouldn't."

The child had thrown out her arms in a wide gesture. "It sounds so far away and different. I like different places. I like any place that isn't here."

Milly Pardee had stared at her. It was the father talking in the child. Any place that isn't here. Different.

Out of years of bitter experience she tried to convince the child of her error; tried, as she had striven for years to convince Sam Pardee.

"Places are just the same," she said, bitterly, "and so are people, when you get to 'em."

"They can't be," the child argued, stubbornly. "India and China and Spain and Africa."

Milly Pardee had turned accusing eyes on her amused husband. "I hope you're satisfied."

He shrugged. "Well, the kid's right. That's living."

She disputed this, fiercely. "It is not. Living's staying in a place, and helping it grow, and growing up with it and belonging. Belong!" It was the cry of the rolling stone that is bruised and weary.

Sam Pardee left for Oklahoma the following week. Milly Pardee refused to accompany him. It was the first time she had taken this stand. "If you go there, and like it, and want to settle down there, I'll come. I know the Bible says, 'Whither thou goest, I will go,' but I guess even What'shername would have given up at Oklahoma."

For three years, then, Sam Pardee's letters reeked of oil: wells, strikes, gushers, drills, shares, outfits. It was early Oklahoma in the rough. This one was getting five hundred a day out of his well. That one had sunk forty thousand in his and lost out.

"Five hundred what?" Maxine asked. "Forty thousand what?"

"Dollars, I guess," Milly Pardee answered. "That's the way your father always talks. I'd rather have twenty-five a week, myself, and know it's coming without fail."

"I wouldn't. Where's the fun in that?"

"Fun! There's more fun in twenty-five a week in a pay envelope than in forty thousand down a dry well."

Maxine was fifteen now. "I wish we could live with Father in Oklahoma. I think it's wrong not to."

Milly Pardee was beginning to think so, too. Especially since her husband's letters had grown rarer as the checks they contained had grown larger. On his occasional trips back to Chicago he said nothing of their joining him out there. He seemed to have grown accustomed to living alone. Liked the freedom, the lack of responsibility. In sudden fright and resolve Milly Pardee sold the furnishings of the four-room flat, packed the peripatetic linen and silver, and joined a surprised and rather markedly unenthusiastic husband in Okoochee, Oklahoma. A wife and a fifteen-year-old daughter take a good deal of explaining on the part of one who has posed for three years as a bachelor.

The first thing Maxine said as they rode (in a taxi) to the hotel, was: "But the streets are paved!" Then, "But it's all electric lighted with cluster lights!" And, in final and utter disgust, "Why, there's a movie sign that says, 'The Perils of Pauline.' That was showing at the Élite on Forty-third Street in Chicago just the night before we left."

Milly Pardee smiled grimly. "Palestine's paved, too," she observed. "And they're probably running that same reel there next week."

Milly Pardee and her husband had a plain talk. Next day Sam Pardee rented the two-story frame house in which, for years, the famous Pardee dinners were to be served. But that came later. The house was rented with the understanding that the rent was to be considered as payment made toward final purchase. The three lived there in comfort. Maxine went to the new pressed-brick, many-windowed high school. Milly Pardee was happier than she had been in all her wedded life. Sam Pardee had made no fortune in oil, though he talked in terms of millions. In a burst of temporary prosperity, due to a boom in some oil-stocks Sam Pardee had purchased early in the game, they had paid five thousand dollars down on the house and lot. That left a bare thousand to pay. There were three good meals a day. Milly Pardee belonged to the Okoochee Woman's Thursday Club. All the women in Okoochee seemed to have come from St. Louis, Columbus, Omaha, Cleveland, Kansas City, and they spoke of these as Back East. When they came calling they left cards, punctiliously. They played bridge, observing all the newest rulings, and speaking with great elaborateness of manner.

"Yours, I believe, Mrs. Tutwiler."

"Pardon, but didn't you notice I played the ace?"

Maxine graduated in white, with a sash. Mrs. Pardee was on the committee to beautify the grounds around the M. K. & T. railroad station. When relatives from Back East (meaning Nebraska, Kansas, or Missouri) visited an Okoocheeite cards were sent out for an "At Home," and everything was as formal as a court levee in Victoria's time. Mrs. Pardee began to talk of buying an automobile. The town was full of them.

There were the flivvers and lower middle-class cars owned by small merchants, natives (any one boasting twelve year's residence) and unsuccessful adventurers of the Sam Pardee type. Then there were the big, high-powered scouting cars driven by steely-eyed, wiry, cold-blooded young men from Pennsylvania and New York. These young men had no women-folk with them. Held conferences in smoke-filled rooms at the Okmulgee Hotel. The main business street was called Broadway, and the curb on either side was hidden by lines of cars drawn up slantwise at an angle of ninety. No farmer wagons. A small town with all the airs of a big one; with none of the charming informality of the old Southern small town; none of the engaging ruggedness of the established Middle-Western town; none of the faded gentility of the old New England town. A strident dame, this, in red satin and diamonds, insisting that she is a lady. Interesting, withal, and bulging with personality and possibility.

Milly Pardee loved it. She belonged. She was chairman of this committee and secretary of that. Okoochee was always having parades, with floats, sponsored by the Chamber of Commerce of Okoochee and distinguished by schoolgirls grouped on bunting-covered motor trucks, their hair loose and lately relieved from crimpers, three or four inches of sensible shirt-sleeve showing below the flowing lines of their cheese-cloth Grecian robes. Maxine was often one of these. Yes, Milly Pardee was happy.

Sam Pardee was not. He began, suddenly, to talk of Mexico. Frankly, he was bored. For the first time in his life he owned a house—or nearly. There was eleven hundred dollars in the bank. Roast on Sunday. Bathroom shelf to be nailed Sunday morning. Y.M.C.A., Rotary Club, Knights of Columbus, Kiwanis, Boy Scouts.

"Hell," said Sam Pardee, "this town's no good."

Milly Pardee took a last stand. "Sam Pardee, I'll never leave here. I'm through traipsing up and down the world with you, like a gypsy. I want a home. I want to be settled. I want to stay here. And I'm going to."

"You're sure you want to stay?"

"I've moved for the last time. I—I'm going to plant a Burbank clamberer at the side of the porch, and they don't begin to flower till after the first ten years. That's how sure I am."

There came a look into Sam Pardee's eyes. He rubbed his neat brown derby round and round with his coat sleeve. He was just going out.

"Well, that's all right. I just wanted to know. Where's Max?"

"She stayed late. They're rehearsing for the Pageant of Progress down at the Library."

Sam Pardee looked thoughtful—a little regretful, one might almost have said. Then he clapped on the brown derby, paused on the top step of the porch to light his cigar, returned the greeting of young Arnold Hatch who was sprinkling the lawn next door, walked down the street with the quick, nervous step that characterized him, boarded the outgoing train for God knows where, and was never heard from again.

"Well," said the worse-than-widowed (it was her own term), "we've got the home."

She set about keeping it. We know that she had a gift for cooking that amounted almost to culinary inspiration. Pardee's dinners became an institution in Okoochee. Mrs. Pardee cooked. Maxine served. And not even the great new stucco palaces on the Edgecombe Road boasted finer silver, more exquisite napery. As for the food—old Clem Barstow himself, who had a chef and a butler and sent east for lobster and squabs weekly, came to Pardee's when he wanted a real meal. From the first they charged one dollar and fifty cents for their dinners. Okoochee, made mellow by the steaming soup, the savoury meats, the bland sauces and rich dessert, paid it ungrudgingly. They served only eighteen—no more, though Okoochee could never understand why. On each dinner Mrs. Pardee made a minimum of seventy-five cents. Eighteen times seventy-five ... naught and carry the four ... naught ... five ... thirteen-fifty ... seven times ... well, ninety-five dollars or thereabouts each week isn't so bad. Out of this Mrs. Pardee managed to bank a neat sum. She figured that at the end of ten or fifteen years....

"I hate them," said Maxine, washing dishes in the kitchen. "Greedy pigs."

"They're nothing of the kind. They like good food, and I'm thankful they do. If they didn't I don't know where I'd be."

"We might be anywhere—so long as it could be away from here. Dull, stupid, stick-in-the-muds, all of them."

"Why, they're no such thing, Maxine Pardee! They're from all over the world, pretty nearly. Why, just last Thursday they were counting there were sixteen different states represented in the eighteen people that sat down to dinner."

"Pooh! States! That isn't the world."

"What is, then?"

Maxine threw out her arms, sprinkling dish-water from her dripping finger tips with the wide-flung gesture. "Cairo! Zanzibar! Brazil! Trinidad! Seville—uh—Samar—Samarkand."

"Where's Samarkand?"

"I don't know. And I'm going to see it all some day. And the different people. The people that travel, and know about what kind of wine with the roast and the fish. You know—the kind in the novels that say, 'You've chilled this sauterne too much, Bemish.'"

"And when you do see all these places," retorted Mrs. Pardee, with the bitterness born of long years of experience, "you'll find that in every one of them somebody's got a boarding house called Pardee's, or something like that, where the people flock same's they do here, for a good meal."

"Yes, but what kind of people?"

"Same kind that comes here." Sam Pardee had once taken his wife to see a performance of The Man From Home when that comedy was at the height of its popularity. A line from this play flashed into Mrs. Pardee's mind now, and she paraphrased it deftly. "There are just as many kinds of people in Okoochee as there are in Zanzibar."

"I don't believe it."

"Well, it's so. And I'm thankful we've got the comforts of home."

At this Maxine laughed a sharp little laugh that was almost a bark. Perhaps she was justified.

The eighteen straggled in between six and six-thirty, nightly. A mixture of townspeople and strangers. While Maxine poured the water in the dining room the neat little parlour became a mess. The men threw hats and overcoats on the backs of the chairs. Their rubbers slopped under them. They rarely troubled to take them off. While waiting avidly for dinner to be served they struck matches and lighted cigarettes and cigars. Sometimes they called in to Maxine, "Say, girlie, when'll supper be ready? I'm 'bout gone."

The women trotted upstairs, chattering, and primped and fussed in Maxine's neat and austere little bedroom. They used Maxine's powder and dropped it about on the tidy dresser and the floor. They brushed away only what had settled on the front of their dresses. They forgot to switch off the electric light, leaving Maxine to do it, thriftily, between serving courses. Every penny counted. Every penny meant release.

After dinner Maxine and her mother sat down to eat off the edge of the kitchen table. It was often nine o'clock before the last straggling diner, sprawling on the parlour davenport with his evening paper and cigar, departed, leaving Maxine to pick up the scattered newspapers, cigarette butts, ashes; straighten chairs, lock doors.

Then the dishes. The dishes!

When Arnold Hatch asked her to go to a movie she shook her head, usually. "I'm too tired. I'm going to read, in bed."

"Read, read! That's all you do. What're you reading?"

"Oh, about Italy. La bel Napoli!" She collected travel folders and often talked in their terms. In her mind she always said "brooding Vesuvius"; "blue Mediterranean"; "azure coasts"; "Egypt's golden sands."

Arnold Hatch ate dinner nightly at Pardee's. He lived in the house next door, which he owned, renting it to an Okoochee family and retaining the upstairs front bedroom for himself. A tall, thin, eye-glassed young man who worked in the offices of the Okoochee Oil and Refining Company, believed in Okoochee, and wanted to marry Maxine. He had twice kissed her. On both these occasions his eyeglasses had fallen off, taking the passion, so to speak, out of the process. When Maxine giggled, uncontrollably, he said, "Go on—laugh! But some day I'm going to kiss you and I'll take my glasses off first. Then look out!"

You have to have a good deal of humour to stand being laughed at by a girl you've kissed; especially a girl who emphasizes her aloofness by wearing those high-collared white silk blouses.

"You haven't got a goitre, have you?" said Arnold Hatch, one evening, brutally. Then, as she had flared in protest, "I know it. I love that little creamy satin hollow at the base of your throat."

"You've never s—" The scarlet flamed up. She was human.

"I know it. But I love it just the same." Pretty good for a tall thin young man who worked in the offices of the Okoochee Oil and Refining Company.

Sometimes he said, "I'm darned certain you like me"—bravely— "love me. Why won't you marry me? Cut out all this slaving. I could support you. Not in much luxury, maybe, but—"

"And settle down in Okoochee! Never see anything! Stuck in this God-forsaken hole! This drab, dull, oil-soaked village! When there are wonderful people, wonderful places, colour, romance, beauty! Damascus! Mandalay! Singapore! Hongkong!... Hongkong! It sounds like a temple bell. It thrills me."

"Over in Hongkong," said Arnold Hatch, "I expect some Chinese Maxine Pardee would say, Okoochee! It sounds like an Indian war drum. It thrills me.'"

Sometimes Maxine showed signs of melting. But she always congealed again under the influence of her resolve. One evening an out-of-town diner, on hearing her name, said, "Pardee! Hm. Probably a corruption of Pardieu. A French name originally, I suppose."

After that there was no approaching her for a week. Maxine Pardieu. Pardieu. "By God!" it meant. A chevalier he must have been, this Pardieu. A musketeer! A swashbuckler, with lace falling over his slim white hand, and his hand always ready on his sword. Red heels. Plumed hat. Pardieu!

How she hated anew the great oil tanks that rose on the town's outskirts, guarding it like giant sentinels. The new houses. The new country club. Twenty-one miles of asphalt road. Population in 1900, only 467. In 1920 over 35,000. Slogan, Watch Us Grow. Seventeen hundred oil and gas wells. Fields of corn and cotton. Skyscrapers. The Watonga Building, twelve stories. Haynes Block, fourteen stories. Come West, young man! Ugh!

Sometimes she made little rhymes in her mind.

> There's Singapore and Zanzibar,
> And Cairo and Calais.
> There's Samarkand and Alcazar,
> Rangoon and Mandalay.

"Yeh," said Arnold Hatch, one evening, when they were talking in the Pardee back yard. It was nine o'clock. Dishes done. A moon. October. Maxine had just murmured her little quatrain. They were standing by the hedge of pampas grass that separated the Pardee yard from Hatch's next door.

"Yeh," said Arnold Hatch. "Likewise:

> "There's Seminole and Shawnee,
> Apache, Agawam.
> There's Agua and Pawnee,
> Walonga, Waukeetom."

He knew his Oklahoma.

"Oh!" exclaimed Maxine, in a little burst of fury; and stamped her foot down hard. Squ-ush! said something underfoot. "Oh!" said Maxine again; in surprise this time. October was a dry month. She peered down. Her shoe was wet. A slimy something clung to it. A scummy something shone reflected in the moonlight. She had not lived ten years in Oklahoma for nothing. Arnold Hatch bent down. Maxine bent down. The greasy wet patch lay just between the two back yards. They touched it, fearfully, with their forefingers. Then they straightened and looked at each other. Oil. Oil!

Things happened like that in Oklahoma.

You didn't try to swing a thing like that yourself. You leased your land for a number of years. A well cost between forty and sixty thousand dollars. You leased to a company represented by one or two of those cold-blooded steely-eyed young men from Pennsylvania or New York. There was a good deal of trouble about it, too. This was a residence district—one of the oldest in this new town. But they bought the Pardee place and the Hatch place. And Arnold Hatch, who had learned a thing or two in the offices of the Okoochee Oil and Refining Company, drove a hard bargain for both. The yard was overrun with drillers, lawyers, engineers, superintendents, foremen, machinery.

Arnold came with papers to sign. "Five hundred a day," he said, "and a percentage." He named the percentage. Maxine and her mother repeated this after him, numbly.

Mrs. Pardee had been the book-keeper in the Pardee ménage. She tried some mathematical gymnastics now and bumped her arithmetical nose.

"Five hundred a day. Including Sundays, Arnold?"

"Including Sundays."

Her lips began to move. "Seven times five ... thirty-five hundred a ... fifty-two times thirty—"

She stopped, overcome. But she began again, wildly, as a thought came to her. "Why, I could build a house. A house, up on Edgecombe. A house like the Barstows' with lawns, and gardens, and sleeping porches, and linen closets!... Oh, Maxine! We'll live there—"

"Not I," said Maxine, crisply. Arnold, watching her, knew what she was going to say before she said it. "I'm going to see the world. I want to penetrate a civilization so old that its history wanders down the centuries and is lost in the dim mists of mythology." [See Baedeker.]

Sudden wealth had given Arnold a new masterfulness. "Marry me before you go."

"Not at all," replied Maxine. "On the boat going over—"

"Over where?"

"Honolulu, on my way to Japan, I'll meet a tall bearded stranger, sunburned, with the flame of the Orient in his eyes, and on his thin, cruel, sensual mouth—"

Arnold Hatch took off his glasses. Maxine stiffened. "Don't you d—" But she was too late.

"There," said Arnold, "he'll have to have some beard, and some flame, and some thin, cruel, sensual mouth to make you forget that one."

Maxine started, alone, against her mother's remonstrances. After she'd picked out her boat she changed to another because she learned, at the last minute, that the first boat was an oil-burner. Being an inexperienced traveller she took a good many trunks and was pretty unpopular with the steward before he could make her understand that one trunk to the stateroom was the rule. On the first two days out on the way to the Hawaiian Islands she spent all her time (which was twenty-four hours a day in her bed) hoping that Balboa was undergoing fitting torment in punishment for his little joke about discovering the so-called Pacific Ocean. But the swell subsided, and the wind went down, and Maxine appeared on deck and in another twelve hours had met everyone from the purser to the honeymoon couple, in the surprising way one does on these voyages. She looked for the tall bearded stranger with the sunburn of the Orient and the thin, cruel, sensual lips. But he didn't seem to be about. Strangely enough, everyone she talked to seemed to be from Nebraska, or Kansas, or Iowa, or Missouri. Not only that, they all were very glib with names and places that had always seemed mythical and glamorous.

"Oh, yes, Mr. Tannenbaum and I went to India last year, and Persia and around. Real interesting. My, but they're dirty, those towns. We used to kick about Des Moines, now that they use so much soft coal, and all the manufacturing and all. But my land, it's paradise compared to those places. And the food! Only decent meals we had in Egypt was a place in Cairo called Pardee's, run by a woman whose husband's left her or died, or something. Real home-loving woman she was. Such cooking.... Why, that's so! Your name's Pardee, too, isn't it! Well, I always say to Mr. Tannenbaum, it's a small world, after all. No relation, of course?"

"Of course not." How suddenly safe Oklahoma seemed. And Arnold Hatch.

"Where you going from Honolulu, Miss Pardee?"

"Samarkand."

"Beg pardon?"

"Samarkand."

"Oh, yeh. Samar—le' see now, where is that, exactly? I used to know, but I'm such a hand for forgetting—"

"I don't know," said Maxine, distinctly.

"Don't—but I thought you said you were going—"

"I am. But I don't know where it is."

"Then how—"

"You just go to an office, where there are folders and a man behind the desk, and you say you want to go to Samarkand. He shows you. You get on a boat. That's all."

The people from Iowa, and Kansas, and Nebraska and Missouri said, Oh, yes, and there was nothing like travel. So broadening. Maxine asked them if they knew about the Vale of Kashmir and one of them, astoundingly enough, did. A man from Milwaukee, Wisconsin, who had spent a year there superintending the erection of a dredge. A plump man, with eyeglasses and perpetually chewing a dead cigar.

Gold and sunlight, myrrh and incense, the tinkling of anklets. Maxine clung to these wildly, in her mind.

But Honolulu, the Moana Hotel on Waikiki Beach, reassured her. It was her dream come true. She knew it would be so when she landed and got her first glimpse of the dark-skinned natives on the docks, their hats and necks laden with leis of flowers. There were palm trees. There were flaming hibiscus hedges. Her bed was canopied with white netting, like that of a princess (the attendant explained it was to keep out the mosquitoes).

You ate strange fruits (they grew a little sickening, after a day or two). You saw Duke, the Hawaiian world champion swimmer, come in on a surf-board, standing straight and slim and naked like a god of bronze, balancing miraculously on a plank carried in on the crest of a wave with the velocity of a steam engine. You saw Japanese women in tight kimonos and funny little stilted flapping footgear running to catch a street car; and you laughed at the incongruity of it. You made the three-day trip to the living volcano at Hilo and sat at the crater's brink watching the molten lava lake tossing, hissing, writhing. You hung there, between horror and fascination.

"Certainly a pretty sight, isn't it?" said her fellow travellers. "Makes the Grand Canyon look sick, I think, don't you?"

"I've never seen it."

"Oh, really!"

On her return from Hilo she saw him. A Vandyke beard; smouldering eyes; thin red lips; lean nervous hands; white flannel evening clothes; sunburned a rich brown. Maxine drew a long breath as if she had been running. It was after dinner. The broad veranda was filled with gayly gowned women; uniformed officers from the fort; tourists in white. They were drinking their after-dinner coffee, smoking, laughing. The Hawaiian orchestra made ready to play for the dancing on the veranda. They began to play. Their ukeleles throbbed and moaned. The musicians sang in their rich, melodious voices some native song of a lost empire and a dead king. It tore at your heart. You ached with the savage beauty of it. It was then she saw him. He was seated alone, smoking, drinking, watching the crowd with amused, uneager glance. She had seen him before. It was a certainty, this feeling. She had known him—seen him—before. Perhaps not in this life. Perhaps only in her dreams. But they had met.

She stared at him until her eye caught his. It was brazen, but she was shameless. Nothing mattered. This was no time for false modesty. Her eyes held his. Then, slowly, she rose, picked up her trailing scarf, and walked deliberately past him, glancing down at him as she passed. He half rose, half spoke. She went down the steps leading from the veranda to the court-yard, down this walk to the pier, down the pier to the very end, where the little roofed shelter lay out in the ocean, bathed in moonlight, fairylike, unreal. The ocean was a thing of molten silver. The sound of the wailing voices in song came to her on the breeze, agonizing in its beauty. There, beyond, lay Pearl Harbour. From the other side, faintly, you heard the music and laughter from the Yacht Club.

Maxine seated herself. The after-dinner couples had not yet strolled out. They were waiting for the dancing up there on the hotel veranda. She waited. She waited. She saw the glow of his cigar as he came down the pier, a tall, slim white figure in the moonlight. It was just like a novel. It was a novel, come to life. He stood a moment at the pier's edge, smoking. Then he tossed his cigar into the water and it fell with a little s-st! He stood another moment, irresolutely. Then he came over to her.

"Nice night."

In Okoochee you would have said, "Sir!" But not here. Not now. Not Maxine Pardieu. "Yes, isn't it!"

The mellow moon fell full on him—bronzed, bearded, strangely familiar.

At his next question she felt a little faint. "Haven't we—met before?"

She toyed with the end of her scarf. "You feel that, too?"

He nodded. He took a cigarette from a flat platinum case. "Mind if I smoke? Perhaps you'll join me?" Maxine took a cigarette, uncertainly. Lighted it from the match he held. Put it to her lips. Coughed, gasped. "Maybe you're not used to those. I smoke a cheap cigarette because I like 'em. Dromedaries, those are. Eighteen cents a package."

Maxine held the cigarette in her unaccustomed fingers. Her eyes were on his face. "You said you thought—you felt—we'd met before?"

"I may be mistaken, but I never forget a face. Where are you from, may I ask?"

Maxine hesitated a moment. "Oklahoma."

He slapped his leg a resounding thwack. "I knew it! I'm hardly ever mistaken. Name's—wait a minute—Pardee, isn't it?"

"Yes. But how—"

"One of the best meals I ever had in my life, Miss Pardee. Two years ago, it was. I was lecturing on Thibet and the Far East."

"Lecturing?" Her part of the conversation was beginning to sound a good deal like the dialogue in a badly written play.

"Yes, I'm Brainerd, you know. I thought you knew, when you spoke up there on the veranda."

"Brainerd?" It was almost idiotic.

"Brainerd. Paul Brainerd, the travelogue man. I remember I gave you and your mother complimentary tickets to the lecture. I've got a great memory. Got to have, in my business. Let's see, that town was—"

"Okoochee," faintly.

"Okoochee! That's it! It's a small world after all, isn't it? Okoochee. Why, I'm on my way to Oklahoma now. I'm going to spend two months or more there, taking pictures of the vast oil fields, the oil wells. A new country. An Aladdin country; a new growth; one of the most amazing and picturesque bits in the history of our amazing country. History in the making. An empire over-night. Oklahoma! Well! What a relief, after war-torn Europe and an out-worn civilization."

"But you—you're from—?"

"I'm from East Orange, New Jersey, myself. Got a nice little place down there that I wouldn't swap for all the palaces of the kings. No sir!... Already? Well, yes, it is a little damp out here, so close to the water. Mrs. Brainerd won't risk it. I'll walk up with you. I'd like to have you meet her."

THE END

www.ingramcontent.com/pod-product-compliance
Lightning Source LLC
Chambersburg PA
CBHW050951120626
46552CB00001B/492